TOO MUCH TOO YOUNG

by Steve Piper

An Old Dogs Publishing Paperback

First published in Great Britain in 2015 by Old Dog Publishing
5 Hogshill Lane, Cobham KT11 2AG

5th Edition reprint
Copyright © 2015 Steve Piper

Printed with love by
www.booksfactory.co.uk

Too Much Too Young is a work of fiction. Admittedly a fiction coloured and scented by historic happenings and the authors experiences, memories and feelings but fiction all the same.

Steve Piper October 2015

A hefty nod is given to Gareth 'Garfus' Richardson, my
2 Tone brother-in-arms who shared some of my formative years.
I have much affection for Dave Fleming and Justina Dewhurst-Richens.
Thank you for your positivity, belief and unquestioning friendship.
For encouragement, youthful enthusiasm, advices and diplomacy I raise a
pint to Comrade Paul Hallam Esq (Old Dog books).
Much love goes to Dot and Al, two great parents. Sorry for all the worry I
may have caused you both over the years.
A massive respect goes to Terry, Neville, Lynval, Roddy, Brad, Jerry,
Horace and Rico (RIP). Thank you.
My deepest affection and love is reserved for my long-suffering 'doll'
Melissa and our two cracking kids, Charlie and Rebecca.
xxxx

CREDITS
Cover: Pip! Pip!
Cover Star: Christian Jonasson and Matt Price
Photographer: Andrea Locking

A fifth reprint

When I agreed to attend a joint 50th gathering somewhere in the east end of London over a year ago little would anyone outside my immediate family have guessed the effort and energy required and encouragement from my long-suffering 'Doll' and kids that had been needed to get me there.

Sat in our little garden in Essex earlier that summer, my daughter Bex had enquired what I had done with my 'book'. It was stashed away in drawer somewhere. Bex, like a dog with the proverbial bone (except she's a vegan!), nagged me. After much nagging I dug it out and after more nagging I put out feelers once more.

PjH was a face from old. Someone I liked. A fact which may not seem relevant to many but those that know me will recognise it is being an essential one. We had not been in touch for a very long-time but our mutual friends and acquaintances ensured that we had connection. PjH had started up a publishing company called 'old dog books'. He wanted to see the manuscript.

'Come to my 50th birthday party.' He insisted. 'Bring the book with you.'

I count myself as fortunate. I have attributes, skills, experience and personality traits that work for me. That is why I have survived these 47 years but that is not why I am fortunate. I am fortunate because I have folk in my life who are the 'cement to my bricks', filling in those gaps, complimenting, strengthening and binding.

Thank you all for believing in me and for buying this little story.

Steve Piper January 2017

Foreword
By Neville Staple

When I hear stories about the 2Tone era, I get a sense of pride that I would never of thought about back then. We were there in the thick of things, beating the crap out of skinheads on a Wednesday night, then singing and partying with them on the weekend. We were infighting with ourselves in the band, behind the scenes, then coming together for the masses, with our mash up blend of ska, punk and reggae music. I used to hate it when old people said about the 50's or 60's, 'those were the days' but to rhaatid, those really were the days..! The 70's and 80's were the days of the youth. The days of the real hardcore subculture. Occasionally, I do some talks for colleges and universities and I couldn't count how many times the students have asked me about my social awareness in the late 70's and early 80's. They especially single out 'Ghost Town' lyrics, as it was so apt, for a time where the UK was depressed and broke, unemployment was at record levels, Thatcher became the Anti-Christ, yet we were subjected to the biggest, lavish pomp of a royal wedding ever known to that generation of kids! It seems that, that was a period of time that was so significant. Politics were crap and harmful, riots were a regularity, caused predominantly by the ridiculous miss-use of some bomba claat vagrant law from ancient history, called 'SUS Law'. So apart from black youths like my friends, getting regular racist kickings and bullying, by Babylon's'Jancro' [vulture police]; my white working class friends took a lot of shit too. So kids were listening more than kids have probably ever listened. Our music was fun, harsh, in your face - but tidy and so very relevant, with a real message in each song. Most of the songs were about me. They were about you. They were about your mates or your sister. I was a dad at 15. I did too much too young! I was a troublesome rudeboy, who got 'lock up' in borstal, who needed 'A Message..' We all did. We all had a 'stereotype uncle' or knew a 'Pearl' in the local cafe. But let me tell you, I blood claat loved it! Fighting, performing, spreading messages, getting in trouble. It was all about living. It was all about living through the crap of a dodgy Government system. We wasn't ready to back down. We was ready to fight. We united. The Specials - we gave you black and white, we gave you politics, social injustices. We gave you style. And a subculture of music that the kids today would never understand, or are only just tuning into. Mod, punk, reggae and ska all blended together like a fish and chips, with salt and vinegar!

The youth now have similar issues around them but they don't seem to notice like we did. We didn't twerk, we didn't gyrate or get our tits out. We were at a time for dressing up, looking hard, looking sharp, wearing better clothes than our parents. We danced and skanked and showed off our vinyl records. We'd spend our last pound towards shiny new loafers or sta-press trousers, rather than worry about having no job, or not knowing if mum could afford tomorrow's dinner. But most of all, we fought back against the system. With a punk attitude, with a skinhead toughness, with a mod suaveness, with a reggae togetherness. We were rudeboys and rudegirls; and we took no shit. I tell you man, those were the raas claat days.

Neville Staple November 2015
http://jamaicanpatwah.com/term/Jancro/1019#.VkJsU9yLTIU

You CAN teach an old dog new tricks   .

Nick A   Danny DC   PjH

We would like to mention: Nicky Porter, Alan Handscombe, Rob Murphy,
The Camden Stylists, Dave Wakeling, Garry Bushell, Pauline and Gaps,
Dax Britton, James Travis and James Gilmour plus
Ollie and Alfie - IOW Rude Boys
Sonia, Joseph, Mary and Hannah Hallams (all Chingford and proud)
and all rude boys and girls everywhere
who have bought this book in their thousands. We salute you.

Foreword

November 1979. The lines are clear. Things so black and white, at least to the eyes and ears of Britain's youth.

The ragged edges of punk rock had been smoothed in to the sound of new wave and inner city housing estates had yet to decompose in to the crumbling and neglected smack and crack saturated slums of the '90s.

Britain's tribes were defined by differences in attitude, attire, musical allegiance, philosophies, territories and behaviour.

Mods were mods, punks were punks.

The Labour party was the Labour party and the Conservatives, Conservatives.

The workers kept working and the bosses planned their retirement.

That November on BBC's 'Top of the Pops' three bands performed. Conceived by different mothers; the Midlands of England and its capital, and yet intrinsically linked by the same sire; ska music imported from the West Indies, they signal in a new era and the arrival of the 2 Tone records gravy train.

Championing a stable of fresh fledgling upstarts pumping out a punchy hybrid of ska-punk tunes, 2 Tone records grabbed the pop charts by the throat.

That same year Britain went to the polls.

The nation tired and tested after two terms of turbulent Labour government voted in a Conservative administration; at its head Britain's first ever female Prime Minister, Margaret Thatcher.

And she was out to spoil the party.

I
Blank Expression. Spring '79

'Are you a mod or are you a skinhead?'

It actually sounded more like; 'Are yuh mod or skin'ead?'

Grimacing, Julian quickly analysed the intent of the snot-garbled question.

And there the question hung, in that corridors claustrophobic air, like a phlegm-baited fish hook.

The mechanism of time had come to a grinding halt. Julian, goldfish mouthed and stunned into a temporary paralysis, absorbed the question. Suspended in the moment, he stared with as un-emotive a look as he could muster, back in to the face of the feral, a face that was flecked with scabby, dry skin and smeared with malevolence.

Julian fought desperately to suppress any outward expression of the fear that soaked his gut. Desperately trying to offer neither weakness nor resistance, neither trigger nor target, it was of an imperative that he maintained an air of reasonable calm.

He required as much thinking time as he could muster to find the appropriate response to situation.

He could not believe that he was in as compromising a situation as this already.

It was not unusual for him to get into the odd scrape but he had only just started at the school that morning.

No, it was fair to say that he had been in his share of predicaments already in his short life and that these had usually been caused by his naivety and an innate ability to speak before thinking through any consequences.

There was the time he had lied to his Mum about going to the woods with some of the boys who lived just down the road from him.

Arriving home later that day, the drying plaster of the black and smelly bog mud and a feathering rip in the knee of his jeans had given the game away. That oversight had cost him a long grounding after a severe tongue-lashing from mother.

The snuff sniffing incident, however, had required no punishment from his elders.

After sneaking into his Grandad's shed and swilling the remaining dregs of Guinness from a sticky half-pint glass left upon the work bench he had reached up to the little blue tin on the windows ledge and took himself a quick snort of the fine brown powder it contained.

He had been incapacitated for what had seemed like a week by the lethal mentholated ground tobacco powder contained therein. Brown, frothy snot had leaked from his burning irritated nostrils throughout the day and into the night, soaking his white cotton pillow.

He had wondered if it would ever stop at the time.

It had been a blur of a morning that had preceded this current predicament.

On arrival at classroom 5B, his new form tutor Mr Boddy, the pupils called him Mr Bogey when out of earshot, had been far too harassed and possibly in the throes of a nervous breakdown to ensure that Julian was given any induction required to settle in. Clammy faced and anxiety riddled, Mr Boddy was not unduly concerned with something as trivial as over-seeing the settling in of new pupil. Waving a nylon sleeved-forearm, he had hurriedly delegated that role to Henry Swansong.

Henry, in turn, made it quickly obvious how disinterested he was with his newly apportioned responsibility by giving what can only be described as a minuscule grunt of recognition before turning his back on Julian so that he could resume his football match analysis with the lad on the adjacent desk. As if Henrys lack of concern for the well-being of Julian, his new and vulnerable classmate, were not enough the boy's terrible personal hygiene also brought tears to Julian's eyes.

Suffice to say, Henry, the chosen one, had then dumped Julian at the sound of the first break bell without apology leaving him to find his own way around the maze of look-alike corridors and classrooms.

Back and forth he had shot like the silver ball in a pinball machine, slamming into pillar and post, the cacophony of youthful shrieks and bellows replacing the bells and buzzers of the arcade game.

A consolation of Henrys disappearing act meant that Julian could once more breath through his nostrils, no longer having to suffer the stench of the boys particular brand of 'eau de testosterone' and for that small mercy alone, Julian had been grateful enough.

It had all seemed so simple.

Mr Boddy had thrust the weekly lesson timetable into his palm after that morning's tutorial neglecting to acknowledge that he, Julian, had no idea of where anywhere was. Julian's concerned enquiry had fallen on deaf ears. Desperate for his fix of black coffee and nicotine the teacher had simply waved him off down the corridor.

All so simple?

All Julian had to do was find his way to the technical block where he would find the metal work room. Once there he was to introduce himself to Mr Lears before settling in for an hour of metal forging. With a bit of effort he had thought, he could turn out a nice key ring for his mum or alternatively fashion himself a useful set of knuckle dusters.

Lord knows he could have made use of them sooner than he anticipated.

Unfortunately, the only simple parts were the numerous simpletons who for their own banal enjoyment deliberately sent him the wrong way down the long unforgiving corridors and into the wrong classrooms. He quickly tired of interrupting home economics classes full of giggling pubescent females and science lessons presided over by the most short-tempered and least tolerant teachers imaginable.

Other more aggressive-looking Neanderthal types had met his requests for assistance with undisguised expressions of pure disgust as they checked him out. Their cold gaze had lowered, scanning him, down to the level of his new school shoes then back again. Up and down they had checked him out while a stifling blend of tobacco and threat secreted from their pores like some toad-like poisonous defence mechanism.

Julian felt as if he were infected.

Diseased.

It was as if he had contracted new boy-itis, a highly contagious ailment.

It would have been foolhardy for other pupils to have acknowledged or responded to his presence. An act of sensitivity would have almost certainly guaranteed them having to endure some cruel ridicule in the changing room showers about being a gay-lord.

At worst they may have even had to face the real possibility of receiving a well-practised dead arm or Chinese burn for daring to help out someone in obvious need.

That was just how it was.

Julian was just a stickleback in a river swarming with piranha fish.

And that was how, confused, frustrated and naïve, he came to be there at that particular moment in time. Caught, snared and cornered in that empty, echoing corridor with no chance of anyone interrupting the interrogation.

Teaching staff and pupils would all be in lessons and oblivious to his predicament just yards away from the classrooms.

Julian felt exposed and vulnerable, his beating heart drumming a deafening tattoo inside his ribcage.

His only company, uninvited and unwelcome, were the two reincarnate Hitler youth stood before him oozing with menace and spiteful intent.

Was he a mod? Was he a skinhead? Why, what, where?

'Christ.' Julian thought he wasn't even sure what a mod or skinhead was, let alone being able to decide to which of the two cults he should nail his colours.

He had heard his Grandad use one of the monikers in reference to the local group of teenagers who hung around the local off-licence

'Bloomin' Skin'eds'. He had muttered as he exited with his two bottles of stout rattling in the carrier bag.

What was the difference?

He scrambled through the selection of possible responses that had popped up in his mind. He knew that a 'don't know' was not going to cut it.

He guessed that any cop out on his part would expose his lack of knowledge and judging by the vibes he was getting from the boys he would probably end up get a kicking anyway just for being a 'div'.

Maybe he should he ask for a question on sport or literature instead?

A grin almost erupted across his jaw as he pondered this option deep within the grey matter.

Common sense prevailed and he quickly decided to save his comedic response until a safer and more appropriate opportunity presented itself.

Imminent threat quickly stifled the urge to smirk. A sense of humour was definitely not in this lots make-up and a roughly applied head lock could soon wipe any further mirth from his face.

Was there a hybrid of the two? What about a ' mod-head' or a 'skod'?

He quickly dismissed that as silly. They would not find that answer even mildly amusing; stupid, provocative and inviting maybe but certainly not amusing.

Somehow he knew that this was all something to do with preferred fashion choices and therefore probably linked to loyalty, an allegiance to a gang of some sort.

He had not lived in cave for the last three years and he had read stuff about punks and teddy boys.

And yet the two reprobates in pincer movement waited. Their postures ready and intimidating, shoulders rounded forward, arms held cocked by their sides.

They made stupid look clever as his step-dad would have said, so Julian knew he was on very dangerous ground.

He needed to avoid looking too smart or flash. He needed to avoid making them feel inferior. That sort of approach would easily provoke a violent response from the thugs.

Julian had quickly ascertained that there was no escape available to him. Their triangle approach had cut of any means of a sprinted escape. His gift of the gab and endless wit, the envy of many, were not going to get him out of this hole. The large proverbial spade he may have used to dig the proverbial hole would have been useful if only to whack them over the head with it.

Julian carefully scanned the stoutest figure at about one o'clock, front right.

He searched for clues, something obvious, a button badge confirming allegiance to a band, a youth cult maybe. He looked for the giveaway sign of a particular haircut.

The fat boy's tatty snorkel parka, shiny-skinned and too tight, was completely zipped and buttoned to under his chin. The coat was greasy and snot-soiled particularly around the lower sleeves. He reeked of recently smoked fags.

The lad's head sat atop the collar of the coat like a golf ball on a tee.

Below this cocoon of a coat he sported a pair of inexpensive blue jeans. These were certainly not on any school uniform list Julian could remember.

The jeans were short in length exposing a pair of regulation grey ribbed school socks wrinkled in to a pair of scuffed, black school shoes.

These were sensible shoes, the kind that were deemed good for your feet and hard-wearing. They were the kind of shoes that seemed to have been specially designed so that parents could make their children wear them to weddings, funerals and, of course, to school. These looked like they had been used to kick footballs and heads around an asphalt playground.

Julian winced as he imagined the unforgiving hard plastic welt around the sole and hard leathered toe cap being booted into his nether regions.

He quickly glanced at the boy's chest.

No badge. Bugger!

He raised his eyes and looked at the hair again taking care not to catch the boys stare.

To be caught staring him out would only invite quick and nasty retribution.

Julian prayed for the graded crop of the skinhead but instead saw a mass of unruly locks, wiry and unkempt, somewhat resembling a well-used Brillo pad that had been left bent out of shape and rusting by the kitchen sink.

Snorkel boy wasn't smiling. Far from it. His appearance was one of glaring intent.

Julian could sense the eagerness in the boy's eyes. The eagerness borne out of an innate need to cause someone pain for his own gratification.

In desperation Julian turned his blank expression to the grinning chimpanzee stood just to the left of his own shoulder mirroring the ready stance of Snorkel boy.

Chimp boy was revelling in Julian's discomfort, thoroughly enjoying the mental torment they were inflicting on him. An appetiser for the main course of physical torment they were cooking up for him.

Bingo!

Chimp boy and his closely shaven scalp had given Julian the lifeline he craved. It was not a thing of beauty, just a roughly shorn dome laced with numerous nicks, scabs and abrasions. Just a boiled egg balanced upon a knotted Arsenal football club scarf, but it was a lifeline all the same.

Julian breathed in slowly, he took a second, he had been always taught to think before you speak, to think before you act. It was a saying that he had heard from time to time from those a lot older than himself and it was one which he had never really used to great effect.

It was quite possible that the haircut was not a fashion statement but that the Chimp could have had a serious nit infestation recently which had required the drastic action of a good set of sterile hair clippers.

Julian's gut twisted and turned, he felt the dizzying effect of anxiety creep up his body.

Snorkel boys breathing had quickened and Chimp boy's eyes had widened with anticipation.

Julian's instinct told him that an answer was needed and that he had seconds left blurt it out.

Say what you see and it could not be denied, the Chimp was bald.

'Skinhead'

Julian was either incredibly lucky or Snorkel boy was a lousy shot.

Levering off his toes Snorkel boy drove his head towards Julian's face. Julian instinctively flinched, drawing his shoulders up and neck down, an action that changed the target area allowing the clumsily performed head-butt to thud into his lower forehead and the very top of the bridge of his nose.

There was a bit of dull thud then an instant numbness but other than that there was no real adverse effect apart from the shock of receiving a face full of greasy hairs that somehow snaked into his mouth too.

Naturally the aggressive action had sent Julian's adrenal gland into over-drive but thankfully his bodies fight or flight mode was aborted, as mission fulfilled, Snorkel boy and Chimp barged him aside leaving him cupping his face and checking for blood.

They swaggered away from him, away down the long grey linoleum-floored corridor. Their footsteps clacked and echoed as their clumsy plastic soled shoes made contact with the cold, highly polished surface. When they reached the two heavy brown swing doors at the end of the corridor, the Chimp turned back and looked at Julian.

His face still bore the same sadistic, twisted grin.

'Welcome to hell, new boy!' He cackled.

And with that footnote, they both heaved themselves through the opening and disappeared, leaving the heavy doors swinging and sighing until they slowed to an eventual, groaning and protesting halt.

Welcome to hell. McEntee secondary school, April 1979.

Hell indeed, if you had no friends, couldn't fight and didn't understand the importance of being a somebody or even an anybody.

None of these usually applied to Julian. He was a cheeky chancer. It was always tough starting a new school mid-term but there had been no option really.

He could be adaptable, chameleon-like even. Maybe he was not possessed with the combat skills of Bruce Lee but he was definitely a quick enough learner and, more importantly, a quick enough runner if the situation required such evasive action.

He could usually talk anyone into a verbal-induced coma for long enough to make a quick getaway.

Shy and retiring were two words that did not normally apply to Julian.

'You can talk for England' His Nan had often said.

'You've got verbal diarrhoea.' His granddad had often observed.

Julian brushed things off quickly and moved on. He was that type.

Gerry though was a different animal altogether.

A solitary figure, he didn't seem to have or need the shield of a posse of peers. This dark and brooding figure was not built for sprinting and luckily he never needed to call upon such athleticisms anyway.

He managed to keep away from the fights and bullies but that could have been due to his genetics.

At fifteen years old he was built like a brick outhouse and heading the top of the school puberty league, a fact that had been evidenced by him owning more body hair than the whole population of McEntee school put together and that sum included the moustached physical education teachers and the hormonally afflicted girls hockey team.

Most of the other boys tended to keep him at a respectable and safe distance with good sense. They thought he was a bit weird anyhow so why rattle the behemoth's cage.

Gerry was going to be Julian's mate, his best mate, only he didn't know it yet!

Two weeks prior Julian found himself struggling to find another position to park his painful buttocks. The agony of sitting on the plywood flooring of the van, feeling every pothole in the road grind the muscles of his arse cheeks to mincemeat had long ago destroyed any machismo he had possessed. He felt like crying.

Stuck in the back of the well-used and abused Luton van, squeezed in amongst mattresses, wardrobes, white goods, boxes of rattling kitchen utensils and coupled with the company of his two recently acquired and very noisy, squealing younger step-sisters who just seemed to find the whole thing highly exhilarating, Julian felt he knew what hell would be like.

The back of the van had heated up like an oven. The early April sunlight had been magnified to an alarming intensity by the glass fibre walls and roof.

Sweat had appeared in crevices he did not know existed on the human anatomy. His tongue had become adhered to the roof of his mouth, swollen useless, rigid, through lack of hydration. Rather like a slug with too much salt on its lettuce lunch.

Any request he had wished to make for Jenny and Jessica to quieten down on the journey had been nigh on impossible.

The two step-piglets had seemed unperturbed by his pain and discomfort as they had squealed and squawked their way through their second rendition of 'Hooray, it's a holiday' which Julian surmised was only marginally worse than the version released by those German hit making machines, Boney M.

So it was with a blessed relief that he heard the chugging of the diesel engine come to a shuddering halt.

The muffled voices grew louder and close, there followed an almighty clatter as the van's steel shutter shot upwards, the chain rattling angrily metal upon metal.

The sudden exposure to daylight once more blinded Julian and his two step sisters, it took a good couple of minutes for them to acclimatise before they were all able to see clearly again.

Looking up at their well-cooked faces stood Julian's Mum, her hands planted on her hips. Her face was lit up with a beaming radiant smile. By her side was Joe, her new husband, the girl's father and Julian's newly acquired step-father.

Joe flexed his shoulders ready to get on with the heavy work.

'Come on son, hop down, then you can start to give us a hand while your mum opens up and gets these two squeaky things out of our way.' He grabbed the girls under their armpits helping them down to the ground leaving Julian to clamber about in the vans bowels.

The piglets tucked their trotters into his Mum's hands. Walking away from the van she turned and looked over her shoulder and smiled at him approvingly, adoringly even.

The girls dangled off her arms, trying to spin her like a maypole.

Then they whirled her around and they all skipped off quickly to wherever, leaving Julian rubbing the blood back into his plasticized buttocks contemplating a full van.

Julian jumped out of the back of the van on to the hard, unforgiving ground. The shock hurt his shins and he winced.

His senses were immediately enveloped in a sea of grey.

A hard and utilitarian grey.

Grey, lifeless brickwork, blockwork and rendered mortar. Tall walls, short walls, fat walls, skinny walls. The flat ground, sloping ground, steps and stairs were all grey.

Different shades of grey, Julian would concede, but still grey nonetheless.

His eyes flit over the terrain, consciously looking for that elusive flash of colour.

Searching for a glimpse, a break in tone, a small imperfection in the grey canvas that was laid out before his eyes.

A flower petal. A crisp bag. A tin can. Something that was not grey.

A slogan, fat and bold and white, had been daubed on to one of the walls.

Tottenham FC YIDS.

The graffiti cut across the urban background like a slashed wound.

Evidence that the deed had been done hurriedly with gloss house-hold paint was obvious. He could make out where the drips and runs had oozed off the bold lettering and headed towards the ground before they had hardened and set in permanence.

A scrawny sapling in a square concrete planter pointed accusingly skyward. Like some crooked, geriatric digit it drew attention to the monstrous concrete creation twenty one stories high that dwarfed its existence.

The faint tang of burnt tingled Julian's nostrils. It seemed to hang in the air. It was a subtle lingering smell that appeared to be etched into the very atmosphere of the estate.

Burnt rubbish.

Certainly.

Not the cosy smell of burnt wood or coal like you experienced when walking through country villages or Victorian housed streets but the dirty stinking smell of bins set alight.

'See, son, not as bad as you thought it would be is it? '

Julian peered out at Joe. 'That would depend on how bad I thought it could be,' he thought. Some spittle formed in his mouth loosening his paralysed tongue.

'No, it looks okay, Joe.' He fibbed forcing a short tight smile. 'Let's get unloaded, yeah? '

Julian grabbed a Golden Wonder crisp box with the word kitchen scrawled over the top and passed it down to Joe. It clattered noisily. He wondered if anything had been broken. He would not have been surprised.

Luckily Julian and his mum had never been great hoarders and the small amount of material possessions they owned were sparse. He guessed unloading would not take too long. Looking despondently at the bulkier items of furniture, he prayed the lift in the block was working.

Joe was a nice guy, Julian had liked him from the beginning, but even Joe could not begin to understand the feelings of fear and dread that coursed through his body at that precise moment.

Previous to this latest house move, Julian had been living with his nan and grandad in Essex for as long as he could remember. His mum, Doreen or 'Rene as those familiar liked to shorten it to, had moved back in with her parents soon after Julian's father had left them.

At the first opportunity he got, so he had been told, his father had hot-footed it, disappearing when he was around two years old. No one had heard from him since.

This had never been a major issue for Julian. He accepted his mother's version of events in good faith, after all why would he doubt her?

He preferred to spend his energy on the people close to him. His mum never bad mouthed his father; in fact, they very rarely discussed his whereabouts. He could have been the next door neighbour for all Julian knew or cared.

Julian and his mum especially welcomed the support of her parents and both enjoyed living with them. There was always plenty of room in the three bedroom mid terraced house, the rooms were a good size and they were bright and airy.

He had grown to appreciate the familiarity and warmth of the home's very outdated fifties style décor and the basic amenities within it.

The street itself was spacious and traffic quiet.

The school Julian attended was just a minute walk away, turn the corner at the bottom end of the road and there it was. A bustling, jostling menagerie of youthful screeches and hollers.

The school boasted large playing fields and goal posts, an amenity which the groundsman allowed the pupils to roam and play on without fear of reprimand.

The Wreck was a small wooded area with a tiny stream running through it which the locals called The Ditch; as good a place as any to get well deserved booty full of stagnant ditch water. Close to home and safely away from main roads, Julian and his friends had constructed many a den there.

Imaginary battles had been fought and wars been won amongst the vegetation, over the ditch and across the field.

Julian's nan was always around, over-seeing things. Mainly from the vantage point of her kitchen she could see right across the back garden and on into the field where the ditch ran alongside. The wide double window spanned the breadth of the enamel sink and beyond. The kitchen was her domain and god help anyone who got in her way.

And his wise old grandad kept well out of the way.

He kept himself busy usually tending to his vegetable plots and geranium beds or tinkering with stuff in the shed.

The shed was an absolute wonder to a young Julian. It had been built from reclaimed timbers his granddad had collected from old bombsites dragging them home on an old go-cart with hard rubber pram wheels.

His grandad had spent a summer erecting the impressive workshop at the back of the garden.

Julian loved the shed and spent many an hour there, sitting on a tall stool, watching and listening as his grandad worked away with antiquated carpentry tools, making small tables, shelves and other things. Quite who he gave them to Julian was never sure.

Often the radio would be on in the background, especially if there was a cricket test match on.

His granddad would suddenly stop whatever he was doing at a pivotal point in the match listening intently to a wicket being taken or great batting stroke being played before either grimacing or nodding approvingly depending on the outcome of that particular bowl or stroke before carrying on where he had left off.

Life was not without its usual hiccups and hurdles to get over but most would describe the family as living quite an idyllic existence there.

Julian's mum Doreen never one to shirk her responsibilities worked at Woolworths chain store in the local high street.

It was there one day at work where Doreen had first met Joe.

He was the single father of two young girls, an unusual set up for the time. Most single parents Julian knew were women, not that he knew many anyway.

Joe's wife had died about a year before. She had suffered from long-term heart problems which she had eventually succumbed to leaving Joe to pick up the pieces and soldier on. After all, as Joe had often said, what else can you do?

He was probably making a delivery drop or something like that when he had taken his chance and made a play for Doreen and she had certainly found him agreeable enough to let him take her out.

Joe was a proper Cockney. He was born and raised in the East End of London, all, 'gawd blimey, guv' and everything's a laugh.

The name Cockney, Joe had informed Julian was alleged to have been derived from the phrase 'a cocks egg', which was apparently a descriptive for a misshapen egg.

It was a name that had been applied to Londoners by rural dwellers, who remarked that 'these cocks-eggs' tended to live by their wits and were ignorant of country ways.

'Folklore says,' he had continued, 'that a true Cockney must be born within the sound of the Bow bells but the reality is that being a Cockney is more about your attitude and accent, the descriptive being earned by a period of time,' and he never specified quite how long a period of time,' living within an East London post-code from a young age.'

Combined with a tendency to drop your t's and h's and to use flowery phrase in conversation and you were pretty much a Cockney.

Time and experience taught Julian that Joe's was pretty much the best explanation for what and how a Cockney came into being.

A hard working, uncomplaining man, Joe drove a lorry around London and its suburbs making sure that the loads of hardware and fittings made it to their destinations in one piece.

He was a genuinely nice bloke, always polite and respectful to most people. Julian thought he was unflappable really. The 'salt of the earth' to use a favourite Cockney descriptive.

In fact the only time Julian remembered him getting agitated and quite angry was at a family wedding reception.

An older cousin of Julian's thrice removed or something as remote as that was getting a bit too over familiar with his mum. Joe had been patient with the very inebriated and irritating cousin and for Doreen's sake he had tried to sit back and let her handle the situation on her own, after all, she had done a good job of looking after herself so far.

Unfortunately the intoxicated and thoroughly tedious relation had failed to grasp the very clear message being put out and it was when he tried to pull Doreen down onto his lap causing her enough concern to swear loudly at him that prompted Joe to intervene by grabbing the man's jacket lapels and hauling him up on to his tip toes.

Luckily a few of the other men at the party got between them and drunken cousin was escorted out before real fisticuffs ensued.

Joe must have done something right because he and Doreen were all over each other for the rest of the evening and they danced real close, his hands on her bum and her head resting on his shoulder much to Julian's embarrassment.

They did look a well suited and handsome pairing though and many people said so. Julian was pretty sure that was the night Joe had asked mum if they would move out of nan and grandads and set up with him and his two girls in East London.

It was not quite a whirlwind romance but neither of them hung around playing hard to get. It was obvious that they got on great together.

It wasn't too long before Doreen broached the subject with Julian. What did he think about them moving in with Joe and his girls; lock, stock and barrel.

She was concerned that changing schools just before the start of his last year would interrupt his exams so to be fair he was given the choice to stay with his grandparents until he had completed them. Given that Julian was totally unfazed by the looming presence of studying for his O-levels, he always seemed to get high grades despite the little effort he applied to study and revision, he chose to ride shotgun with his mum.

All for one and one for all, besides Julian was always game for a bit of a new adventure and hopefully, some excitement too.

Most importantly though for Julian, his mum seemed genuinely happy and he knew she really deserved that at the very least.

II
Dawning of a new era. Late Spring '79

'Well now, this should all be very interesting son. ' Joe was cramming the remainders of a slice of toast into his already over-filled mouth and trying to slip an arm into his padded nylon work coat while reading the headlines on the front of his newspaper at the same time.

'What will?' Julian asked drowsily, he was not fully awake.

'She went and did it mate, got in with a majority of forty four. Maggie Thatcher is now Britain's first female prime minister. God 'elp us.'

So that was it. The general election of Great Britain had been and gone. The population of these fair isles had decided yesterday.

May the third, 1979.

Julian could vaguely recall the last few weeks and hear the floated comments and hypothetical questions directed towards the television screen by Joe particularly during the news broadcasts. He had seen the banners in windows; the signposts erected in front gardens. He had even noticed and heard the occasional discussion or debate, at home, in the café, at bus stops and wondered what exactly the fuss was all about.

Weren't all the politicians the same? What difference would it make whether a woman, man, martian or monkey was in control of the country?

Did it really matter if it was the Tories, Labour or anyone else in charge?

Wouldn't they all lie and screw it all up for everyone?

As far as Julian could tell it was only the National Front who had policies that were completely different from all the other common or garden political parties.

What was he supposed to think were the implications of this bombshell being in charge for the next four years?

More to the point, did he even care for that matter? He had to be in school in just over an hour.

'Who did you vote for then, Joe?'

'That's for me to know and you to find out.' Joe was having a laugh; there was that recognisable twinkle in his eye as he tapped the side of his nose with his finger.

Julian thought it looked like Joe's eyes were smiling sometimes.

Didn't anything get to him or worry him? He often wondered.

'Bet you voted NF or raving loony!' He quipped, pointing the glutinous cereal spoon in Joe's direction. Milky sludge dripped onto the perforated silver top of the salt cellar smearing its shine.

'You cheeky blighter! Mind you it'd be hard to tell which of those two are the real loonies anyway I reckon!' Joe checked his watch.

'Better get a move on, can't afford to be late, being new there. Important year this is comin' up, remember, you should start studying hard. Y'mum's got high hopes for you, exams will soon be loomin' an' all that. Don't want to end up drivin' lorries around the smoke for a livin' like me!'

'Yeah, I know,' came the understanding yet weary response from Julian's Weetabix smeared mouth. He could barely summon up the effort to swallow it.

It was not the exams he was bothered about, it was the 'all that' that he found distracting; taking up valuable head space, sometimes keeping him awake all hours of the night. He craved stimulation both physical and mental, some form of immersion in a hobby or interest that would stop his mind galloping off in different directions.

He needed something to focus on to stop the distraction of uncertainty that seemed to inhabit his mind. A gutful of anxiety about the future and what it might hold for him.

It had the horrible effect of making him fidgetty, particularly at night when all was quiet save for the odd snort or snore from a sleeping relative. Sometimes it felt like a load of people having a party in his head, so many voices and noises.

Different images going round and round. The more he tried to block it all out, the more irritating and insistent it all got.

What are you going to do with the rest of your life? Have you thought about a career? Why don't you join the Army? What exams are you taking? What grades do you think you'll get? Have you made any friends yet? Have you got a girlfriend? Why is it taking you so long to brush your teeth? What are you doing in there all this time?

A million and one questions.

Oh yes, the pleasures of late adolescence and not only that, to top it all off, Britain's only gone and elected a woman called Maggie as their prime minister.

Well, like he gave a toss!

He made it to school and only just on time.

He had managed to muster up enough energy from his hormone racked body to get himself looking half respectable for another day in the most important year of his life; the year he would 'never get another crack at' by all accounts according to his elders.

'Don't waste this chance, boy. Regret's a terrible thing.'

That was his grandad's favourite.

The old man would pop this one out while not even lifting his head to meet Julian's bored glazed look as he continued with whatever he was doing at the time. It was an art, a skill. Julian guessed the message was supposed to inspire and encourage somehow.

'Ooh, if I had your opportunities, my lad.'

That wistful one was his nans and there were plenty of other supposed motivational one-liners from different members of his now extended family.

Julian had already filed them away in his mental filing cabinet for future use and labelled the folder ' no regrets' .

That night, after an arduous day at school which he had mostly spent avoiding the opportunist teeth collectors and nose-bloodiers while also trying to get some education in between, Julian stared at the flickering television screen with his usual distracted boredom.

Picking at his nails with his teeth, he listened to Joe's pearls of wisdom, his clipped opinions punctuating the news items.

If he had something else to do he would have been doing it but he did not, so watching the news with Joe was the best he could come up with.

Why anyone would actually set time aside to watch the early evening news was a mystery to him. Yet for Joe this was part of his whole routine despite Julian knowing that he had already devoured his newspaper over the course of the day..

Like clockwork, Joe would arrive home; hang his anorak on coat peg in hallway, peel off the heavy leather work boots, slip on the tartan slippers then give his 'Reen a peck on the cheek after slipping a hand around her waist before settling down into his favourite spot on the faded, brown corduroy cushions of the well-worn but surprisingly comfortable sofa to catch up on the news.

Politics, religion, war, economics and death; all with a bit of sport and a weather report thrown in to spice things up; that seemed to be the formula for a satisfactory news broadcast. Admittedly there was the occasional cheerful piece about animals and babies but generally Julian found the usual content of most news programmes to be quite depressing and, on the whole, incredibly uninteresting.

Margaret Thatcher on the other hand was looking pretty pleased with herself though. Standing outside number ten, Downing Street, in front of the gloss black door with a shiny brass one and nought fixed to it, she looked like a stern headmistress to Julian.

Flanked by black painted railings and policemen, she addressed the nation after her victory in the polls successfully ousting the battle-worn Labour party opposition from the famous address where, now she was the countries leader, she would be at the helm with her hand-picked Tory colleagues in cabinet.

She was a smartly dressed lady, a quite serious looking fifty something year old with a very stiff hair do, probably a can and a half's worth of holding spray Julian thought.

'Where there is discord, may we bring harmony.'

'Where there is error, may we bring truth.'

Julian thought she had said 'this cord' at first and expected her to hold up a ceremonial rope or some sort of stringy prop to aid her delivery.

He looked over at Joe feeling confused but he was too busy concentrating, listening intently to the remainder of the Iron Maiden's speech.

Julian eventually found out that discord was actually just a posh word for conflict and disharmony!

'Where there is doubt, may we bring faith. '

'Where there is despair, may we bring hope. '

She ended her speech, an efficient enough orator it seemed to Julian. He later learnt at school that the content of her speech had been originally spoken by a historical figure by the name of St. Francis of Assisi.

He glanced sideways at Joe again expecting to hear some educated insight or well-thought out criticism bleated into the room for anyone that cared to listen but unusually for Joe he said nothing.

'Jeremy Thorpe; former liberal leader' at least that was what the blurb read on the screen, said; 'I am horrified, she makes Jim Callaghan (her predecessor by all accounts) look like a moderate!'

'Better watch out for the skinheads then!' Julian quipped, 'Get it? Mods, moderate?' He thought this was rather witty.

Joe just raised his eyebrows and shook his head good naturedly.

Of course, Mr Thorpe's comment had nothing to do with youth culture but was an obvious swipe at the new prime ministers perceived lack of restraint and fairness but Julian thought it was funny anyway.

The gnarled, unforgiving concrete surface of the estate made sure you were awake by the time you left its perimeter. Like an ugly sea of corrugated sand, cement and rough aggregate, it spread outwards to the estate boundaries. Every step over it violently massaged the soles of your feet and jolted your joints into submission. Running over the surface seemed an inconceivable idea.

It was as Julian was making his way down one of the many slopes towards the main road leading away from the estate that he first noticed him.

He was a tall, grizzly bear of a figure with dark black hair, his head was down and his hands thrust deep in his jacket pockets.

Julian knew he was of school age, of that he was sure. The bear was wearing grey school trousers shiny with added Teflon and Julian could see the bottom of his blazer jacket sticking out below the knitted hem of his bomber-type jacket.

Julian guessed that he must attend the same school and was almost certainly in the same year. That was unless the bear was even more a freak of nature than he already appeared to be.

Julian needed to know more.

He was quite huge. Much heavier set; taller, wider and hairier than any youth Julian had encountered and, Julian thought, quite possibly more developed than most young adult males that he knew as well.

Julian quickened his pace until he was almost running in an effort to draw up alongside the bear.

As Julian fell into step beside him the bear made no acknowledgment of his arrival, not a lift of the head or a glance sideways to where he was trotting alongside him.

Julian had to throw in the odd skip and hop to keep up with the bear's stride pattern as the pace and length threatened to leave him behind.

He was breathless with effort but managed to gasp a greeting anyway.

'Alright, mate?'

The bear grunted. It sounded like a yes but Julian couldn't be certain. He took this as a green light to continue his attempt to communicate though.

'Do you go to McEntee?'

Again, even though he didn't see his lips move he was sure he recognised an acknowledgement of sorts.

Maybe he had just farted? Julian was unsure.

He ploughed on.

'That's cool. Do you mind if I walk with you then?'

There was no audible noise or answer to this request. Julian thought rather worryingly that maybe he had gone too far, rushed in as usual and offended the bear.

Maybe he had made him nervous or even worse disturbed him in some way. 'God help me,' Julian thought 'if I've had upset him.'

He really would make mincemeat of him, the bear being about three times his size and weight.

Julian imagined it would be just like that nature programme he had seen about grizzly bears in Canada fishing for salmon out of a fast flowing river. With their great big paws they snatched the fish from the shallows before they tore the flesh free from the live and flapping silvery prey with ease.

Julian tried to sneak a peek at the bear's paws but they were firmly planted in his trouser pockets.

Julian deliberately kept quiet for a hundred yards or so until the pair rounded a corner heading towards the bus stop where the number 42 bus stopped and loaded its cargo of juvenile delinquents for delivery to McEntee Secondary.

Julian was surprised and somewhat perplexed when the bear did not break stride or peel off to join the bus stop queue full of bustling, boisterous youths.

The term queue may have been slightly misleading. Some were puffing away on illicit contraband most likely liberated from their mum's handbag or scrounged from mates. Many of the youths favoured the age old style, reminiscent of borstal boys and convicts, of holding their fags pinched between thumb and index finger and held reversed so that the glowing tip of the cigarette pointed inwards towards the palm of the hand.

Some had their blazer jacket collars turned up, one boy even had his whole blazer on inside out exposing the shiny lining and outfitter's label.

School ties hung like discarded dish rags from their grubby collars in a bizarre display of different knots, thickness's and lengths, the synthetic material pock-marked with fag-tip burns.

They were a rabble of street urchins and with a recognisable hierarchy, the leader being easily identified by his looming dominant body language as he presided over the others in the ragged, multi-coloured bunch.

The bear continued on past the scene without as much as an upward glance. Julian chose to follow him, unsure of why but he was intrigued and that was reason enough.

No one walked to school as far as he knew but then again, he did not know anyone, certainly not anyone that could be bothered to communicate with him without verbal, physical or actual threat to his well-being.

Julian was confident that they were headed in the right direction but he was also reasonably sure they would struggle to make it to school on time for registration.

Julian voiced his anxiety.

'Don't you want to get the bus? We might be late.' He offered.

The bear shook his head lightly but there was still no verbal response as such. He seemed in no mood for conversation that fine morning.

Julian had caught his breath and though it was still an effort to keep up as he was using at least one and half strides to the bear's one, his heart rate had settled into a more realistic and sustainable rhythm which afforded him a touch more comfort when trying to speak and so he rattled on.

'We'll probably get detention an' have to stay behind after school and all that. Have you had one yet? I haven't. I think you have to do lines or copy out of a really boring book. Some kids get loads! I never got any at my last school. I went to a school in Epping. Do you know Epping? It's like the country, lots of trees and stuff. No black kids there. Not that I've got a problem with black people or foreigners. Not even Irish people. I mean, not all Irish are for the IRA are they?' Julian paused thoughtfully.

'Where are you from? I mean, you're really…..'erm …..Kind of …..tall…..big, bigger than anyone I know!'

Julian quickly realised how pathetic he sounded. He made amends.

'My mum always said not to ask personal things about people so no offence meant, mate'

Not normally a quitter Julian began to doubt even his persistent verbal prodding would not be sufficient to crack the bear's exterior.

He had hoped that babbling away like he had known the bear for ever and a day would have triggered him into some sort of response and that maybe they could have at least enjoyed a nice chat on the way to school which might have sweetened the impending mention in the late book and an almost certain detention.

On they trod, side by side in silence. Julian found the space uncomfortable and fought his innate tendency to fill the air with noise.

They breezed past the newsagents next to the dry cleaners.

Julian breathed in the heady aroma from the cleaners. He always liked the smell that wafted out from the cleaners. Tinged with a chemical pungency it always smelt warm to him, he took a lungful feeling the aroma invigorating, waking him up as they passed. It cleared his stuffy sinuses.

Julian's mum just thought he was a bit weird.

Julian had heard lots of people call the newsagents, 'the pakis'.

The people who owned it were Asian but Joe, who never called the shop by that name, said that was racist and that they couldn't be 'pakis' because the owners came from India not Pakistan. He said they would be very offended to be called 'pakis' and had proceeded to give Julian a history lesson regarding the border conflicts between India and Pakistan. He had explained to Julian how the majority of Indians happened to practise the Hindu and Sikhism religions and that most Pakistanis were Muslims following the religion of Islam.

He said that some people were ignorant and should get their facts straight.

Some of the urchins at the bus stop bought their cigarettes from there because the shopkeepers never asked your age even if you had school uniform on and would sell you a single cigarette imaginatively called 'a single' rather than a whole packet.

Julian and the bear trod on. Occasionally he took a glance across but the bear did not seem to notice anything or look up at any of the shop fronts.

He appeared oblivious to the people who passed them on their way to whatever the day had planned for them.

Julian wondered what he was thinking. Was he happy or sad?

He looked a bit down in the dumps to him, fed up maybe, but he could not be sure.

Julian really liked the bear's jacket.

It made him look heavily muscled, like a body-builder, the fibrous filling of the jacket padding out his already substantial frame.

'What d'you think about Sid Vicious dying?'

He had absolutely no idea where the comment came from or why. It was as much a shock to him as to anyone else that he often blurted out statements, questions and other oddments related or otherwise to the situations or conversations he was in.

Suffice to say he heard the words emanate from his lips before he had even had the chance to consider their relevance, evaluate their necessity in this instance and therefore avoid making a complete idiot of himself by blurting them out to someone who, at the moment, was a complete and potentially dangerous stranger that appeared to have absolutely no intention of meeting his acquaintance yet, in any way, shape or form.

The bear halted.

He turned to Julian; a somewhat quizzical expression creased his face.

Julian was taken aback by the face. It was soft, not at all how he had envisaged. There was a dark fuzz of facial hair around his jaw line and his top lip. His skin looked a bit grubby but Julian was sure this was down to his age and the hormones of which he was positive the bear had more than his fair share of, hence the abundance of blackheads peppered around his nose and chin.

Greasy patches of skin on his forehead and chin shone out from his rounded face.

And yet despite his imposing physique there was a definite softness, a calmness to his features.

His hair was thick and dark, a bit lank looking but healthy enough besides.

The most eye-catching part of the bear's whole appearance was his amazing set of sideburns.

Full-blown, shag-pile carpet, mutton chops. Trimmed and shaped they would have given Slade's Noddy Holder a run for his money.

A very impressive facial adornment for an adolescent not yet out of school.

'Sid Vicious died in February,' Grizzly corrected him, 'ages ago. That's old news mate.' He sounded a touch exasperated but didn't look annoyed or threatening.

'Yeah, I know. Killed himself, didn't he?' Julian rolled with it.

'Not 'til he'd killed his girlfriend Nancy first he didn't.' The bear returned, 'Idiot.'

Julian was unsure whether the insult was aimed at Sid or him.

The bear set off again.

Julian took this as an invitation to continue in his company if he could just keep up with the energy sapping pace.

'Have you heard of The Specials?'

Julian was taken aback by the change in Gerry's tone. Gerry explained that he had heard the group's debut single called 'Gangsters.

Gerry had discovered them; he had been reading about their early gigs in the music papers; they were making quite a noise in the press and he had heard the single played over the airwaves on the small radio in his bedroom. Obviously smitten by their sound he wasted no time in telling Julian more about it.

'Gangsters' was a rehash of a 1964 Prince Buster single 'Al Capone'. The Prince was not a real prince but was actually a successful Jamaican recording artist. The hit had been very popular on its original release particularly among the young mods of the '60s. The intro, a teeth-grating cacophony of screeching tyres conjured up scenes of mafia violence; the instrumentation providing an exotic rhythm for youngsters always searching for the new sound.

Cleverly adapted by The Specials, that original composition now formed the backbone for the bands self-penned lyrics; an angry rant at being stitched up by some unscrupulous businessman.

It had shot into the top ten in the early summer of that year, peaking at number six.

Julian had listened with a child-like curiosity; he reckoned that if Gerry liked them there was a good chance that they would be worth a listen.

The bear had a glint of passion in his eye. Julian got the strong feeling that he knew what he was talking about and what the hell did Julian know about pop or rock music anyway!

The bear had lit the fuse. He had managed to intrigue Julian even more. He was eager to spend more time with this knowledgeable behemoth of a youth.

'I got nutted the other day.' Julian blurted.

'That doesn't surprise me. Who'd you upset? '

'I don't know their names but they asked me a question and I must have got it wrong' Julian went on to retell the incident in detail as they scuffed along the way.

A short snigger from the bear punctuated the end of his tale of woe.

'Sounds like you met Jeffers and Jonesy. A right pair of dickheads.' He paused. 'Come on, we'll be late for school if you don't get a move on!' He prompted.

'It's Gerry. Short for Gerald.' Gerry informed Julian as they continued with the forced march towards school. 'I was very lucky. Me mum wanted to call me Dylan'

'Dylan? What? Like that rabbit out of The Magic Roundabout? '

'Don't be so stupid. She wanted to name me after Bob Dylan, some bleedin folk singer! '

'Bob Dylan?' And he was genuinely ignorant.

The only music Julian got to hear was usually playing quietly in the kitchen at home on an old transistor radio that his granddad had given his mum and he could not say he had paid too much attention to who or what sang or played whatever.

'What bands he in then? '

He really had not got a clue who Bob Dylan was or what he did.

'He was a folk singer, you know, protest songs, hippy stuff, 'time's they are a changing' was one of his ditties. I don't suppose you would have heard his stuff. I only know it 'cos me mum used to play it.' Gerry chuckled. 'She was listening to him a lot when I was born. Just glad me old man had a say in it to be honest.'

'Nope, still haven't the foggiest who you're talking about, mate. Do you mind if I just call you Gerry, short for Geraldine!'

Gerry laughed and gave Julian a friendly barge with his rather considerable cannon ball of a shoulder. This sent Julian sideways, stumbling into the path of a very pretty and young secretarial type who had to stop dead in her tracks to avoid him becoming cocooned between her bosoms.

Gerry, some way ahead, glanced back over his shoulder, enjoying every second of Julian's embarrassing predicament.

After a quick and awkward attempt to apologise and looking desperately like the red faced, clumsy oaf that he appeared to be, Miss Bosoms allowed him off the hook with what little dignity he had left. A loud tut leaving Julian to straighten his tie and toddle off after the great bear who was chortling away to himself up ahead.

Gerry the bear had the route to school and timing of their arrival completely sussed.

Julian need not have worried himself. The bell call for registration rang as they entered the cloakroom much to his relief.

He had only been at McEntee for a couple of weeks and he was worried how his Mum would have reacted to his first ever detention. So it was with some degree of relief that he was able to defer that potential banana skin to another time and place.

And the jacket Julian had admired so much?

That was 'an American issue, olive green, MA-1 flying jacket with bright orange, reversible lining' as Gerry had proudly explained. He had got it for his fifteenth birthday, purchased with the money he had received from his Dad in addition to the cash he had saved in his plastic TSB money box shaped like a globe of the world.

He had bought it from an army surplus stall at the Sunday market and it was so expensive that it was all he had to open on the day but he did not mind because he knew it looked great, the business in fact and now Julian wanted the same.

III
Concrete Jungle. Summer '79

That summer of '79 would pass in a speeding blur of exploration as Julian roamed his new environment and continued with the all-important task of building on his initial encounter with his newfound best friend.

In June that year, the film star, the old cowboy and one-man army, John Wayne passed on into the great western in the sky and Joe had mourned for a week, forcing them all to watch re-runs of the gung-hos and shoot 'em ups that Marion had made his own.

In August the Irish Republican Army murdered Lord Mountbatten, a cousin to the Queen, by blowing him up with a bomb planted on his fishing boat.

This incident in particular had prompted Joe into a long and drawn out thesis on the political intricacies of British involvement in Northern Ireland and the possible consequences of the army's continued presence there.

Julian would not have minded but he had only asked why the terrorists would want to blow up a cousin to the Queen and kill a couple of kids who were unlucky enough to be there at the same time.

Julian's mum always said 'deaths always come in threes' and so he had waited, expectantly, wondering whether it had to be a famous death or if any old dear popping their clogs would be suffice to fill the prophecy.

Gerry and Julian yelled their rendition of the Sex Pistol's 'friggin' in the riggin' as they made their way across the estate.

Julian just hoped there were not any pensioners about to take offence at their filthy choral exhibition. They might tell his mum.

Julian took every opportunity to spend time with Gerry even subtly forcing his presence on him on days when it appeared Gerry really wanted to be on his own doing absolutely nothing.

He watched, questioned and listened to Gerry rather like a younger child would hang on to its elder siblings every word and movement. Gerry was a fountain of information.

He seemed to be remarkably well read on things that Julian had only just begun to discover. He had an uncanny ability to absorb and store facts and figures about music, fashion, films and other topical, worldly matters in his grey matter.

Gerry even had opinions. Something Julian had never had to bother with up until then.

Julian came to know the estate rather like a tribal younger comes to know the jungle or plains his tribe inhabits.

He gained an intimacy with its myriad of nooks and crannies, its numerous different blocks and dwellings, the stairways and corridors flecked with cigarette butts, lighter-burnt scars, lewd graffiti and phlegm.

There was what appeared to be a random scattering of twenty one storey towers and four floor high maisonettes over the sprawling council development. Julian's family shared a flat in one of the maisonettes. Pine, Yew and Spruce were the other three lower height dwellings, theirs was called Sycamore.

The other vertigo-inducing and up-ended boxes of concrete and steel, forever a mystery of construction to Julian, were comically named St Fabian, St Albans and St Francis. Julian and Gerry had joked that one of the tower blocks should have been named St Rastafari, in honour of the dread-locked brethren who congregated on the compact, jaundice coloured communal landings, filling them with a lingering haze of sickly-sweet blue smoke and the bass-heavy rumblings of home-built amplifiers and speaker boxes.

Gerry always light-heartedly called the blocks; scab, boil, zit, mole, wart, bogey and pile. Pile as in haemorrhoid that is although it could easily have been argued that pile, as in pile of shit, would also have fit the bill.

These were Gerry's alternate names he had applied as he insisted these were de-scriptive of those unwanted and embarrassing blots on the human body that had much in common with the mostly unloved lumps the planning department in their infinite wisdom had bestowed upon the common man.

Julian thought this was very funny and very clever.

Most estates of this type had been hurriedly erected in the fifties and sixties.

Seen as a suitable and convenient solution to the war-ravaged, low on mod-cons, high maintenance East end slum problem, families had been encouraged to give up their decrepit terraced housing to take up the offer of moving onto the new and com-pact, 'innovatively' designed housing estates of the future.

And as a huge selling point the flats boasted their own hot running water, hot air heating systems and toilets that you did not have to put your coat on to visit!

Just through following Gerry around and paying attention to the architecture and landscape they inhabited, Julian learnt something new every day about urban survival. Picking up everyday skills and learning the safest routes that could be used to avoid turning the wrong corner at the wrong moment and finding oneself at the mercy of the local soul boys, with their tight afro hair styles and pronged fork-like combs stuck in the back of their pompadours like an apache feather, was of paramount importance if you were to avoid colliding with those who would chase you, hunting you down like a pack of rabid Doberman dogs. The adventure park was to be avoided. That was their fortress. You entered at your peril.

They could be relentless in pursuit of their prey, persistent in the man-hunt until they had satisfied their bloodlust by dishing out a bit of a slapping to those who were too slow to outrun them, applying a well-worn warning to 'stay off their manor'.

The fact that most of their victims happened to call the estate home, their manor too, was irrelevant.

Julian followed Gerry's slow ascent climbing the forty two flights of piss smelling, aluminium-nosed stairs to its very peak. They sucked in much needed air as they climbed, their need for oxygen overcoming any aversion they had to the stale, acrid stench that engulfed the stairwell.

Gerry had recently discovered a loose bar in the heavily pad-locked railings on the roof of the block on one of his many reconnoitres. These areas had been designed and fitted out to deny access to those who desired illicit access to the tower blocks apex and true to the art of any design, a flaw in the design youth had found.

After gaining their breath, composure and pondering why they had not just taken the lift, Gerry freed the ill-fitting pole from its fitting. Lifting it high up through the holes and placing it to one side he just about managed to squeeze his large frame through the gap and stepped out onto the flat roof beyond.

Julian, no invite needed, was right behind him and through in an instant.

The bitumen surface of the roof felt slightly softened and a touch tacky due to the copious good weather they had been enjoying and the flat areas proximity to the sun ensured that it copped the full effect; the gritty, non-slip covering crunched underfoot. Julian was immediately aware of a deep pulsating hum, not unlike the sound a fridge freezer makes, only multiplied by about a thousand decibels.

The two mammoth boxes constructed from grey steel that the noise emanated from were shielded by tall wire fencing. The sign fixed to the wire read ' Danger high voltage risk of electrocution' with a silhouette of a man keeling over with a lightning bolt piercing his chest. Julian looked nervously at Gerry.

'They're just generators, they supply power for the lifts and stuff, I think' Gerry answered.

'Wouldn't want to be stuck up here if there was a fire, would you?' Julian attempted to hide any nervousness.

'What would you do? Jump or be burnt alive.' Gerry teased.

'We could re-enact The Towering Inferno!' He grinned, 'the one about the sky-scraper set in New York. Can't remember the name of the hero in it, think it might have been Steve McQueen.'

'Did he get them out in the end?' Julian was not familiar.

'Some of them,' Gerry chuckled, 'not all were so lucky though!'

'Well I hope for our sake there's a Steve about if we get into strife because I don't fancy jumping from up here.' Julian quipped.

They had reached the far end parapet which formed part of the solid concrete perimeter to the roof space. It was rough rendered, a bonus as it helped Gerry gain some purchase as he reached up to his full height, gripped the slab overhang and begun to haul himself up, his training shoes giving him adequate purchase against the coarse face. Julian watched in disbelief as his mate virtually disappeared up onto the walls thick summit.

'Gerry!' Julian fretted, concerned that he may have gone straight over and was now spread over half of the estate. 'What the bloody hell are you doing, you nutter!'

Gerry's grinning moon of a face appeared over the edge of the wall looking down at Julian stood below. Squinting up at the precipice the sunlight created a fuzz of bright white around his head, a Ready Brek glow, a fiercely-glowing halo.

Gerry was spread on his front.

'What's the matter with you? You big girls blouse.' He jibbed.

'You're mad.' Julian squinted up at Gerry, the powerful sunlight blinded him, 'You might fall you idiot.'

'Been up 'ere loads of times,' he dismissed Julian's concern, 'come on, get up here. You've got to see the views, mate. Here reach up, I'll give you a hand.' Gerry reached down offering his outstretched palm for Julian to grasp.

Julian reluctantly placed his hand and his trust into Gerry's shovel of a hand, feeling himself lighten as he rose up onto the balls of his feet and begun his own ascent. The cheap vinyl coating on the toes of his trainers was quickly feathered by the scuffing and scraping as he scrambled up to be alongside Gerry.

Julian's elbows dug into the hardness as he hooked himself over the lip and heaved himself up and over onto the top. He sprawled alongside rubbing his wounded elbows.

The top was wide and flat, at least two metres in breadth of concrete slab with enough area to rest and get his bearings in relative safety.

'You really are raving mad Gerry.' He gasped.

'Just copy what I do.' Gerry rolled back over onto his stomach before shuffling like a commando towards the outer edge of the slab. Julian mimicked Gerry move for move until his head, like Gerry's, was in position, he peered downwards over the outer edge of the slab.

The ground shot up towards Julian at an unexpected rate of knots. His legs became as light as feathers. A sensation not unlike someone lifting them up and trying to propel him headfirst towards oblivion and the bold front page headlines of the local paper overtook him.

Julian froze stiff. His breath stuck like a golf ball in his throat before self-preservation kicked in and sent him scuttling back a few safe inches like a crab pulling itself back into a rock's crack before flopping over onto his back.

He squeezed his eyes shut in an attempt to stop the spinning vertiginous giddiness he experienced and folded his arm over his face to shut out the too-bright sunlight.

He swallowed the sticky acidic spew that had lurched into his mouth, the bile burning his throat on its downward passage. The acrid, metallic taint lingered in his mouth as he fought to regain his senses.

'Are you alright, mate?' Gerry sounded concerned but Julian could see the effort it was taking him to suppress his amusement, 'It can take a while to get used to it. Take a minute to get your bottle back then have another go, it won't be such a shock second time.'

After a few minutes, with his equilibrium regained, curiosity and some amount of pride convinced Julian to try for another look.

It was with some trepidation that he eased himself forward for the second time of asking. He felt more prepared this time.

The enormity of what he experienced then left him speechless.

The whole estate was laid out before them both, like a poor man's miniature village made of grey modelling clay and grey cardboard. He could see minute figures of people going about their business, quite oblivious to the sky-high pair of watchful eyes that monitored their movements. A stray dog, tiny, like an ant, wandered aimlessly.

The sky was clear and summer blue, cloud cover was nil, conditions perfect for sightseeing.

Gerry pointed, 'If you look hard over that way you can see the Post Office tower over in the city. '

He was right. There it stood tall, clear as day, pointed upwards like a rocket ship out of a science fiction movie ready to launch.

Julian scanned, taking in the recognisable and the anonymous architecture of London spread out for miles like an opened, pop-up A-Z map. The dome of St Pauls cathedral, its roof visible and eye-catching, like a well-rounded breast, the spire its erect nipple, Julian could just make out through the hazy skyline of the city.

'Tallest building in London, that is.' Gerry nodded towards the Post Office tower.

'You were right G, it's an amazing view' Julian had no trouble agreeing.

After a few minutes spent basking in the special view and soaking up the rays from the warm summer sunshine, Gerry sat himself up. He swung his legs under him then edged forward until his legs were dangling over the edge of the building.

Julian's heart skipped a beat.

'Come on, Gerry, you're pushing your luck a bit now, be careful will you.' He urged.

Julian wondered why Gerry was trying to impress him. He would have known that he clearly did not need to do that as he was already under his spell.

'You worry too much. It's a confidence thing, you see. If you watch cats and monkeys they are so sure-footed, quite deliberate when they move about. They don't fear heights or distance, the only thing they have to worry about are possible predators and dangers like that. So if you're confident and focused in what you're doing then you'll probably be safe, see?'

Julian did not see. Gerry's bravado had unnerved him spiking adrenalin into his own gut. Gerry slowly and deliberately lifted himself up out of his seated position and raised himself up until he was standing upright.

'Christ, Gerry!' Julian hissed through a clenched jaw. 'Sit back down you idiot!'

Gerry paid no mind, Julian's pleas for sanity a waft of wind. He turned away before walking a few deliberate paces along the sky-scraping aerial footpath.

He stopped, turning again, back to face Julian.

Julian found it excruciating to watch but even harder to look away.

'Seriously Gerry, mate, what if a gust of wind blows you off or you slip or something?' He tried to reason, 'Get down, please.'

'Ain't no chance of wind today.' Gerry looked untroubled, relaxed even.

'Talking of wind though did you know that in strong winds these blocks can sway and flex? I'm sure I've noticed it when I've watched 'em out me window. It's a deliberate design to stop them sustaining damage, like how trees move with the wind instead of resisting so they don't snap. You can 'onestly see the buggers move.'

How he appeared so calm and collected, holding a conversation while suspended who knows how high above sea level, Julian could not fathom.

'Remember what I said earlier Jules, it's all about bein' calm, you got to have confidence.' Gerry physically relaxed before lifting one of his legs until he was stood on one looking like a large and hairy but somewhat demented flamingo.

Julian shook his head in disbelief. 'You are really are a hamper short of a picnic.'

Gerry resumed to standing on two legs and returned to his perch next to Julian.

After a couple of quiet minutes and some steady breathing Julian finally plucked up enough will and courage and stupidity to join him on the edge, he allowed his legs to hang over.

Initially he kept his eyes shut tight keeping a death grip on the lip las if his life depended on it, which it clearly did.

As he became more confident, acclimatised he relaxed more. Listening to Gerry's observations on life helped take his mind of the fact that they were precariously perched atop a tower block. Slowly he found the urge to open his eyes too difficult to resist. He blinked them open.

'D'you know, that if you drop a coin off the Empire State building which is a bloody sight taller than this block and it hit a bloke on the top of his head, it would go right through his body like a bullet, shoot out of his arse and still embed itself in the ground!' Julian allowed a sideways glance presenting Gerry with a mildly bemused expression though to be fair he was no more well-informed to challenge the stupendous statement.

Gerry caught the glance. 'See, not so scary now is it, bruv.'

And he was quite right. It was somehow possible to acclimatise yourself to being in or on very unfamiliar and challenging terrain if you allowed yourself to. Despite this realisation Julian continued to ponder why anyone would normally want to put themselves in such a sketchy predicament.

Gerry leant forward encouraging a globule of saliva to ooze slowly off his bottom lip, carefully controlling its release before allowing it to begin its unstoppable and accelerating descent. He monitored the fluid's speeding fall; it's swirling, it's twisting, it's breaking up into smaller particles until it finally disappeared from view.

Julian heard him clear his nasal passages with a deep snort and hawk as he pulled more phlegm up into his throat and in to his mouth before starting the firing sequence again.

Julian joined in. He found himself hypnotised by the different shapes the flob made and the unique path of flight it took as his spittle made its way down to terra firma.

From that day Julian came to understand why Gerry found solace and peace up there on their own private roof terrace. He himself grew to enjoy the escape of spending time there; hanging out, sunbathing, listening and chatting to Gerry without interference, interruption or threat from others.

He became more and more confident, joining Gerry on his mad, death defying jaunts around the precipice and gaining his high altitude flobbing certificate.

It was there up on the roof of the block that they would regularly discuss with growing enthusiasm the rumblings of the pioneering sound emanating from Coventry.

Gerry always picked up new information from his furtive forays into the newsagents. He would pop in every day where he would read as much of the New Musical Express paper as he could before being ejected to his great amusement by the shop owners.

Julian noticed that Gerry's block was much more exposed than his own.

Being on the periphery of the estate, Gerry's maisonette was one of those that skirted its outer circumference; it could act like part of an enormous grey windbreak protecting the more central blocks from the buffeting autumn and winter winds and the driving side-ways rain that often came with them.

Gerry had an annoying habit of taking three steps at a time as they climbed the exterior fire escape to the fourth floor where he lived. This left Julian chasing his shadow, playing catch up as he disappeared around each ninety-degree turn and onto the next flight.

His head spun, dizzy with exertion.

He heard the loud groan of the heavy glassed door, its industrial-strength closer arm complaining through years of poor lubrication, as Gerry shoved his way in to the corridor.

He caught up with Gerry as he ambled along the fluorescent-lit hall.

Virtually identical in lay-out and décor to Julian's own communal dwelling, the walls boasted similar, impulse-driven and banal graffiti.

'suck my cock'.

'Jackie woz ere '79'.

'Deano is queer'.

Julian wondered who the hell Deano and Jackie were. Maybe Deano wanted Jackie to suck his cock? No, apparently he was queer.

Nonsense.

The flooring was the same dull red cigarette-pocked marble-effect linoleum in his block and the whole interior bore the evidence of the superficial vandalism of the bored generation; scratched, marked, gouged, poked and spat at.

Gerry turned the key in the lock of another non-descript light-wood door, the frayed lace from which he hung the key from his neck was wrapped around his turnip-sized fist.

He stepped over and into his home, leaving the door ajar and Julian stood on the threshold. Julian was always told to wait to be invited in. It was habit.

He eyed the aluminium letterbox identical in design to that on his own front door apart from the different black numbers; Gerry lived at number 125.

'Come in you muppet!' Gerry's voice beckoned from within. The echo-like sound hinted at the interiors hollowness.

Julian stepped into the poorly lit hallway and immediately his nostrils began to itch, irritated by a lingering smell of stale cigarette smoke and full ashtrays.

Walking into the lounge, he scanned quickly looking for furniture and everyday living. There were a couple of threadbare armchairs.

A chair was skirted by a solid glass ashtray advertising John Bull bitter which was full to overflowing with cigarette butts, a couple of days' worth of carelessly-folded newspapers and an assortment of chipped mugs with the dried-up dregs of strong tea encrusted in their bottoms.

A heavy brown television set was sat, looking important, on top of a white melamine bedside cabinet. The cabinet's door was hanging on to the last over-loaded hinge, bent and twisting in desperation.

The browns and oranges of the room's mid-seventies décor were faded, the original boldness having been hidden beneath years of nicotine-staining, mould-infestation and unrestrained sunlight.

A couple of forlorn-looking and greying net curtains hung lop-sided in the window space. Some would have called it the minimalist look.

'Sit down, mate.' Gerry called out from the kitchen. ' I'm just knockin' up some grub. D'ya want anything ? '

'Can I have a drink please mate?' Julian glanced back at the unwashed cups on the floor and feeling parched after the hike across the estate decided he would risk it anyway.

'No problem, mate. Sure you don't want some beans and cheese on toast? ' Gerry poked his head around the doorframe joining the two rooms. 'It's me speciality!'

Julian felt his stomach gurgle. The portion of chips he had devoured around lunchtime had long ago been spent in his body's furnace.

He caved. 'Yes please.'

It all felt odd. Nobody under the age of twenty-five had ever cooked Julian dinner before. It would have been polite to offer to set the table but there was no table. He guessed he would have to wash up afterwards instead.

The meal was a taste sensation. The hot beans melted the strong cheddar cheese, the stringy goo mingling with the sweet, orangey tomato sauce that had soaked into the thick-buttered white toast.

Julian offered to wash the dishes but Gerry was insistent that Julian stay put, switching the television on for him before going into the kitchen. 'Blimey mate, it'll only take me a minute, just two plates an' a saucepan.'

The local news was on but Julian did not take much notice. He felt a bit conspicuous sitting by himself in the lounge.

Just as he thought about joining Gerry in the kitchen he heard the front door open. There was the scuffling of movement and the thumps of someone kicking off heavy footwear from the small entrance hallway. A deep cough followed by throaty man's voice echoed out from the hall.

'Alright, son?' Came the enquiry, 'Get the kettle on will yuh!'

The dark, stocky physique of Gerry's dad shoved open the lounge door. He stopped in the doorway, raised his eyebrows at Julian for a moment before stepping fully in to the lounge.

'Well, who've we got 'ere then?'

Julian stood up from the armchair which was a real feat as the seating had long ago lost any support and had swallowed his puny rear end in to its bowels.

Offering a handshake the man introduced himself to Julian. Julian's milk-white skinny hand was enveloped in the man's warm, calloused palm. Strong black hairs carpeted the back of his hand from the wrist to the knuckles; the man smelt strongly of cigarettes and damp, musty clothing.

'Very pleased to meet your acquaintance, young man!' He raised his voice for Gerry's benefit. 'Nice to meet someone with manners.' Stan winked at him.

Julian guessed that Stan was in his early fifties despite the youthful and thick head of hair, a legacy of which Gerry had certainly inherited.

He wore a surprisingly clean, pale-blue work-shirt and a pair of striped braces clipped on his jeans 'Sit yourself down, son. No need to stand on ceremony 'ere.'

Stan cast his eye around the floor area. ''Scuse the mess. I weren't expectin' company.'

Stan bent by the armchair hooking up all the cups with his index finger. Julian spotted the chunky and ornate silver rings rattling against the china. There was a fox head on one and a thick belt buckle design on another.

'Why didn't you tidy up, Gerry?' Stan called out in light reprimand.

Gerry appeared between the door frame drying his soapy hands with a tea towel.

'He don't mind. Do yuh?' Gerry nod towards Julian.

'No, of course not!' And it was true, Julian never minded.

Gerry threw the tea towel back in the kitchen before heading for the hallway and bounding up the stairs. 'Won't be a minute, nature calls.'

'Same time, every day!' Stan enlightened.

Julian wrinkled his nose. Stan chuckled, his upper body giving a short shimmy.

'So where d'you live then? '

'Over at Sycamore.' Julian watched as Stan settled down into the other chair after he had the plonked the cups down in the kitchen.

He had slipped his braces down off his shoulders with his thumbs so that they hung around the seat of his jeans.

'Oh yeah, so you're from the rough side of the estate, are yuh?' Stan grinned as he pulled a pack of Embassy number 6 from his shirt chest pocket, teasing one of the stubby cigarettes out of the pack with his lips.

He flicked the lid of a pewter coloured Zippo lighter. Julian caught the pungent vapour of lighter fluid.

'We've moved in with Joe, Joe Walcott. You probably know him; he's lived here for a long time.'

Stan gave a short laugh. 'Oh, I know who you mean, Joe, short bloke about six foot six, skinny with a weight problem, bald with hair down to 'ere!' He tapped his shoulder with his fingertips to emphasise his point.

'I'm just teasing, son. Do you know how many people live on this estate? '

'No I don't.'

'Nor do I,' Stan admitted, ' but suffice to say, it's bloody thousands.' He dragged on his number 6. 'Jeez, I hardly know me neighbours.' He let out a long plume of smoke. 'What does Joe do for a living? '

'He drives; drives delivery trucks. '

'Locally? '

'Yes, I think so.' Julian was vague. He had never really spoken with Joe about his work.

'Whereabouts?

'I don't know. ' Julian shrugged his shoulders self-consciously. 'Sorry.'

He gazed absentmindedly as Stan took another long drag of his cigarette, his attention was held by the inch-long length of grey ash that clung to the white stick. It curled downwards and yet seemed to defy gravity and fate.

Stan broke the spell as he deftly flicked the orange butt of the cigarette, decapitating the head of ash and dispensing it into the glass ashtray perched on the arm of the chair.

'Suppose you'll be studying for yuh exams soon?'

Gerry had reappeared in the doorway.

'Yeah, he will be, he's a boff though!' Gerry interrupted.

Gerry often teased him about school work and Julian had never quite worked out if being described as a boffin was a good thing. The adults he knew seemed to think it was a compliment but the other lads at school just wanted to flush his head down the toilets.

Julian did not consider himself a boffin. He laughed good-naturedly.

Julian knew that Gerry struggled with academic pursuits. It was a boredom thing certainly not a lack of intelligence. His attention would waver and he would gaze out of the window or read a music paper he had brought in. He was often caught by teachers and any intervention would spiral as Gerry retaliated with sarcasm and non-compliance.

He was not thick or work-shy, his basic maths and literacy were fine but lessons were torture for him. An hour lesson for Gerry was fifty minutes too long.

Despite having to endure the embarrassment of getting called out of the main classes to be cooped up in a glorified cupboard with a well-meaning but patronising special needs teacher, who tried different methods to get Gerry to focus more energy to his schoolwork, he had still yet to complete a project or hand in a piece of homework. When he did hand something in, his handwriting looked like a spider staggering on crutches across the page and Julian had often wondered if this was down to Gerry being left-handed.

Detentions, which Gerry hardly ever attended, and summonses to the head's office were common place.

'C'mon boff,' Gerry was sliding into his jacket, 'let's go an' mug some old grannies!'

Gerry ducked the crumpled cigarette packet missile Stan had thrown at him. Julian excused himself.

'Nice to 'ave met you son, maybe you can educate young Gerry 'ere how to stay out of trouble in the future.'

That is one hell of a responsibility, Julian thought. He joined Gerry making his way out of the front door. That was one responsibility that he was not confident of upholding.

'Don't be too late home, son.'

'Sure, Dad '

Julian felt the affection in their exchange.

Unexpectedly yanked sideways Julian yelped as the Air-wair soles of his boots gouged and twisted in the rough hide of the concrete surface. A dark shadow exploded to his right with a loud, deep pop. Way too close for comfort.

Gerry let go of his sleeve.

Julian stared at the crumpled bin bag hearing it wheeze as previously trapped air squeezed out through impact-torn holes and splits. The shiny black skin spilled its guts out on to the ground like a hurriedly disembowelled carcass. Chicken bones, soiled disposable nappies and the jagged remains of a tomato sauce bottle hung from the tears.

The detritus of everyday life.

Mixed smells of excrement, food rot and emptied ash trays wafted into the surrounding air space.

'Jesus!' Julian looked upwards, 'That could have killed me!'

The stacked balconies of St Francis block appeared uninhabited, odd pieces of laundry fluttered like flags of surrender over the rails in the high breeze that tickled the uppermost sections of the tall blocks.

No faces checked outwards, guiltily, concernedly or otherwise, from the occasional open window that he could see.

'You were lucky, mate!' Gerry seemed unfazed by the aerial assault, 'I've seen armchairs an' allsorts lobbed out.'

'Oh, that's bloody alright then!' Julian looked up instinctively, checking for the atom bomb of furniture being released from on high; maybe a fridge freezer or soiled mattress this time. He was pleased to find the sky above them empty apart from a squawking gathering of seagulls that had spotted the gutted remains of the bin bag.

'They can't be bothered to drag stuff down the stairs, especially when the lifts out of order.'

Julian looked again at the sprawled remains as they walked away leaving the seagulls to their fill.

Gerry offered final insight.

'I expect the rubbish chute was full up.'

'Buster he sold the heat,'

'with a rock steady beat.'

The nutty boys from Camden Town sounded great if a little tinny on the old record player Julian's mum had bought for him from the local junior school's jumble sale.

He was sprawled out on his back on the lumpy bed, topless, his jeans hung low on his waist.

He was trying to dry off after getting a rare and long soak in the bath; rare because waiting for the immersion heater to get hot again after someone else had been in the bath meant a lengthy wait and even then the water often turned out to be lukewarm.

The hot, humid summer air that circulated around him in the room caused sweat beads of moisture to appear on his body hindering the attempted drying process.

Occasionally a welcome cool breeze would waft into the room through the aluminium framed windows he had opened wide which helped to temporarily lower the intensity of the close, stifling climate within.

His hands were linked behind the back of his head and he found his hips gyrating in rhythm with the irresistible beat coming from the miniature single speaker sound system.

With their unique take on the ska revival sound, Madness had created another hybrid by adding, what sounded to Julian like, traditional fairground music into the mixing pot. He had taken a liking to this jovial bunch of Londoners and their first 2 Tone release.

As the forty-five rpm single came to an end, he heard the first sirens.

Not an unusual sound around the estate, he did not stir from his position initially preferring to continue his relaxation but within minutes the wailing sirens had multiplied becoming more apparent and definitely closer.

He began to identify raised voices and the sound of human and vehicle movement. The estate had that odd characteristic of amplifying whatever noise was being made, the noise rebounding off the high, flat-sided buildings, the masonry refusing to absorb the sound waves and instead bouncing them back with a vengeance.

God help you if you were trying to sleep and a young lady begun screeching and brawling with her often drunken aggressive male or female escort at two o'clock in the morning.

Julian's curiosity got the better of him, prompting him to raise his still damp, lethargic figure off the bed and pad barefoot across the tacky tiled floor to the window.

He hung his upper torso out of the opening to get the best view he could.

There were a lot of people milling about in groups and chatting excitedly, all animated expressions and body language. Kids and teenagers had stopped their football matches and others had brought their bicycles to rest as they sat astride them and surveyed the scene from ground level. Something was definitely up.

He noticed an abnormally high amount of emergency vehicles; ambulances, police cars and fire engines, some parked up and others arriving. Uniformed servicemen moved amongst the vehicles. He saw policemen trying to herd groups of people away from the scene. Whatever had happened they did not want anyone close. The crowd's hard-done-by whinging was apparent even as high up as he was.

He could not see or smell smoke and that quickly discounted fire in one of the blocks.

He wondered if a lift had broken down trapping inside its steel casing whoever was using it at the time but there were too many police and firemen around for it to have been such a common and boring occurrence as that.

He could see policemen unfurling plastic ribbon around the base of Camomile block as if to fence off the area or keep whatever it was in.

It was no good he had to investigate.

Pulling on a t-shirt and slipping on his old training sneakers that were close to hand he was soon out of the front door and headed across the estate to where all the commotion was taking place.

He quickly spotted Gerry sat ungracefully on the surrounding brickwork of one of the large planters. The planters were filled with quite robust but unattractive bushes and shrubs which, starved of essential nutrients, never seemed to flower.

He held up a hand in greeting.

'What's going on?' Julian motioned with his chin in direction of the activity.

'Melanie Barcroft killed herself.'

'How do you know that? ' Julian leant on an elbow next to Gerry..

''cause she's lying over there.'

And it was a matter of fact.

'What's left of her is anyway.' He nodded towards a couple of scruffy urchins perched on the skeletal remnants of their Raleigh Grifter bicycles. 'Those two told me they saw her land.'

He pointed his chin towards the larger group of youths, the match ball tucked tightly under a tall ones arm. 'They reckon they heard it. Said it was loud, like a cannon going off .' Julian wondered what a cannon going off would sound like.

'You mean she jumped off ?' Julian looked up to the blocks apex.

'Yep. Twenty one stories, all the way down without stopping, without passing go, without collectin' two hundred sovs.' (For 'sovs'; see 'notes', pound notes.)

'Why did she do that? That's horrendous.'

Julian looked towards the bustling scene of the apparent suicide in quiet shock, unable to comprehend the enormity of what he was hearing and seeing.

He knew he did not want to see anything. His mind was already morbidly fantasising, imagining allsorts.

Imagining her limbless body; all flayed and lacerated by the impact; her appendages scattered around its frame, legs, arms and head separated from her torso.

He imagined the scene as a formless blob of blood, just a mass of flesh and guts pulped into an unrecognisable mush by her impact with the cheese-grater concrete below.

He tried to erase the thoughts from his head.

'Wasn't she a druggie or something?' He looked for a reason for such a violent act.

'Yeah, a skag head.'

Julian knew Gerry would know, he knew almost every character on the estate.

'I think she was a prozzy an' all.' Gerry's description of Melanie as a heroin-addicted prostitute seemed over-simple and flippant but real all the same.

Even though he knew that Melanie was no longer able to take exception to their discussion, Julian felt intrusive, disrespectful, and insensitive even. He felt decidedly uncomfortable with the subject matter. Heroin and prostitution were yesterday's news to many but it was all still quite new and shocking to him.

'I always felt a bit sorry for her really.' Gerry reflected.

Melanie had always looked a bit lost and vulnerable when they had seen her around the estate. Always seemed to either be on the verge of crying or looked like she had been. Her expressions suggested a pain that was both physical and emotional.

Her body's posture belied her youth. Her limbs were tight and inward, her shoulders rounded and her arms tucked in at her sides. This gave her a foetus-like appearance.

She was always stopping people and asking for a light, her hand trembling as she held the remnants of a wrinkled cigarette at a hover around her thin, dry, cracking lips.

Gerry let out a small sigh. 'She was just a victim, I suppose. Blokes used and abused her. She was always getting beaten up by boyfriends and punters, always sportin' a shiner or cut lip and that's just the injuries that you could see I reckon.'

Julian remembered seeing Melanie with black eyes and bruises though he had never pondered as to how they got to be there. He felt some guilt, some regret and an odd sense of loss.

'Have you seen a suicide before?' He looked sideways at Gerry.

'No. Not around 'ere. There's been others, on other estates I think but not 'ere, not in my time anyway.'

'Do you think she's in one piece?' Julian was unnerved; his imagination was still too active for his liking.

Gerry pondered the question for a moment. 'Dunno, but I bet it's not a pretty sight.' Gerry went quiet, thoughtful even.

All sorts of questions were flooding into Julian's head.

'Do you think she had family?'

'Not sure but she was only young weren't she, so chances are there's someone out there who's related or knows her well.' Gerry paused, 'At least, I hope there's someone, somewhere, who cared a bit, just someone to go to her funeral an' that. It wouldn't be nice if no-one turned up would it? '

'No it wouldn't.' Julian agreed.

The police had managed to successfully cordon off the area around the ground floor and the rubber neckers and nosey parkers had been eased back albeit reluctantly to allow the services to do whatever it was that they had to do. A canopy had been quickly erected over the body of Melanie to allow the investigation and clear-up operation to be carried out with some sort of dignity and without interference from prying eyes.

'Blimey! I've just had a thought.'

Gerry looked across at Julian expectantly, waiting.

'I bet they've found the way we get on to the roof,' the whinge escaped from Julian's mouth with his usual blatant lack of sufficient thought. 'They'll go and fix it now, won't they.' He whined on.

Gerry shook his head with pursed lips. Then with an obvious disappointed air, he stood and stepped away from Julian before turning back.

'That was a down right dick'ead thing to say. I never had you down as a selfish bastard Jules.'

Reprimand administered, Gerry strutted off without looking back, leaving Julian to reflect on his moment of insensitivity.

Julian was left alone to wrestle with his gutful of discomfort and to wonder if Gerry would ever speak to him again.

They were sitting together on the sofa watching nothing in particular when Julian sloped through the front door that evening.

Not exactly 'nothing in particular' to be fair. The vibrant blue screen was emitting a surreal glow over the low lit lounge. Julian squinted to focus on the writing across the blue sheet of nothingness.

'ITV apologise for the lack of programmes due to industrial action.'

He gazed at his parents for some form of explanation. Joe looked up from his crossword.

''Ello mate. Had a good day?'

Julian nodded confirmation despite having spent the most boring and uneventful day on his own.

The day had dragged and stretched after Gerry had left him by the planter allowing him far too much time to think and ponder depressing and banal thoughts.

He had missed Gerry's company, his enthusiasm, wit and endless itinerary. His absence had gnawed at Julian's gut making him nauseous. Eating had been impossible, he had no appetite. He had wandered back and forth across the estate in the closeness of the dry, hot summer day like a lost foreign legionnaire trying to find the oasis.

He had deliberately avoided the area where Melanie Barcroft had brutally and desperately parted company with her own life that morning and where he had upset Gerry.

He had played out different scenarios in his stupid, thoughtless mind, trying to think of ways he could make things up with Gerry. Only his childish embarrassment and fear of rejection had stopped him from knocking on Gerry's front door and apologising for being a dickhead.

It was only after the hours of solitary reflection had frazzled his brain and given him one massive headache that he realised that Gerry would not expect an apology for his selfish comments. Julian offered that to Melanie instead, choosing a moment to look up high in to the heavens.

'I'm sorry!' He bellowed and he meant it.

He hoped there was a heaven after all and that she was being better looked after up there. He hoped she was at peace.

'No programmes on ITV, they're on strike.' His mum smiled at him.

'Why don't you watch BBC then?' Julian offered the obvious.

'Nothing on at the moment.' And Joe wasn't joking.

Later that night as Julian lay awake desperately trying to find some solace in sleep that would not come, the happenings of the day tormenting his over-stimulated mind. He ruminated.

Surely if anyone required salvation it was the poor, the vulnerable, the ill, the tortured, the wasted. Where were the churches? Where were the sanctuaries? Where were the safe havens? Where were the bosoms of comfort and hearts of unquestioning benevolence?

He kicked at the claustrophobic tangle of sheet and bedspread that strangled his lower limbs. His eyes involuntarily searched the darkness of his room, wide open and alert, refusing to close and award him the safety of sleep.

His heartbeat and racing thoughts were his only company that long night, deafeningly loud and torturous.

He racked his brain trying to remember if he had seen a church or place of worship near the estate. He could think of none.

Had God forsaken this place?

'Alright mate? Where you off to then? ' Gerry's long-legged stride was an attribute to be envied. His cadence must have eaten up Julian's puny pigeon steps with ease as he had caught him up.

Julian's previous stupidity had obviously been forgotten or forgiven, maybe both. Julian felt relieved, Gerry's convivial air nullifying Julian's initial flush of embarrassment.

'Got to go and get my hair cut.' He ruffled his unruly mane with the palm of his hand.

'Hey!' Gerry's eyebrows lifted. 'So 'ave I. Dad's orders. Said I look like a bleedin' hippy. We can give each other some moral support,' Gerry grinned, 'and we can take the pee out of each other !' Gerry was a dab hand at lightening what could have a chore.

'What you gonna 'ave done then? '

Julian felt his cheeks redden again. He fiddled with the cutting in his trouser pocket he had surreptitiously torn out of that months Jackie magazine in the newsagents that morning.

'I'm not really sure, I wouldn't mind something a bit different from the short, back 'n' slap I usually end up with though.'

'Yeah, I reckon you should go for a Suggsy would suit you.' Gerry alluded to the flat-top cropped style of the lead singer of Madness, Suggs otherwise known as Graham McPherson.

'Really?' Was Gerry ribbing him? How could he have possibly known? Julian pulled the scrap of magazine out of its hiding place.

'What about a Chas Smash?' He passed Gerry the small picture of Carl Smythe,

the master of ceremonies and on-stage nutty dancer from Madness. Not quite Suggs but close.

Gerry seriously studied the creased image; he looked back at Julian, tilted his head slightly then returned his attention back to the picture before giving me him the eagerly-awaited verdict. 'Yeah, I think that would really suit you mate.'

Julian's apprehension about his choice of coiffeur disappeared with Gerry's thumbs up.. He felt more relaxed now he had the vote of confidence from Gerry. It was a huge decision to make after all. He did not want to look like a knob.

Gerry pulled a piece of scrunched piece of paper from his own pocket and offered the fluff-adorned picture for Julian's inspection. The pictures sheen had been depleted by too much finger-tip sweat but the image was instantly recognisable. Terry Hall stared out at Julian; serious, unsmiling, stony-faced.

'D'yuh think I could carry off a Terry?'

The jangle of bell alerted the Greek owners of the barber shop to their arrival.

With a wave of a hand and a dip of the shoulders they directed them to wait their turn. The boys plonked themselves down on to long black vinyl-covered bench seating. Both barbers were busy styling a couple of follicle-challenged elder statesmen who had hair that lay in waves across the top of their heads in a style reminiscent of corrugated cardboard.

Suitably seated, Gerry picked up the copy of the Racing Post trying to find names of horses that were double entendres for their amusement while they waited.

The smell of sucked mints and medicated shampoo wafted around the shop. Julian nudged Gerry and discretely brought his attention to a cardboard advertisement for Durex condoms; a left-over relic from the early seventies judging by the man in the pictures hair-style and the flare of his shirt collar.

Other portraits that hung crookedly on the walls seemed even more ancient; the black and white portraits being damp-stained and yellowed by years of hanging around.

'Yes boys.' Both of the brothers barber gestured for them to take a seat in the prospective chairs.

Julian spied Gerry advising Steve, quite a John Belushi look-alike. Steve was squinting at the picture he had handed to him, lifting his glasses and replacing them as if to focus more clearly while Gerry tried to make his wishes clear.

Julian was glad that Andy, his John Travolta wannabe, did not wear glasses but then wondered if maybe he should when he flicked a vinyl cape sending hair trimmings all over him.

Andy cranked the chair up to a workable height. Julian handed him his picture of Chas.

'He's a handsome, yes?' Julian guessed that he meant that Chas was a good looking fellow.

'Err, yes, I suppose he is.' Of one thing Julian was certain; Andy's English was better than his Greek.

'Can you do my hair like that?' Julian prodded the picture emphasising his point.

Julian searched Andy for some affirmation, some recognition, as he busied himself plugging in the clippers.

'No problema.' Andy fitted a graded guard to the heavy electric clippers before switching them on. His whole arm seemed to vibrate, his heavy gold identity bracelet jangling on his tanned wrist.

He did not glance at the picture again.

Exiting the shop Julian's scalp tingled with exposure. He looked at Gerry's grade four all-over crop. Julian decided he looked like a dark-brown tennis ball.

'It is a sort of Terry Hall I suppose.' Julian offered diplomatically.

Gerry was rubbing the bristly fuzz, sending tiny hair trimmings out in a spray like grass shooting out the back of a lawn mower.

Julian looked hard at his own reflection in the shop window, the tiny remnants of shorn hair felt like thorns as they irritated the skin of his neck.

He also sported a grade four all-over crop, almost identical to Gerry's bar a difference in hair colour.

Gerry gave his new style the once-over, slightly nodding his head knowingly as he circled him.

'Yeah,' He finally offered. 'looks cool.'

He really was a good mate, was Gerry.

The walk home from school could take any amount of time. They tended to amble homewards at a leisurely snail-like pace, chatting, singing and generally fooling around.

Normally it was just Julian and Gerry that kept each other company but sometimes they were caught up by Mo.

They did not mind Mo and it was quite nice to have alternative entertainment for a change. Anyway both agreed, Mo was a laugh a minute and he loved 2 Tone.

His insights into the school day were hilarious. The tales of his encounters with various psychopaths and frustrated teaching staff were Monty Python-esque, his feigned naivety and simplistic outlook setting him up for bizarre misunderstandings.

Bullies avoided Mo. He could twist them up in knots with surreal responses to their aggressive approaches. They obviously found it easier to find someone they could understand to steal dinner money from. It was a great defence mechanism even if it was not meant to be.

Gerry and Julian loved it when Mo exaggerated his inherited Pakistani accent. He would wobble his head as he gave a big cheesy grin while performing in his best broken English.

Mo was British-born with Pakistani heritage; second generation. He spoke excellent English with a hint of accent. Mo had explained that his mother spoke no English so they spoke Urdu in the home.

At that time, those in the community of Pakistani origin were seen by many as the runts of the litter. Amongst the population of the estate, not many made them welcome. Many treated them with utter contempt, complaining about them, insulting them even assaulting them and their property.

They had become the scapegoats, easy targets, for whatever ills an individual may be experiencing.

The prejudice did not come solely from the white British, not many of the black community integrated with the Asians either.

Julian and Gerry did not care about any of that, they had no axes to grind and they liked having Mo around even if with hindsight it was his self-deprecating humour that got the loudest laughs.

He was never allowed out after school.

'Got school.' He had informed them when they had invited him out one evening.

'But you've been at school all day!' The thought of more classes made both boys baulk.

'No this is different type of school. It's studies.' Mo looked a bit uncomfortable by the inquisition.

'What do you study then?'

'Qu'ran.'

'What?' Julian should have been more attentive during religious education lessons.

'It's our bible, we have to learn it by going to study classes; it's part of our religion. We go to classes in the mosque and sometimes teachers set up study classes in their homes.'

'So you're a Muslim, aren't you?' Maybe Julian had learnt something after all. He had some knowledge of world religion, it could hardly be avoided. He knew that the national religion of Pakistan was Islam. Joe had told him that.

'Yeah. Allah, is our God, and we follow the prophet Mohammed. Peace be upon him.'

'So 'ave you got a bird lined up then?' Gerry chimed in.

'What? I don't get what you mean.'

Gerry explained himself. 'Arranged marriage an' all that. Do you already know who you're gonna 'ave to get married to when you leave school?'

Mo grinned. 'Not yet, but probably, yeah, my family will try and find me a suitable wife.'

'Jesus!' Gerry grimaced. 'Don't you get a choice? What if she's ugly or something?'

'No!' Mo chuckled at Gerry's concern. 'It don't work like that man! They'll find suitable matches then I get to check them out before anything gets decided. I get the final say. My family would want me to be happy, it's not a forced thing.'

Gerry nodded resignedly. 'Suppose it saves spending a load of dosh taking a bird out an' all that only to get left on the doorstep without reachin' first base!'

As the group walked on, Julian could not contain the burning impulse to ask the one question he had been dying to ask Mo ever since starting at Oakfield.

He bit the bullet and fired away.

'Why does Mr Devers call you a mummy and daddy's boy when he calls register?'

Gerry erupted with laughter, a grin stretched across Mo's narrow, brown face spreading his fledgling moustache across his upper lip.

Embarrassment and confusion scrambled Julian's thoughts; his face must have been a picture.

Mo slapped Julian across the shoulders.

'That's my name you idiot!' He explained. 'Mohammed Dhadabhouy.'

Gerry was not looking at Julian as he handed him the one foot square piece of card over for his perusal.

Sat on Gerry's bed, the wavy strands of the yellow candlewick bedspread the wavy threads plucked and pulled bare by bored hands, Julian held the record cover lightly; as if it represented something so precious. The light from the naked cobwebbed bulb dangling from the ceiling reflected in its semi glossy surface.

Gerry had already taken out the circular slab of lustrous black vinyl and placed it on the chunky wooden-bodied turntable. He lowered the stylus on to the 12 inch disc's run in and plonked himself next to Julian.

Julian stared intently at the record cover in his hands.

It was so mesmerising in its black and white simplicity. No fancy or bright colours to distract the eye.

No clever or ornate lettering, just a bold statement of fact.

A chequer board detail led into strong open block lettering.

Specials.

Julian and Gerry had been following The Specials since hearing the group's debut single called earlier that year.

They had eagerly awaited the release of the group's first long player. They had devoured any information about the band and the 2 tone movement like a pair of starving waifs around the bins.

They had developed a style; a rude boy style and attitude.

By encouraging each other and gaining confidence from the others qualification they did all they could to dress differently; desperate to stand out, to make their mark. Shortening their jeans and trousers to expose their socks and after much begging; after convincing their parents that they would make sensible school footwear they had got a pair of black Dr Martens each.

Their hair was short, cropped and they turned their school ties skinny-side out to make them narrow; rude boy style.

Julian was immediately taken aback by the glaring omission of their first hit.

'Gangsters' was missing from the track listing.

He liked it so he thought it an odd decision but also a rather brave and rather cavalier thing to do.

He felt a little cheated, sold short.

At least he owned the 45.

The list of tracks sprawled down the right hand side of the sleeve almost to the bottom; simple typography but memorable in its directness.

There was just enough space in the bottom right hand corner of the sleeve for the logo that would become his colours; his standard, his flag, colours to which he would swear allegiance.

The badge he would wear with pride.

2 Tone records.

The crackle and pop of the needle run-in woke him from his musings. He lifted his head. The harmonica intro made the few hairs on his body stand to attention.

The drum roll rat-a-tat beckoned in the blasts of the trombone, trumpet and horn.

'Stop your messing around'

The deep voice that sung was most definitely British but tinged with a strong hint of West Indian lilt.

'Time you straightened right out.'

A Message To You Rudy.

Track one; side one of The Specials debut long player.

As Julian gained some musical knowledge of his own, he would discover that 'Rudy' was in fact another cover song. A cover of an early reggae release by a Jamaican singer called Dandy Livingstone. Dandy's music had been popular with the original skinheads and West Indian community in the late sixties and early seventies.

The Specials penchant for the original sound of Jamaican music was glaringly obvious; its influence was smeared across the long player's contents.

Eventually released as a single from the album that October, Rudy would climb to number 10 in the pop charts.

Still, none of that meant anything to Julian that day.

Like Gerry he fell in further.

He felt like he was listening to and experiencing a direct message, a personal message to him through the miracle of stereo.

He was being baptised into the church of Two-Tone. He was to be a monochrome warrior, a disciple of the prophets Dammers, Hall, Staple, Golding, Radiation, Panter and Bradbury.

A message to Julian, Rudy.

He focused on the cover of the album again.

A more rough and tough looking bunch would have been hard to find. Looking like recently released prisoners in sixties style suits they looked back up at him with serious and disdainful expressions. Five white men and two black, just like the cover, black and white together, like hard and soft, hot and cold, yin and yang, they complemented each other, all about the balance, he thought.

A couple of the group had their hands in their suit jacket pockets, another appeared to be just about to take his dark shades off, one of the black men looked quite menacing, some wore trilby type hats but it was the younger looking man at the front of the group who demanded Julian's attention.

His eyes were dark, he looked like he had eyeliner or something on and he had the kind of stare that made people feel nervous, like he didn't care what anyone else thought, like he was at odds with all and the world.

Julian turned to the back of the sleeve, his eyes scanning to the bottom where he read the names of the band members; Horace, Terry, Neville, Jerry, Roddy, Lynval and Brad.

Terry - vocals.

His guess being that was who old scary eyes would be. He found it difficult to match the others from the list to their pictures as much as he pondered.

That electrifying and all enveloping sound as Julian experienced right then was a raw blend; a blend of bouncy ska music of the sixties and the power punk of the seventies. Jamaican in its origin, ska was also known as Blue beat in Britain.

The earliest recorded mention of the word ska in print was in 1963; it being used in the title of a Tommy McCook forty-five released on Island records called 'Ska-ba'.

The origins of this sound were in the imported rhythm and blues of the United States to Jamaica encouraging those resourceful Jamaicans to manipulate the structure to form their own home-grown dance music.

Now those vintage musical arrangements were being recycled and cleverly combined with the working class raucousness of punk-rock delivery and doused in youthful attitude for what was becoming a post-punk party.

The singers laidback delivery supported by the rhythmical toastings of another; an accompaniment that was almost conversational in style not sung, the machine gun stutter of the trebly rhythm guitar, the stabs of the mad eccentric electric organ and the beefy backbone of the brass ensemble all combined to hypnotise Julian through the unique and collected sound, hypnotising, mesmerising, until the blips and hops of the side coming to an end woke him. He watched the stylus lift off the record returning the arm to its cradle.

'D'yah wanna hear the other side?' asked Gerry.

Julian just nodded.

He heard them as they eased door open enough for them to access his dark room, its hinges squawked. The gap allowed a shaft of light to illuminate the space and they could make out Julian's comatose form buried beneath a jumble of sheets.

He first felt the cold hands wrap around his left ankle, goosebumps erupting on his skin as the impatient tugs began, jerking and yanking his legs exposing his uncovered flesh and thin striped pyjama bottoms to the frigid winter morning air. The sheets fell away from his body. A metallic crunch disturbed him from his slumber as the extra weight upon the mattress compressed and twisted the inner springs, lolling him across to the depression made in its surface. He smelt the Daz washing powder-infused flannelette and felt the heat of morning breath on his face.

'C'mon, get up Julian. It's Christmas day!' They on the bed bounced in time with each excited syllable.

Realisation bit, remembering his oft repeated hints as to what he would have liked Father Christmas to bring him that year, he was soon up out of his nest, ignoring the chill, the cold harshness of the bare floor and was chasing the two girls down into the lounge.

The hot air heating system was humming away in a sorry attempt to raise the temperature a couple of degrees, the waft from the louvered vent rustled the multi-coloured foil decorations hanging from the ceiling threatening to detach them from their drawing pin anchors.

The dimmer switch was set low giving the room a nice subdued light. Their parents entered; hair in disarray, cocooned in their dressing gowns.

They looked at the gold sun-burst clock fixed to the wall.

Seven o'clock in the morning, 25th December 1979. Christmas day.

'You lot might've waited 'till the sparrows got up!' Joe plonked himself on the sofa covering his modesty with the flaps of his gown.

'Robins not sparrows dad! It's Christmas silly!' Joe ruffled the girl's heads.

Doreen filled kettle in the kitchen, the kettle began its roar as she fished among the cutlery for a spoon. There was the loud rattle of metal on china as she gave the cups of tea a stir.

The girls dug out the brightly covered parcels from under the lop-sided tree threatening to topple it as they rooted around beneath its base.

Reading out the name on each of the labels they passed the presents to their respective recipients. Julian feigned his patience, trying to act cool, hiding his excitement, careful to avoid looking immature or silly. And yet inside he was full of anticipation, the nervous energy and expectation threatening to blow a hole in his chest.

What had Santa left for him?

'Yes, thank you, thank you, thank you!' Jessica, surrounded by the confetti of coloured wrapping paper, held the box to her chest. 'My own Tiny Tears!' Through the cellophane window the eyes of the ugly doll flicked up and down, open and shut as she tipped the box back and forth. She scuffled across the corded carpet eager to display her appreciation with a kiss and a hug for Joe and Doreen.

'Go on then, son! Don't stand on ceremony.' Joe gave Julian a deft nudge.

Julian surveyed the three parcels in front of him unsure of which one to open first.

Two were labelled from 'mum and Joe' and the other one was from the girls.

He reached down and picked up the limpest and flattest of the three.

As he peeled the Sellotape off tearing a reindeers head free from its torso, his heart leapt as he caught a glimpse of the black cotton drill beneath it.

He tore the remainder of the covering off in one fell swoop; jumping to his feet he held the garment by the shoulders holding it up for all to see. It was impossible to hide his glee.

'Yes, yes, yes, thank you!'

His very own Harrington jacket complete with red woollen tartan lining.

He jumped on to the sofa, smothering his mum with kisses then flinging his arms around Joe's neck before realising what he was doing and quickly standing up and offering a handshake .

Joe grabbed him and pulled him into an embrace.

The two girls shook their heads, pulling faces at his display.

'It's only a jacket!' Jessica was not impressed.

'Hope it fits.' Doreen said. 'It doesn't look very warm. You'll freeze to death'

The infamous Harrington jacket; a proper design classic, an Ivy League staple.

A sports jacket. Light-weight in design, simple and yet timeless, smart and functional. Loads of lads had them and now he owned one too.

Julian stood in front of the full-length mirror fixed to the wardrobe in his parent's bedroom.

Slipping the new itchy lining over his bare torso felt fantastic. The jackets new uncreased stiffness hung off his shoulders perfectly.

Zipping the metal zipper up to within six inches of its full length and feeling the snug fit felt even more splendid.

He fiddled and unclipped the metal fastener on the small disc before placing it carefully on the left side of his chest and gently easing the pin through the new material, refastening it as it appeared back through.

Slipping his hands into each of the flapped, slanted pockets he checked himself.

His new jacket was finished off with a gleaming new 2 Tone records logo button badge. He had bought the badge nearly a month ago from a stall at the local Sunday market in anticipation of this day.

He felt like the luckiest and best-dressed person in the world at that moment.

And the jacket looked great with his striped pyjama bottoms!

Julian loved the Christmas holidays.

He knew that some liked to knock it but he enjoyed the build-up, the gaudy bright colours of the over-the-top decorations scattered through shops, schools and homes; the exotic and luxurious foods, jellied fruits, dates, nuts; seeing the bottles of spirits brought out of cupboards; the secrecy involved in buying, wrapping and hiding presents.

He even secretly liked the cheesy Christmas songs that were played to death and hearing his mum absent-mindedly singing along.

He looked forward to the ceremony of sitting at the table for an enduringly prepared roast dinner with the family, pulling crackers, reading the rubbish jokes, trading the toys and trinkets that flew out of the cardboard tubes as the explosive strip cracked and wearing the tissue paper crowns until the sweat of their foreheads made the colours run, staining their skin.

The family never missed the Top of the pops special. Joe revelled in the fact that 'the Floyd' were the Christmas number one that year with their haunting 'Another Brick In The Wall' and Julian was over the moon to get a glimpse of The Specials performing 'Rudy' in all their exuberant skanking glory.

The late afternoon he spent, as the adults relaxed and chatted drinking their choice of poison, listening to The Specials on his record player trying to drown out the clack of Tiny Tears eyes as she was put to bed and woken every quarter of an hour by his sisters.

He joined the family for the evening tea and traditional fun and games. They would have an intermission in the frolics to catch the Morecambe and Wise Christmas special His parents allowed him a sniff of a snowball or slosh of Joe's ale before well-stuffed and exhausted he retired to bed late, happy and contented, listening to the alcohol-fired hum of conversation and laughter among the adults left downstairs.

That year during lulls in the festivities his thoughts often drifted across the way.

As he sat admiring his new jacket; in the quiet straight after dinner; after he had watched The Specials; he thought of Gerry.

He wondered what Gerry would be doing. He wondered if he was enjoying the day, aware of the fact that it would be just the two of them opening their presents together that morning then most probably sitting on the sofa with their dinners on newspapers on their laps rather than at a set table.

Julian loved the day and all its trimmings but he could not help but look forward to tomorrow when he would be allowed out.

He could not wait to show Gerry his new jacket.

Julian knew that Gerry would be annoyed if he felt pity for them.

He remembered the day when Gerry had explained in one of the many conversations they had when they had first met that his mum had died two years previously; this being after a short and rapid decline of health to a particularly aggressive ovarian cancer.

He had spoken without bitterness. There was sadness evident in his eyes as he spoke but otherwise he showed no obvious anger or venom or unresolved issues.

Pictures of Carol were potted around their flat, on walls and the window sill. She looked healthy in them and pretty too. Julian had admired them; pictures of Carol dressed in mini-skirts in the sixties, getting married to Stan in a flowing white satin dress, holding baby Gerry.

Stan had continued with the responsibility of raising Gerry the only way he knew how; with uncomplaining independence.

A proud man he had 'never looked to the state for hand outs', 'never asked for charity'.

Gerry's grandparents on both sides had passed away before Carol had died. The men from complications in health; one of which had brought it home from the war. The women's demise was less clear but Julian wondered if it had been through exhaustion. Gerry's dad had described a very poor and tough childhood; long working hours in terrible factory conditions, trying to manage a home and family in challenging living conditions.

Stan continued to clock on at the factory where he operated enormous, deafening and incredibly dangerous multi-ton presses which stamped out parts for electrical fittings, fixtures and components.

Gerry by necessity had become a 'latch-key kid' overnight. His dad's shifts ensured that he rarely got home before six o'clock in the evening. The gaffers had been as accommodating as they could be with his rota but there was work to be done.

Stan would sometimes take the offered overtime particularly at Christmas when needs required it but it never sat right with him.

Gerry had quickly got used to the scribbled notes left on the side in the kitchen with suggestions for tea and the odd pound note left to get some milk and bread in. The notes always, without fail, ended with the sentiment; 'Love as always, dad, X '.

Gerry had never complained. Never, not once had Julian heard him complain.

A basic but capable cook, well-schooled by necessity, he could rustle up beans or sardines on toast easy enough before checking the washing pile and throwing a load in the machine if needed. He could do his bit.

Julian had come to admire and at times, envy his independence.

IV
Stereo-types. January '80

Was it the weather closing in? Joe wondered if it was thunder. He checked out through the grimy window scanning up at the clear skies, he frowned, not a dark cloud could be seen and yet he thudding persisted.

Joe concentrated his hearing detecting the muffled but unmistakable sound of music accompanying the dull repetitive noise.

He stepped in to the small lobby of the flat pausing at the bottom of the stairs. The racket was coming from one of the bedrooms and he knew which one.

Joe swung the door open to be halted in his tracks by the tinny distorted noise of a volume set to max and the disturbing sight of two bouncing-soled, Dr Marten clad youths hopping from one boot to the other in time with the jaunty beat.

The floors in the flats did not flex like a traditional wooden floorboards like you would find in an average terraced house. This fact allowed the record to play without the worry of the needle jumping and scratching the precious vinyl.

They came to a stuttering halt sweat beading off Gerry's forehead.

Julian could not tell if the glow on his cheeks was through the exertion of dancing or in embarrassment of being caught in the act of dancing.

'What the bleedin' 'ells going on 'ere!'

'We're dancing!' Julian shouted breathlessly back across the room.

'What?' Joe cupped his hand around his ear. Julian turned the music down.

'It's called the moon-stomp.' Julian handed Joe the cover of the extended player.

Joe glanced down at the record cover turning it over then back again. In his hands he held the latest release from The Specials, a live recording boasting the group at their best. Joe looked unimpressed.

The glossy cover was a shot from the stage, a black and white exposure of the audience at one of the gigs. The rude boys and skinheads were there in numbers.

The title track 'Too much too young' was a turbo-charged alternate take of the same-named but slower rendition off their debut album. It was a blunt-instrument attack, a reality check for listeners who dabbled in copulation without giving sufficient thought for consequences or considering contraception.

'You've done too much..'

'you're much too young..'

'you're married with a kid when you could be 'aving fun with me..'

'Oh no, no, no gimme, no more pickney!'

The other live recordings were covers of early reggae and ska classics, side one being recorded at the London Lyceum and the flip at Coventry's Tiffanys.

In the bands absence the single stormed to number one in the UK charts in the bands while they toured the United States.

Julian eagerly replaced the needle at the beginning of the 45.

'I wan' all you skin'eads, rudeboys, rudegirls, get up on yuh feet..'

'Put yuh braces together an' yuh boots on yuh feet..'

'An' give me some of that ol' moonstompin'.. '

Julian nodded towards the sleeve still in Joe's hands.

'Are you ready?' The master of ceremonies Neville Staple continued his introduction, winding up the audience.

'Yeah!' The crowd screamed back at him.

'Are you ready? ' He teased, imploring a louder response, building the crescendo.

'Yeah!' You could hear the anticipation and excitement in the voices.

'Start stompin'! '

Julian started stomping.

'I'll tell you what,' Joe whipped the needle off the record, he gestured with his thumb for emphasis, 'you can go an' bloody well moon stomp on the bloody moon, you noisy bloody buggers!'

'An allotment, that's what you need.'

Julian looked up from his lovely roast dinner; his mouth was full of sticky-skinned roast potato and sweet chicken infused with thick gravy all mashed together in a pulpy blend.

He liked having his grandparents over for Sunday lunch. He knew that his mum enjoyed seeing them both and particularly liked to spend time with his nan chatting and catching up while preparing the dinner for them all.

Julian looked over at Joe with raised eyebrows.

'Then you could grow your own veg and allsorts.' His grandad explained.

He watched as his grandad sliced into a plump potato impaling the morsel on his fork then layering it with vegetables and meat. It looked precariously balanced but with one swift movement he swung it up in a well-practised loop, up and into his mouth without losing any baggage.

Julian almost applauded.

'Just think, you'll save yourself money and have the reward of knowing that it was all cared for and nurtured by your own hands.' He stabbed at his peas. 'You can pick a cabbage and have it in the pot in less than an hour and you don't get much fresher than that, believe you me.' His grandad gestured with his fork spraying droplets of gravy over the table cloth in the process. 'Need to make a start soon mind you. Get 'em in before the summer.'

Joe had put down his knife and fork. His elbows were on the table and his fingertips touching forming a steeple. He rolled his tongue around his gums clearing the remnants of this dinner. Julian was sure he could hear Joe's cogs turning.

'That's another fine mess you've got me into, Stanley!' Gerry poked Julian in the shoulder. Julian grinned back at him. Gerry's dad Stan often referred to them as Laurel and Hardy or the 'dynamic duo' in reference to the superhero's Batman and Robin.

The nettle and bind-weed jungle before them looked impregnable. Forgotten bamboo canes poked out of the dense, tall growth like paralysed serpents, their forms strangled to rigidity by the relentless advance of the weed. Twine flapped from the poles like tentacles. Black car tyres lay scattered like sleeping pythons, their middles packed full with thick-stemmed greenery.

A shed, lopsided with age and timber-rot looked unreachable beyond the green curtain.

Julian glanced around. He looked across to where an Asian man was tending his own allotment. Neat rows of onion stalks stood at attention, the soil around their bases weed and stone-free. A row of long canes, angled and tied at the top formed a long upside-down vee. Young runner bean plants were wrapped around the lower portions of the structure. The man was fixing twine between the canes to support the climbers. He caught him looking and smiled. Julian self-consciously returned his smile.

'Shouldn't take long for two young stallions like you to hack through that lot, should it now? ' Julian's grandad was dressed for the weather. A thick anorak zipped to the neck and a woolly hat pulled over his ears. His navy and red striped braces hung loosely from the waistband of his tan coloured slacks. Julian wondered why he bothered with them; his trousers had stayed up without them. His grandad wiped at his nose with his handkerchief.

Julian studied the serrated bread knife in his hand with contempt. His hands were freezing. Gerry, who had won the toss of the coin, boasted an odd-shaped but quite lethal-looking gardening implement in his possession. He grinned at Julian.

'C'mon lightweight! We will soon warm up' With that, he swung the sickle in a wild arc chopping into the vegetation.

'Watch out for them adders!' Julian's grandad wheeled the barrow towards the whirling dervishes. 'They can get a bit tetchy this time of year! '

Julian knew it was meant as a tease but he could not stop himself looking around his ankles for signs of reptilian life.

'He's a right wind-up, your Grandad, ain't 'e?'

Gerry was right. They soon warmed enabling them to whip off their head gear and jackets, sweat chilled on their brows.

Julian's skin stung and angry red blotches appeared on his limbs. Checking his forearms the shapes were uncannily formed, like the countries on an atlas. Julian recognised one shaped like the Americas.

The plant-life was sinuous and tough. Left to grow unchecked it had thickened and hardened. It dragged at their slashes almost pulling the blades from their grips as it recoiled. It lashed at any exposed skin, snarling itself around their forearms and hands, leaving reddened welts in its place.

Some was sticky, some was coarse and some bled its green onto their bodies and jeans. Some was barbed and hooked. Some stung; any stings being heightened by their skins youthful sensitivity and the frigid air.

But the time flew by and it was with some relief that his grandad called them out for a well-earned break.

The cheese and pickle sandwiches tasted like heaven, a taste to behold.

The sweet tang of the pickle and the tingle of the mature cheddar seemed amplified on the roof of Julian's mouth, his senses having been sharpened by the mornings graft.

A hot mug of sweet tea helped wash the food down into his stomachs furnace. Plumes of steam came from their mouths. Julian thought the tea tasted odd, almost alcoholic.

With a loud belch he expressed his gratitude to the gods before leaning back against the wheel barrow, legs stretched out along the manicured strip of grass. Resting his work-sore palms behind his head he closed his eyes and rested.

The smell of freshly-cut vegetation perfumed the air.

'It's my turn to use the gardening thingy now, isn't it?' Julian muttered.

Gerry was sprawled out nearby, close enough for Julian to hear his snigger.

Assuming an accent that was meant to sound upper class he replied, 'If you mean the sickle then I would remind you that it was I that won the toss and therefore I am the sickle-master!' It was a sorry attempt.

Julian responded adopting as posh an accent he could adopt, 'Technically that is correct, my good sir, but as a question of fairness and in a display of gentlemanly conduct I ask you to show compassion towards your fellow worker and relinquish the aforementioned tool as an offering of solidarity and good will.'

Gerry's body began wobbling like a large blancmange as his chuckle gurgled in his throat.

His grandad glugged the remnants of his mug and screwed the cap back on the thermos flask and the small brandy bottle. He gave a satisfied smack of the lips.

'Come on you two. Mum and Joe are hoping this lot will be cleared by sundown. It'll be a nice surprise for them.' He encouraged them back to their feet.

It was late afternoon before they reached the shed's door.

Despite the structures list and its scruffy outward appearance it was in fact very solid. The layers of paint although peeling and curling like a crusty skin seemed to have awarded it some protection against the elements.

The door was firm and well and truly locked. A substantial padlock, welded shut by hard rust built up over time, barred the way. Julian rattled the offending lock, yanking at it as if it would make a difference. His grandad gently eased him aside.

The boys looked on as he forced a formidable looking flat-bladed screwdriver behind the latch. Tapping the handle of the screwdriver with a hammer, he managed to jam it in behind the toughened steel plate before pulling at the screwdriver handle. The action seemed to have little effect. A rhythmic squeak came from the hinges as his grandad forced his weight on the screwdriver in an attempt to pop the latch clear of its fixings.

In a last ditch effort his grandad and Gerry using their combined body weights gave it a last great tug. The effort resulted in a loud crack which sent his grandad flying backwards onto his backside. The door swung open with a loud begrudging yawn as the tight hinges gave way.

'Blow me that took some doing, didn't it?' Julian was relieved to hear that his grandad had picked himself up and had joined them both at the doorway. He was a bit breathless but luckily unhurt.

Musty, stale air wafted out of the shed into their inquisitive faces. Cloudy cobwebs cloaked the sheds interior, moths and bluebottles mummified in the clouds of silken threads. Huge black spiders scuttled for cover disturbed by the intrusion.

It had become a dumping ground, the interior now full of yesterday's forgotten items. Paint pots, plant pots, rusted tools, boxes of screws and nails, tarpaulins, slug pellets, weed killer, old decaying cardboard boxes spilling their contents.

Exactly the kind of debris you would expect to find in an abandoned shed.

Gerry clambered inside. The floor was hidden beneath compost bags, fallen pots, newspapers and magazines, a couple of mummified pigeon carcasses.

Julian required no warning. He was already taking evasive action as the rigid, feathered remains were flung in his direction. His grandad stood behind was not so quick, the bird bounced off his shoulder covering him in dead bird feathers.

'Oi ! You little bleeder!' He picked a feather free from his lip, 'I'll 'ave you for that!'

Gerry, in the meantime, was busy kicking out wildly at a plastic plant pot that had attached itself onto the toe of his boot. A final flick of the ankle sent said pot off upwards where it bounced off the shed roof, came back down and hit Gerry on the head.

Of course Julian found this hilarious. 'That's karma for you!'.

There was a lot of scrabbling and scuffling about while Gerry continued his expedition into the sheds darkest inner regions. Feeling emboldened by Gerry's show of grit, Julian inched carefully inside.

It was like a Tardis. Julian could not believe how much junk could be squeezed in into a space of that size.

'D'yuh think there's rats in 'ere?' Already committed and awkwardly positioned, Gerry twisted his head towards Julian.

It was quite a bizarre sight to behold. Gerry's jeans had slipped so low you could have parked a bicycle in his bum-crack. He kept trying to hitch them up but every time he attempted to release a hand to complete the task the precariousness of his body position threatened to up-end him and send him crashing to the shed floor.

'Quite possibly.' Julian tried to flick a sticky clump of spider's web off his fingers.

Smiling to himself he realised that he had discovered Gerry's Achilles heel.

Julian had always been envious of the fact that Gerry seemed genuinely fearless and unfazed by things that most others would run a mile from.

Gerry now was looking quite vulnerable, some anxiety etched across his face.

Julian watched as he scrambled around the sheds innards for a moment more before picking his moment.

'What was that!' He yelped.

'What was what?' Gerry snapped, he fired a look back at Julian..

'Over there,' Julian pointed towards nothing in particular, 'I saw something, something like a mouse only it looked too big.'

'Don't mess about mate!' Gerry was hovering, suspended somehow, he seemed to be levitating. 'You're joking with me ain't yuh?'

'No, serious, mate, I honestly saw something.' Julian made as if he was surveying the inside of the shed, looking past Gerry's peculiarly positioned form and at nothing else in particular.

Then, with great drama, he yelped. 'There it is, quick get out!'

The noise was apocalyptic as Gerry hurled himself towards the door like a man on fire. Gerry floundered through the accumulated debris aiming towards the door, slipping, sliding, scrambling, slipping, cursing as he stumbled and clattered his way through.

Julian stepped aside at the last moment as Gerry flew past him out into the light where he staggered like a newly- born mammal before collapsing to the floor. He grasped at his shin, wincing with pain.

'You alright boy?' Gerry squinted up in pain at Julian's grandad stood over him with some bemusement. Gerry rolled over in the dirt and caught sight Julian laughing himself into a stupor.

'You knob'ead! I could've killed meself!' Gerry groaned.

Julian lauged harder, he thought would pass out from the exertion.

While Gerry regained his composure, rubbing at the grazed welt that had appeared on his shinbone with a spit-moistened finger Julian stuck his head back inside.

'There's something in there.' Gerry called over to Julian as he scanned the interior.

'Yeah sure!' He retorted, 'Already done that joke!'

'No, I'm serious you idiot,' Gerry remonstrated, 'something bigger. I think it's a motorbike or something.'

Grandad hearing their exchange stopped loading the wheelbarrow and ambled over to investigate. Gerry picked himself up and joined Julian at the doorway.

'There's a bike or something under that tarpaulin.' He pointed past Julian's ear towards a large cloaked lump against the back wall.

'How could you get a bike in there?' Julian ran his eyes over the inside of the shed.

'I think it would have been a squeeze to get it through the doorway and to turn it but with a bit of determination you could probably manage it.' His grandad offered.

'Well, what are we waitin' for. let's 'ave another butchers shall we?' Gerry, pain and fictitious rat forgotten, was eager. He almost pushed Julian over in his rush to get back in the shed.

It took some considerable effort but they eventually cleared access to the covered article. Passing the detritus to Julian and then waiting for him to return after offloading it was slow but the only realistic way of going about the task. There was no room inside for two with all the clutter.

Julian joined Gerry inside for the unveiling ceremony. He felt the buzz of anticipation. His grandad who had let them go about the mission without interference stood beside them, his hand resting on Julian's shoulder.

Gerry tugged at the tarpaulin. It had hardened stiff with time and grime, like a huge warped sheet of hardboard. Years of previously undisturbed dust wafted around them and the smell of dirt, damp and mould filled their nostrils.

As Gerry bundled the heavy cloth away it became quickly obvious that it was not actually a motorbike as such. It certainly boasted an engine; that was easily recognisable as it was exposed in the open rear of the machine. Its bodies curves were made of pressed steel and its handlebars encompassed a clear round headlamp. A fixed mudguard protruding from the front legshields covered the small front wheel.

'That's a scooter.' Grandad explained. 'I haven't seen one of these for years.'

He wrapped his fingers around the twist grip. 'You see,' he pointed at the left hand grip, 'that's the gear shift over there.' Julian just nodded like he knew what he was talking about. 'and down there,' he continued, pointing to a pedal protruding from the floor pan, 'is the back brake if I remember rightly. I don't think they make them anymore'

Julian nodded again.

The powder blue of the body work, its sheen long ago dulled flat, gave away the scooters age. Cars and bikes were not sprayed in those colours anymore.

'How old is it?' Julian asked.

His grandad bent to look at the back of the machine. 'E reg, that's definitely sixties I'd say. Seems to be missing its side panels though.'

'It's a Lambret.' Gerry had been looking over the front of the bike.

'You mean a Lambretta.' Grandad corrected.

'Says Lambret 'ere. LI 150 aswell.' Gerry added.

'The badge must be damaged.' Grandad offered. 'Let's wheel it out. If someone got it in here, we can get it out.'

Metalhead Mike was a harmless type despite his tough biker jacket and studs. The leather jacket; oil-stained and scuffed to a grey on the elbows and shoulders, boasted allegiances to AC/DC, Black Sabbath, Motorhead and Whitesnake, noisy guitar-driven heavy metal bands. He wore band t-shirts with gaudy skull and snake graphics emblazoned across the front.

Mike's long, lank greasy hair tickled his shoulders and there was a wisp of a moustache in its infancy gracing his top lip.

His jeans were quite possibly water-repellent that much oil had been wiped on them.

Mike took a drag of his sorry looking roll-up, oily fingerprints decorated its thin paper skin. Julian noticed that his hands were filthy, the lines and creases of his skin highlighted by ingrained dirt. His ragged nails were tipped black with grime. Passers-by probably wondered what a couple of sharp looking rude boys were doing skulking around the estate with a greaser. Well, the clues were all there if you cared to look hard enough.

Since they had discovered the scooter on the allotment, they had spent fruitless hours tinkering with it trying to get it started but it was fair to say that they had not got a clue about the finer points of motorcycle mechanics. There seemed to be petrol in it, they had peered in to the tank and it certainly smelt like it but if they were honest that was about the extent of their expertise.

Julian's grandad had explained to them that the scooter had a two-stroke engine and that it required oil added to the petrol at a ratio of 2 % but he had then refused to help them get the machine going, claiming that motorcycles were death traps before going on to tell them unnecessarily descriptive horror stories of friends he had known who were maimed and killed while out riding two wheels.

They had tried to bump start it after a lad at school had explained how to do it but all they had done was succeed in knackering themselves out as they repeatedly shoved the ancient bulk across the estate, letting out the clutch when they felt they had acquired sufficient momentum to encourage it into life.

Their only reward for all the effort they had exerted had been deep gurgles from the scooter's mechanical bowels, but alas, no hint of ignition.

And that was why two sharp looking rude boys had ended up hanging out with Metalhead Mike.

Julian gave silent thanks when they arrived back at the scooter's resting place. Mike's toolbox was heavy and the metal handles cut into his palms. Gerry carried a petrol can containing the required pre-mixed petrol and oil.

They had hidden the scooter in one of the rubbish bin stores below Julian's maisonette. Normally locked, they had discovered an open one and there was plenty of space to the rear of the bins to hide their mean machine.

Gerry wheeled the Lambretta out of the store into the light. Mike shook his head dismissively.

'What am I meant to do wiv that peace of shit?' He nodded his head towards the offending machinery with obvious distaste.

'You know about engines, don't yuh?' Gerry countered. 'It's still an engine ain't it?'

'Yeah, but it's a pile of crap.' He held out his hands in question. 'C'mon look at it!'

'Look, Mike,' Gerry pleaded, 'it's all we've got and it don't run. A pouch of Old Holborn says you, the two-stroke king, can get it hummin' .'

Gerry paused for effect.

Julian looked on at the negotiation, he was quietly impressed. Gerry's patter would most certainly have convinced him to help if he had been a 'two-stroke king' instead of a 'two squirt Bert'. The Old Holborn should seal it he thought. Julian knew Mike had a pretty severe tobacco habit to support.

'Suppose I've got nothing' better to do at the mo', pull it up onto its stand.'

Julian glanced at Gerry. His cheeks reddened.

'Oh, come on! Please tell me it's got a bloody stand!' Mike shook his head. 'Get us a couple of bricks then will yuh!'

Julian did not know what Mike was fussing about, they normally just leant it against a wall.

Once supported on fetched bricks, Mike set about his business.

He checked the spark on the plug by touching it on the scooters bodywork and pressing down on the kick-start. Julian witnessed the blue flash of conduction. Mike seemed happy with the result.

He detached the petrol pipe from the carburettor and drained the old petrol from the tank. 'Gone stale.'

They nodded stupidly.

He then removed the carb itself and with a skill bereft of them, stripped it into pieces and cleaned them up in clean petrol before refitting it reassembled.

'Turn the petrol on.' Mike ordered after refilling the tank. Gerry turned the tap before turning to Julian and shrugging.

'I think that's on.' Gerry was not sure if it was and nor was Julian.

'You think that's on!' Mike mimicked Gerry's answer without looking up. 'What a couple of dicks!'

'Make yourself useful and kick this pile of shit over,' Julian was pretty sure Mike meant to use the kick-start and not to actually kick the scooter over onto its side though he would not have been surprised bearing in mind Mike's aversion to their steed.

'Don't give it too much throttle, don't wanna flood it.'

'Yeah of course, sure, Mike.'

Flood what? Julian thought.

And so Julian set himself up and gave the kick-start a good push downwards with his foot.

Nothing, just that familiar death rattle.

'And again.' He barked.

After a sequence of kick-starting which, for Julian's valiant efforts had rewarded him only with a hefty kickback that had cracked into his shin causing a wave of pain through his body like he had not felt since catching his shins on the pedals of his bicycle going too fast down a hill when he was younger. He had cried then, snot bubbles and all, but managed to stifle the urge to blub this time.

Mike stopped the activity with held up palm.

'Time for drastic measures and as we've no cliffs nearby to push this crap-heap off,' he reached into his toolbox, 'I'm gonna have to try the old faithful.' His hand reappeared clutching a can of spray lubricant.

'Gerry, kick the bike over again while I spray this into the carb.'

Mike gave the can a vigorous shake before giving Gerry the nod to resume kick-starting. Mike gave a strong squirt of the lubricant straight into the mouth of the carburettor.

All were unprepared for what happened next.

The engine almost caught but just would not hold on.

Mike, caught up in the excitement, urged Gerry to keep kicking.

Suddenly there was a huge bang. A flash of flame shot out of the carburettor.

Mike flew backwards off his haunches, launching the can into the air before landing hard on his scrawny, denim-clad arse.

Julian's heart pounded. He grinned nervously at Gerry who was clutching his chest where his own heart was beating an adrenalin-fuelled tattoo. Mike sat shell-shocked, his hands shaking, his complexion turned grey.

Julian and Gerry, as always, were sympathetic. They laughed so hard that they nearly wet themselves. Mike however was not so amused.

To his credit though, after a couple of roll-ups and time to compose himself he got back to the task of fixing old blue. After screwing in a nice new spark plug, settings corrected, she was putt-putting away merrily, the exhaust filling the air with the heady, intoxicating smog of two-stroke fumes that only a teenage boy could appreciate.

The three sat transfixed at the scenes unfolding on the television screen.

Gerry had called round for Julian about half an hour earlier. The intention had been to head over to the playing fields adjacent to a local factory for a kick-about to kill some time but they had been side-tracked by an excited Joe.

His eyes had promised something worth missing a game of football for.

'Lads! Lads! Quick, you've gotta come and watch this!' Joe had called out as Julian had let Gerry in. They had ambled in to the lounge and took a seat on each side of Joe on the sofa. Joe's attention was fixed to the television.

Joe had turned the sound up quite loud, conversation would have been difficult but as it turned out, they were to be rendered speechless anyway.

'It's on all the channels' Joe stepped off the sofa and stabbed at the three buttons in turn to prove his point before returning to BBC1. It was true; the same broadcast was showing on all the stations, all bank holiday entertainment having been suspended to show the dramatic goings-on.

The grandiose white building at which the cameras were aimed was the Iranian embassy. The buildings frontage boasted ornate pillars, large windows and balconies across its breadth.

On April the 30th, a group of Iranian dissidents had entered the embassy and taken twenty six hostages. Most of these were fellow Iranians but there were also tourists, BBC employees and an embassy security police constable, Trevor Lock, amongst those held. The gunmen had demanded the release of ninety one political prisoners held in Iran and safe passage away from the scene in return for the release of the hostages.

Watching the scene five days later, their eyes glued to the real life rescue assault being carried out in real time, the men of Britain's Special Air Service stealthily made their way across the balconies. Clad in dark clothing, cradling their German made assault rifles, their heads encased in black hoods and rubber gas masks, they made their way to the windows where they set a charge on the sill before putting space between themselves and the primed explosives.

The following blast blew a great plume of smoke, debris and a short burst of flame out in to the street.

All three jumped out of their skins. Joe swore.

Trepidation filled Julian's mind as the television picture shaken momentarily by the shock wave of the explosion returned to normal. Joe's eyes were as big as saucers, soaking up the excitement. Gerry was leant forward, his elbows resting on his knees, he was as still as a statue.

Screams and loud shouts were clearly decipherable from the scene as it continued to unfold. The troopers entered through the destroyed openings. Other SAS joined their colleagues by dramatically abseiling down the front of the building on to the balconies. Inside the building contact with the hostage takers was being initiated.

Stun grenades flashed from within the building and the sound of Heckler and Koch machine gun bursts made the hairs stick up on the back of Julian's neck.

Only one of the Iranian dissidents was to survive the raid.

As it became clear that the raid was over and the hostages were allowed out of the building to the waiting ambulances, Julian looked across at Joe. Their eyes met.

'That's it. I'm going to join the SAS!' Joe blurted.

Julian could only agree. 'So am I!'

In the aftermath, the hostages thanked the SAS publicly. The raid and its subsequent success served to save the Special Air Services regiment from the proposed fate of disbandment.

Gerry was always an age in the toilet but Julian never minded too much as it allowed him the privilege of playing at deejay as he chose which records to play next on Gerry's stereo.

Slipping the forty-five out of the trade-mark black and white sleeve, carefully avoiding getting fingerprints onto the clean, glistening grooves, he gave it a quick wipe over with the honey-comb cotton hem of his t-shirt before setting it up on the turntable and setting the belt drive in to action.

The Selecters 'Three minute hero', a recent addition to the growing 2 tone catalogue, thumped out, a stabbing jazzy organ accompanying Pauline Black's clipped vocals.

He shuffled backwards onto the bed until his back was resting against the poster-festooned wall.

There was an art to the way Gerry fixed his favourite pictures to the wall.

There appeared to be no obvious pattern or thought process to his decoration, it appeared haphazard.

Julian had tried many times to emulate the effect on the walls of his own bedroom but even when he had tried to place the posters in position with his eyes shut, the arrangement still looked planned and organised never replicating the desired effect he so wanted.

Pages torn from music papers and magazines were fixed in place by yellowing sticky tape. Other pictures, much glossier and more posed, some from Smash Hits and girl's magazines, filled the gaps.

Terry Hall's eyes, serious and un-amused, seemed to follow him around the room.

The bedside cabinet next to Gerry's bed was piled high, top-heavy with publications.

Tentatively reaching into the pile Julian attempted to extract one from the middle.

He was not sure why he picked that particular one as he had probably read most of what was in the pile and Gerry always placed the latest literature at the top and at a stretch, he almost got away with it.

As he teased the remaining corner of the magazine from its nook in the pile, the rest began to slide in an unstoppable paper-fall, scattering their flapping forms like landed fish across the slippery lino floor.

'Oh, bollocks!'

Shunting himself off the bed and kneeling amongst the carpet of literature he set about scraping it all together into a faintly recognisable pile.

The glossed shine of a folder glinted out at him from the dark beneath Gerry's bed. Along its black spine, tucked into the plastic see-through pocket was a paper label on which Gerry had written 'The Ska Files'. He had chosen a very straight and angular style, black dots centred at the letters angles, made reading the title easier to decipher than if he had used his normal handwriting. Julian had seen this used before as The Bodysnatchers typeface, another 2 Tone band, unusual in there all-female personnel.

Julian looked up, listening for signs that Gerry was returning from his meditations.

The toilet door stayed firmly shut and there was no rattle of the toilet roll holder being spun. Feeling confident that Gerry was deep in the moment, curiosity hung, drew and quartered Julian's cat.

Reaching under the fringe of the bedspread, he grasped the folder. Julian was surprised by its weight and solidity. Easing it out into the open, a copy of Mayfair magazine slid from within, a soft-focus cover model beckoning further inspection. Tempted though he was Julian was already drawn towards the other contents of the folder.

Holding it in both hands, he sat back crossing his legs. All thoughts or concerns around clearing up the mess and Gerry's reappearance had disappeared as he became engrossed in the folder and the need to discover what it contained.

Peeling back the front cover of the ringed binder, his initial reaction was one of momentary confusion as his brain struggled to process the pages before him.

The text was all typed in bold black ink, the first page a list of the folders contents. All the headings, clever with wordplay, referred to the different bands, 2 Tone happenings and record releases. The borders of the page were framed with a hand-drawn and painstakingly coloured band of black and white check.

Turning to the first article Gerry had typed up, spelling-perfect and littered with clever adjectives, Julian began to speed read its content.

The detail within and the sheer maturity of the writing style slowed his pace. Its thoroughness and lucidity were stunning.

Julian felt like he was reading an article written by an experienced hack with a university degree and a fistful of back-stage passes working for the music press rather than a sixteen year old who could barely be bothered to write his name at the top of an English paper.

He had even glued in relevant cuttings and pictures to enhance the in-depth reviews. There were band histories, individual profiles, record release reviews, general news and even fashion critiques.

He fluttered through the abundant content allowing the pages to feather past his thumb like a sketched flicker book. There were at least a hundred pages, maybe more.

Twisting his body to look under the bed again he spotted the small compact type writer pushed deep under.

Returning back to his seated position, Julian felt a presence. Gerry was stood in the doorway.

'That's private.' The statement shamed him. He closed the folder sheepishly. Gerry reached down and lifted it from his grasp.

'Sorry, Gerry,' Julian felt rotten, he had invaded Gerry's privacy and broken his trust, naively maybe but he had broken it all the same, 'I found it by accident.'

Julian glanced around at the mess scattered around him. Gerry held the folder awkwardly, as if looking for somewhere suitable to lay it down.

Julian began to scoop together the collateral damage caused by his earlier clumsiness. Gerry stood over. The folder looked heavier in his grasp.

'Gerry, mate,' Julian started, he trod carefully aware that he had tested the bond of trust they had. 'I don't know if you want to hear this.'

He looked up, Gerry's shadow falling over him like a cloak. A chill ran down his spine. He took a breath.

'But it's good!' Honest it is.' he stumbled for the right words. 'I can honestly say that it's the best thing I've read. You've got a real talent for writing, well, typing, if you know what I mean.'

Gerry said nothing; he bent and pushed the folder back beneath the bed. His cheeks were flushed and he was abnormally quiet and measured in movement.

He broke the atmosphere, 'Just forget it.'

He bent to assist Julian with the clearing up.

'Why don't you send some stuff off? I bet NME would use some of it.'

Gerry shook his head as he lifted a hastily collected pile of magazines in one hand and deposited them back on the bedside cabinet.

'Why don't you ask old Forbes if he knows someone who could point you in the right direction?' Old Forbes was head of the English department at Oakhill.

'Stop going on about it will you?' Gerry quietly requested. He took another scruffy wad from Julian and placed it back on the pile. 'It's just a bit of fun okay? It's just kid's stuff.'

'Show me a kid who can right stuff as brilliant as that and I might agree but I'm telling you, you have got a gift, something special and you should use it.' Julian lifted himself off the hard floor, his knees had locked tight and his buttocks had gone numb. He massaged the seat of his sta-prest with his fists.

'Well, that's as maybe,' Gerry continued 'but it's my writing and what I do with it is my business and I'm asking you to keep it between us okay?'

'Yeah of course I will,' Julian finally conceded, 'but I still think it's a waste!'

It really was quite a sight to behold. Gerry swaying and camping it up around Julian's bedroom. Holding an imaginary microphone to his mouth, he resembled a Las Vegas-era Elvis, gyrating his considerable bulk caused him to perspire and beads of moisture frosted his forehead. His miming was impeccable though, his lip-sync keeping perfect time with the accompanying music.

Gerry pointed at Julian.

They had both picked up their copies of The Specials new release that morning.

Handling the black gold with tender care, cradling the crisp, sharp, black and white paper sleeve with soft hands for fear of staining or creasing its newness, they had headed straight to Julian's.

The lead guitarist Roddy Radiations composition, 'Rat Race', was a sneer at the lack of integrity Roddy felt existed among a lot of university students. It was a galloping jaunt, its bounce punctuated by rockabilly-style guitar breaks. The flip was the raucous 'Rude Boys Outa Jail'. Rat Race would peak at number five early that summer.

Cocking a grin, Julian responded to Gerry's accusing finger.

'Better working for the rat race than ending up on the dole!'

The air was violently forced from his skinny frame as Gerry man-piled him.

Julian was amazed how long it could take to cover about fifty miles.

Cooped up in the rear of the family Ford Cortina estate, the backseat occupants legs stung from the heat reflected back through their garments by the car's vinyl upholstery. They sat, squashed, the four of them; Julian, Gerry and the two J's gazing out of the windows at the other harassed road users. They were all in the same predicament.

Sticking tongues out, making silly faces and shoving digits up ones nostrils as they passed other cars and occupants was only fun for a while.

Despite having left London early that morning hoping to miss the Easter bank holiday rush, they had made good time and yet still managed to get caught up in a five mile queue to enter Southend, a popular Essex seaside town just around the corner from the Thames Estuary, a popular jaunt for those East Londoners eager for some seaside shenanigans.

The bottles of orange squash had been consumed some three miles back and all they had left to offer any sustenance were the withered, hard-crusted cheese sandwiches that the heat had half-baked and half-sweated into a sorry almost inedible state.

All they could hope for was the odd decent tune from the in-car stereo tuned in to BBC Radio 1 and the road-show goings-on in Skegness. Unfortunately for the young but great for Joe; 'Flash' the theme from the new Flash Gordon film was blaring out the door speakers in all its orchestral glory, Freddie Mercury's falsetto filling the car's interior.

'Nothin' like a bit of Queen.' Joe liked his rock music. He nodded his head and tapped the steering wheel. Julian looked at Gerry with raised eyebrows.

'No, nothing like it!' Julian agreed sarcastically adding, 'Thank god!'

'Are we nearly there yet?' The familiar refrain came from the girls squirming in the heat of the interior, digging their bony elbows into Julian's vulnerable ribs and breathing their orange-squash saturated fug over his hot cheek as they whinged.

'Why couldn't we sit near the windows?'

Julian wound the squeaking window down another as they crept right at the roundabout and turned on to the Southend seafront.

He searched the horizon for a glimpse of the ocean, a ripple even but only saw the ever-extending flats of glutinous, sucking silt, a fine moisture-heavy mud-like concoction.

'Best cockles in the world out there.' Joe pointed towards the mud. He was acting tour guide as they crept along the front searching for a rare parking space. Julian wondered how Joe stayed so good humoured.

'Where's the sea?' Julian stuck his head out of the open window allowing the salt-soaked moist air to stir his senses.

'She'll be back later.' Joe assured them all. 'The tide here goes out a long way but when it comes back in it'll come in fast. The silt out there is rich in nutrients making it the perfect spawning ground for the cockle but it's dangerous, some parts'll suck you down like quick sand, without a trace. You'll 'ave to try some, can't come to Southend and not try a cockle.'

Gerry smiled knowingly across in Julian's direction; he had eaten all sorts and was looking forward to introducing Julian to good old seaside fare.

'You lads make sure you're back 'ere by ten o'clock this evening.' Joe gave his orders. 'I don't want to have to come and find you.'

Standing by the car waiting for permission to go they did not argue. They were thrilled to be allowed to do their own thing for the day, to be given independence, set free from restraints of parent-dom.

'And don't get into any trouble.'

Julian fingered the pound notes in his trouser pocket, the paper money licking off the misture from his fingertips. His mum planted a kiss on his cheek and squeezed the back of his arm.

'Have a lovely day, be good.'

'You too!' Gerry replied cheekily and then they were off; the masters of their own destiny, at least for the day anyhow.

They had both dressed for effect and in full complement of each other.

Julian was pleased that the cool sea breeze helped to dry the sweat-damp navy-blue button-down shirt he had put on that morning.

He had developed a little paranoia about sweat, crevices and body odour since sitting too close to a lad in class who was oblivious to the stench that emanated from his own pits and the discomfort this caused to those within half a mile of his vicinity. How could you not smell your own stink he wondered?

As a result Julian could often be found trying to stick his nose under his own armpit in an attempt to check his own whiff.

He had put on a good dose of deodorant in anticipation of the day's events.

Both his and Gerry's black loafers shone in the bright sunlight, creating a nice contrast with their white terry-towelling socks, the tassels on the shoes aprons swung with their step.

Some would have said they were over-dressed for a hot bank holiday Monday but what did they know? You could never be sure who you might bump into.

The wide promenade was busy and bustling with day trippers. Julian drank in the stimulating scenery; on one side the vast landscape of the beach and across the road, on the other side, a medley of kaleidoscope-coloured frontages and amusement arcades, varied eateries festooned with bright signs advertising their wares with hundreds of different coloured light-bulbs peppered around their fasciae.

Drunken men in vests competed young bucks eager to impress, all queuing to slug the mechanical punch-balls suspended outside the arcades, a large comical dial set to measure their efforts with a soaking-wet weakling or heavy-hitting hulk.

Gaily painted clowns faces peered out eerily from everywhere, releasing bursts of maniacal recorded laughter into the street. Loud fairground music that made conversation nigh on impossible blared from out of the arcade openings, hypnotising the young and carefree within reach into copper-spending frenzies.

Julian drank in the sights and atmosphere.

Elderly folk sat on sea-ward facing benches, some with barely a tooth between them, chewing forever on the rubbery, vinegar-soaked whelks they had bought from the famous Tubby Isaacs seafront stall.

Lovingly cared for fifties classics cruised the front proudly driven by James Dean look-alikes, arm dangling out of the window as they puffed on the Marlboro dangling from the corner of their mouth.

Kids skirted the legs of their parents stuffing snot and sand smeared chips in to their mouths while their mothers cackled at the suggestive postcards stuffed in to wire racks outside tacky souvenir shops.

Julian and Gerry were as content as two lads could be at that moment.

'You ready for this?'

Julian allowed himself a glance down into the stubby Styrofoam cup, its innards swimming in vinegar and flecked with pepper. The sea creatures looked like bogeys with tails.

'I don't know if I can.' He felt the trepidation rising within. He made as if to take one of the morsels from the container but jerked back his hand before actual contact with the alien-like flesh.

'Are they still alive?' He had read about people eating raw oysters.

'Of course not, you plonker.' Gerry took a good pinch full of the cockles, tipping his head back before dropping them into his open mouth. He chewed the mouthful vigorously before swallowing theatrically. 'Aah ! Lovely grub!'

He held the pot towards Julian, gesturing him to sample the delights it contained.

'They'll make a man of yuh!'

Julian took one, feeling the small, thin-skinned form between his finger and thumb. He placed it onto his reluctantly waiting tongue. Chomping down on the alien he felt its gritty innards crunch and spill out amongst the vinegar marinade swilling around his mouth.

He flobbed the mess out on to the beach in disgust.

'Why the hell would you do that to yourself!' He waved his hand in deference.' They're all yours. I'll get a portion of chips!"

Gerry tipped the remainder of the pot into his hungry mouth, vinegar, grit and all.

They headed towards the famous Southend pier, the longest pier in Europe at the time, intending to walk the long-timbered boardwalk to its very most end.

Originally 1.33 miles long when built in 1830, the pier had suffered numerous catastrophes, in particular, fires, the last serious one having almost decimated the whole structure in 1976.

It had been set for demolition but this had sparked out-cry amongst locals and admirers. The plans were halted and funds had been diverted into the re-build.

Allowing access to pedestrians since 1889 and boasting an electric railway that ran its length and a bowling alley, the pier was a popular visitor's attraction.

At the pier entrance, a couple of mods, newly revived and looking flash, were perched on their Italian designed steeds, dragging on cigarettes, their eyes hidden by their dark wrap-around shades.

They were quite safe that day, knowing that their skinheaded nemesis had been relieved of their bootlaces and turned back at the train station by the local constabulary.

The mods army surplus coats were draped over the tall backrests of the scooters. Striped boating blazers and bowling shoes completed the look.

The sun glinted off the chrome accessories adorning the motor scooters. They put Julian and Gerry's run-around, old blue, to shame.

A small group of girls walked deliberately by and back again, attempting to draw the attention of the independently-mobile peacocks, hoping for a backie on the scooters in return for a spot of French-kissing and a quick fumble under the pier.

The in-crowd gave the boys lingering disdainful looks as they passed at a respectful distance. Julian guessed they were not looking for trouble when they when allowed them to carry on their way without comment or threat.

The pier walk was pleasant enough and it was truly a feat of engineering, a half mile out the amazingly constructed finger of metal and wood pointed towards the cold North sea inviting visitors to stand at its tip and enjoy the panoramic view.

The small train trundled along rumbling over the timber struts of the pier length offering lazy legs the benefit of its carriage.

It was the option that they had chosen to take having previously spotted the two pretty young things sprawled inelegantly across the seats of one of the open-sided carriages. They had raced to and hopped into the adjacent carriage, stealing quick glimpses of the fair maidens nearby as the train took them landward back towards the promenade.

The girls disembarked and headed for terra firma, all the while glancing knowingly over their shoulders as they sashayed towards Peter Pans playground.

The girl's drain-pipe jeans hugged their youthful behinds, the plastic heels of their patent sling-back shoes clacking on the pavement.

Julian and Gerry followed at a respectful distance but the girls were already wise to the presence of the boys, giggling and nudging each other playfully as they entered the fairground entrance.

'Where've the birds gone?' Despite following them closely the girls had managed to shake Julian and Gerry off their tails leaving them standing beside the toddler's tea cup ride with bemused expressions.

'Maybe they weren't interested?' Julian offered, always the pessimist.

'Why don't you just ask us?'

Both Gerry and Julian turned to face the beauties they had spent the best part of an hour stalking. The voices long fringe hung stiffly across her right eye, a quick flick of her head swung the mane back and away from her eyes, she ran her hand over it to firm it in place. Julian's stomach released a swarm of butterflies.

Her friend, a touch shorter looked to be bit more reserved, she struggled to make eye contact but was cute looking nonetheless. Her t-shirt boasted the three members of the pop group The Police who stared out and accentuated her pert grapefruit-sized breasts.

'I'm Clare and this is Carol. She's a bit shy.' Carol gave Clare an embarrassed shove in response. 'She'll be fine when she gets to know you.'

They introduced themselves in turn. 'We're from East London.' Gerry declared proudly.

'You and every other bloke round here!' Clare teased. She oozed confidence and Julian was already in love. 'We live here. Just down the road really. What d'ya wanna do then?'

'Don't mind.' Julian gazed dreamily at Clare's pretty and enthusiastic expression.

'C'mon then, let's go and have some fun.' Clare took Julian's hand and pulled him towards the swing boats. Gerry followed close behind, chatting to Carol who showed signs that she was beginning to relax.

His arms ached from the exertion of pulling the thick rope in his eagerness to please Clare as she yelled at him to make the boat swing higher. Yet it was worth it to earn the honour of sharing a sweet lurid-pink cloud of candy floss with her as the four rested on an ornate iron bench, the green paint on its armrests thick with the layers of aged paint. His heart missed a beat as she teased a piece of cotton off the stick of candy floss and offered the bud towards his mouth. Julian took the fluffy ball in feeling it dissipate and melt into sugary nothingness.

His heart nearly stopped completely when she offered her lips to his, offering a soft yet experienced kiss, teasing his lips apart with her tongue and introducing him to the world of French-kissing.

He nearly exploded on the spot, in more ways than one!

Gerry and Carol seemed to be getting similarly acquainted.

The day was a heady haze of stolen kisses and embraces as they roamed the sea front, hanging in the arcades, eating steaming hot, salt and vinegar soaked chips that made your eyes water and nose tingle, watching the tide creep in until the pier pilings were wet again, allowing the crustaceans at their bases to forage for food brought in with the seas late afternoon arrival.

That evening, on the only tiny stretch of sand and detritus left dry by the sea, they had paired off, a decision instigated by the girls after they had whispered in each other's ears.

Julian had watched Gerry disappear into the darkness as Clare led him away in the opposite direction.

Close to the pier, hidden from the view of prying or innocent eyes they had kissed hard until Julian was trembling with a combination of lust-full wanting and the chill of the cooling night air.

'Here.' Clare offered him the small rectangular foil packet. It took a moment of recognition but he had seen condoms before. He had even unrolled one, filled it with water and dropped it off the block. Only thing was, he had never put one on!

He tore the resistant covering with his teeth, the metallic tang of the foil setting them on edge. The slimy sheath felt alien between his fingers.

Clare was ready and waiting, leaning back against the concrete sea wall before he had completed the fiddly task of covering his manhood with the baby barrier.

He got the feeling she had done this all before. Her tight jeans and knickers were already in a heap around her shoeless feet. She reached for his hands and drew him towards her.

There was no Olympic love-making session; the act was over in minutes. Yet he was eternally grateful, his day absolutely topped off.

Clare seemed chirpy enough, no sarcastic comments or put-downs or the sparking up of a cigarette.

Meeting back up with the other two they had walked hand in hand until concerned that the girl's older brothers may intercept them on route and give them a pasting for taking advantage of some local girls they all agreed it was time they got home.

After swapping addresses and long embraces, they parted company with their sweethearts and headed off to their own rendezvous.

'Well?' Gerry spoke, breaking the stunned silence, his frozen grin an outward expression of satisfaction.

'Well what? ' Julian replied mischievously. His head still swam from the experience.

'Did you shag Clare?'

'Did you shag Carol?' Julian hit back laughing.

Gerry gave him a friendly shove and added. 'Blimey, you've got a smasher of a love bite on yuh neck, mate!'

Julian rubbed the area where Clare had nibbled.

'Wait 'til the folks see that beauty!'

Julian shrugged his neck low into his shirt collar hoping that his mum and Joe would not notice the purpling bruise in the night light.

That night as the family made their way home along the A127, he gazed light-headed out of the window, watching the broken white lines in their contrast with the charcoal grey tarmac of the dual carriageway merge into one continuous white snake meandering and weaving beside the car.

His forehead, leant against the windows cool smooth surface, vibrated with the throb of the engine hypnotising him into a drowsy state.

The girls were sound asleep, absolutely exhausted from their exciting and active day; their heads nestled under Julian and Gerry's armpits. The aroma of seaside confectionary rose from their sticky faces. He turned and looked for Gerry in the carriageway lamp-lit interior.

'You alright?' Gerry spoke in a low voice careful not to wake the sleeping babes.

Julian nodded with a small smile. Gerry reached across and gave his arm a soft punch, grinning at him, offering a knowing wink before turning back to his window and his own thoughts.

Neither Julian or Gerry heard from the sexy Southend sorts again.

The crash helmet kept slipping forward impairing Julian's vision although having no visor meant that his eyes streamed with tears anyway as the cool wind rushed at his eyeballs. He had found the sticker-clad skid lid in a second-hand shop in the high street and despite the fact that it spun around on his head, it was that big, he paid the fifty pence the man asked for it.

He had particularly liked the two big humorous eyes stuck on the back of it.

As usual he was riding pillion as he was unable to manage the scooter if Gerry rode on the back as his bulk made the bike too heavy for him to control. They had long ago agreed that if they went anywhere two-up it was best if Gerry took point.

He gripped the sides of Gerry's silky flight jacket tight as they putt-putted their way along one of the side streets that circled the estate.

They were heading nowhere in particular but having bored taking turns riding round the estates boundaries they had bravely, or stupidly as some would say, ventured out on to the roads. And it felt exhilarating.

Exhaust fumes floated into the opening of Julian's helmet making him heady.

Gerry was becoming a dab hand at riding the scooter with gear-changes and braking were becoming less jerky. His turning was still a bit tentative especially two-up.

Cruising along the backstreets near the estate, Julian waved at youths he recognised forgetting that as his helmet obscured his features it probably meant that he was un-recognisable to them.

The vibration of the engine filtered up through the metalwork of the scooter, through the decrepit seat, its metal-sprung innards exposed through tears in the vinyl covering and into his numbing buttocks.

Occasionally Gerry would lean slightly back towards him shouting out a comment but the rattle and hum of the engine drowned out his witticisms.

A blue light bounced off Gerry's scuffed white helmet like a strobe breaking the spell. The fact that the light flashed could only mean one thing; the Old Bill.

Gerry eased the scooter over to the kerb where he brought it to a halt.

Deliberately he slapped the clutch out to stall the engine. The police car pulled up in front. Gerry spoke quickly through clenched teeth.

'Stay on the scoot to hold it up and keep yuh helmet on, okay?'

Julian nodded, planting his feet either side of the scooter to compensate for the inconvenient lack of a stand.

Gerry took off his helmet and stood by the bike. A policeman clambered out of the driver's side, flicking his cap up onto his glistening hairless dome as he headed towards them. A bushy moustache hid his top lip.

'Good afternoon sir.'

A polite start.

'I'm afraid you seem to have a brake light out.'

Mr Policeman reached into his top pocket for a small note book.

'Oh you're joking!' Gerry hammed it up, 'I only changed it two days ago. They keep blowing. I must 'ave a bloody electrical fault!'

Mr Policeman seemed oblivious to Gerry's display as he walked over to the scooter eyeing up Julian perched on the back. He began circling the bike.

'This is your machine, sir?'

'Yes.' Gerry stayed close to Mr Policeman.

'Have you any documents on your person to verify ownership?'

'I'm sorry but I've left me wallet on the mantelpiece at home'

Gerry was good. Julian had to give him that.

'I take it you own a full license?'

'Yes I do.'

'Can I take your name please, sir?' Mr Policeman looked up at Gerry expectantly his pencil poised over the notepad.

Without hesitation Gerry answered. 'Gerry.'

Julian's heart thumped, he was sure Mr Policeman would hear it, it sounded like someone hitting a bass drum and he was standing right next to him.

'And your surname sir?' Mr Policeman glanced up at Gerry again after writing in his little book.

'Dammers. Gerry Dammers.' How Julian kept the scooter upright was a mystery to him.

'And your address please Mr Dammers?'

Julian tucked his jaw into his helmet to hide his grin from Mr Policeman.

Gerry gave him a local but obviously false address.

'And where have you been and where are you headed Mr Dammers?' Mr Policeman was being quite thorough it seemed.

'Just picked up my girlfriend.' Gerry pointed to Julian.

Mr Policeman eyed Julian up and down, from his Dr Martens boots up to his saucer-wide brown eyes peering out from his astronaut-sized helmet.

Julian smiled sweetly although he doubt Mr Policeman saw it.

Mr Policeman wrinkled his nose probably wondering what the world was coming to nowadays.

'What's your name love?' Mr Policeman bent his ear towards Julian.

Before Julian could answer Gerry responded. 'Kerry, Kerry Hunt?'

Julian nodded causing the helmet to flop loosely about on his head.

Mr Policeman stared at Julian for what seemed like an eternity. Then with an air of resignation he tucked his notebook away and pulled out a pad of tickets.

'I'm going to have to give you a producer for your documents Mr Dammers. You'll need to bring them with you to the station within seven days so that we can verify all is above board, okay? ' Gerry nodded. 'And I trust you will see to it that the brake light is fixed before you use the bike next?'

'Consider it done officer.'

Julian thought Gerry might be pushing it a touch with the officer bit.

Julian gave Gerry a hefty thump to his arm as he clambered back onto the bike.

'Calm down Kerry or you won't get your oats tonight!'

Then with a hefty kick Gerry started the scooter and they headed off back towards the sanctuary of the estate boundaries.

'Ain't no point is there?' Gerry kicked the crumpled tin can out into the road where it rocked for a moment before a car quickly squashed it to a metallic disc.

All Julian had asked was if Gerry fancied getting together later that day for a revision session. They both had o-level exams looming and he had assumed Gerry would almost definitely need a lot of chivvying along given his application and attitude towards academia.

'Yes, but…' Julian tailed off. Gerry was quite resolute in his own opinion that he had no chance of performing at all well in the exams.

'Why do you turn up then?' Julian persisted.

The pace homeward had slowed somewhat, Gerry's feet scuffling at stones as they walked.

Gerry shrugged.'Dunno. 'Cos you 'ave to, I suppose'

And there seemed to be a kind of logic in Gerry's thinking; a kind of calculated avoidance of interference, of inquisition, confrontation and the agony of reprimand for no-shows. Turn up regardless and no one could hassle him for that.

Since Christmas, the seniors of McEntee had been gearing up for the exam term.

Julian had been fine-tuning his knowledge with pin-point revision, methodically bolstering the odd suspect areas that could possibly let him down in an attempt to achieve top-quality grades for his entry into a technical college he wanted to attend.

He had known where he was heading for a couple of years, blessed with an eye for art and technical drawing, soon to be renamed graphic communication and having the right dominance of grey matter which allowed him to flourish in the sciences and mathematics, a career in some sort of architectural or design firm was what he had in mind.

Gerry though, he lived by the hour. He never really gave any thought to his future with regards to earning a living. More interested in the latest record news or release, the realities of leaving school and carving out a career for himself were the stuff of fantasies.

'Don't know why you bother revising anyway, you'll be okay.' Gerry offered.

'I've got to get the best grades I can, places at college are hard-fought for.'

'Yeah, suppose you're right.' Gerry conceded, 'I'll get down the careers office, soon as this lots over an' try an' get meself a job.' Gerry paused. 'I don't suppose they'll have many openings for a budding music journalist, do you?'

'You would be good at that.' Julian nodded, 'Only one problem though.'

'What'sat?'

'They wouldn't be able to read your handwriting!' Julian jibed and set off in a sprint to avoid Gerry's playful mauling.

It all seemed so sterile. The hall that should have felt so familiar and recognisable had now become formal and foreboding in its officialdom. The busy bustle, the sights and sounds of assembly had given way to the policed silence and order of examination conditions. Teachers press ganged into service as invigilators patrolled avenues between the rows of forward facing desks. Their once friendly and approachable demeanours now cloaked in a veneer of inanimate expression and hands clasped behind backs.

Julian was too nervous to even glance at his nearest neighbour for fear of being accused of cheating. He was pretty sure that it was Harriet Forbouy sat to his right, he could see the vague outline of her profile, her straight clipped hair, thin-rimmed spectacles and Roman nose, and being that she was one of Oakfield's celebrated intellectuals it would not do for him to be caught eyeing her position, even if he did not get accused of scanning her answers, some might think that he was giving her the once over in a romantic sense, and that would make life hell for him at break.

He felt marooned, shipwrecked on his own little wooden island. Its graffito-cut surface was purposely barren save for the essential writing implements needed to complete the exam.

It was just Julian, by himself, alone. He prayed he had done enough preparation.

A waft of air momentarily cooled his flushed face as a hand slapped the papers face down in front of him like a large fan.

'Don't turn them over until instructed to do so.'

He heard the bored mantra repeated behind him as the teacher made his way along the row. Looking up he read the marker-written reminder taped to the wall.

Silence at all times while exam is in progress.

Miss Duboix, the French mistress, stood out front, she was trying to make her voice heard without it becoming a shout as she gave out instructions and wanted to ensure that the masses at the back could hear. Looking up at the main hall clock high up on the wall and then checking her own wristwatch she gave them permission to turn over the exam papers.

The whiteness glared up at him as he gave the questions an initial scan.

There was nothing too daunting there for him but indecision gnawed at his gut and he carefully read them again, and again, before summoning up the courage to put his first pencil mark on the paper. The pencil was uncomfortable to use. Its glossy sides slipped and twisted in his greasy fingertips. Rubbing them on his trousers only encouraged his hands and fingertips to sweat more.

His shoulders ached as time passed, the dull pain created by rigidity as his paranoia stopped him from changing his seating position for fear of being mistakenly observed to be doing something against the rules. Absentmindedly he blew the remnants of rubber filings off his paper. The noise seemed loud and exclamatory in the enforced silence. His eyes strained as he tried to look sideways towards Harriet, she seemed undisturbed as she beavered away at her paper, oblivious to his fidgeting.

Julian wondered whether it was good practice to check over his answers again. He had already been over them twice and all that had served to do was make him even less sure about the answers he was sure were right in the first place.

The problem was that he felt uncomfortable but there were still fifteen minutes of the examination time to go. His mouth was bone-dry, all moisture having being expelled from his body through his clammy brow and hands.

He had doodled on the desk top with his pencil until the point had disappeared completely and had decided against sharpening it again.

He sensed Harriet stealing glances at him as he sat twiddling with the pencil, the looks felt disapproving, he was sure she shook her head in dismissal. She was still scribbling away feverishly which only went towards heightening his anxiety.

Why had he finished before her?

Surely he had missed something out or not embellished enough on some of his answers. He replayed all The Specials songs that he knew over in his head in an attempt to kill more time.

He day-dreamed, imagining that he was at a concert, Terry and Neville reaching down into the audience, helping him up onto the stage where he skanked and hopped along to the performance.

He raised a tentative hand.

Miss Duboix clocked his projected limb, instantly apparent amongst the huddled forms of his peers, like the last man standing amongst a battlefield of fallen comrades.

She approached at pace. Her flowery skirt whipped at the desk legs as she passed.

Her highlighted shaggy perm bounced with each step.

She leant over his desk to whisper her enquiry. The heady perfume of French chemists smeared the air between them. He felt aroused by her closeness. He hoped she would not notice his flushed cheeks as he squirmed in his seat.

He fought hard not to allow his eyes to meet hers afraid that she may somehow be able to read his innermost thoughts. Mesmerised by her natural deep cleavage; a deepness that was made all the more prominent by her forward lean, he admired the texture of the sun-freckled valley browned no doubt by her sojourns to the south of France. He wondered if the absence of milky-white skin around her chest area meant that she sunbathed topless when relaxing on the hot French beaches.

He felt his groin throb.

Miss Duboix had long been the stuff of schoolboy fantasy. Her maturity only added to the erotic image that many a teenage boy had made in his head. The fact that her spoken English was tinged with the sexy drawl of the French added continental spice.

Many an individual's sleepless night had been comforted by the mental image of the sensual and erotic Miss Duboix.

'Yes? What is the problem?' Came the hushed French bark.

'I've finished, Miss.' He held the papers towards her expectantly.

'Well, check through your answers again.'

'Ahh! So pleased you could grace us with your presence, Mr Hanlon.'

The sarcasm was thinly veiled and accompanied by a theatrical bow as Gerry entered the hall.

'I take it you will be staying with us for the duration this time?'

The sarcasm did not warrant an answer and Gerry was not inclined to waste any energy responding. The deputy head was not renowned for his patience and sensitivity and Gerry was well aware what the heads opinion of him was without encouraging the man to actually verbalise his criticisms aloud for all to enjoy.

With the posture of a man heading towards the gallows, Gerry threaded his way through the bustling hordes armed with pencil cases and rulers, approached an uninhabited desk and flopped into the accompanying plastic chair.

He placed his solitary pencil to one side of the scruffy desktop then leant back in his chair and stretched his legs out underneath, almost reaching the chair in front. The boy in front, sensing Gerry's close proximity, turned momentarily to ascertain who or what had encroached on his space. Seeing that it was Gerry sprawled out behind him he chose not to question the invasion of his personal space but busied himself arranging his pens, pencils, sharpener, rubber and ruler in neat rows.

'Looks like he's setting a table for dinner.' Thought Gerry.

Gerry quite liked Kim Kwan even though he was exceptionally studious. He went about his day with little fuss, got on with his work and was always polite and friendly. Gerry could not understand the bully boys who seemed to object to Kims very being, his oriental heritage, taking every opportunity to prod and poke at him, both verbally and physically.

'Show us yuh Kung Fu, chinky.'

'Cat's an' dogs twice please.'

Pathetic idiots.

Gerry had intervened on many occasions but unfortunately for Kim he could not always be there.

The deputy head stood out front droning on, his deep baritone echoing around its walls, reminding all of the do's and don'ts of examination etiquette. Gerry stifled a spontaneous yawn as he listened to the rhetoric for the umpteenth time of late. His gaze wandered around the vast room. Most pupils were busy preparing, psyching themselves up, cocooned in their concentration. He caught the eye of Sally Jenkins three desks to his left. She smiled sweetly but it was all Gerry could do to offer an awkward smile in return.

Gerry suddenly felt envious.

For the first time ever he allowed the pangs of regret to unfold in his stomach. He chewed the inside of his lip and rocked gently in his chair.

In the silence of the hall his thoughts became louder. He was sure others could hear them. Voices of reason reminded him of the importance of his education and the consequences of a lack of effort. He remembered his flippant bravado and the cockiness of his throw-away comments.

For the first time ever, he begun to doubt his long-held philosophy and theories on life but it was all too late.

Hell, he could not remember if it was an English language or English literature examination he was sitting!

'You are flamin' joking!' The head sneered down at Gerry breaking the spell, he gestured to Gerry's lonely pencil, blunted and chewed, like a discarded twig. Shaking his head, he flipped the papers onto the desk top.

'Do not turn over until instructed to do so. In your case Hanlon it may be wise not to turn them over at all.'

Gerry felt the spike of spite and it made him flush with hurt. Kim must have heard too as he peered discreetly over his left shoulder. Gerry noticed the boy's nervous look.

English language it was then.

Gerry felt a rise of some confidence within. Three separate headings. All he had to do was pick one and write a piece pertaining to it.

There was a title; 'the life and times of…' (add subject).

A small starter paragraph; 'The rain lashed and spat at the men as they wrestled with the oars. The waves heaved the boat around like a cork, weightless against the might of the sea. An almighty crack and sudden impact sent the men lurching in unison towards the boats stern.' (Complete the story.)

And the final choice was; 'write an article of interest for publication in a newspaper or magazine'.

Gerry smiled to himself. Now that he might just manage. Creative writing was something he could do.

The sudden snap was like a twist of the testicles.

It sounded like a rifle shot to him but the noise did not register with any of his closest compatriots. Gerry picked up the miniscule remnant of lead and tried to feed it back into the pencils nib. He attempted to resume his writing with the piece of pencil lead clenched between his finger and thumb, the silvery-grey residue coating his fingertips. It really was as pathetic an attempt as it sounds.

With resignation, Gerry linked his fingers behind his head and leant back in the chair feeling it flex with his weight.

Allowing the flex of the seat to rebound him forwards towards the desk and the unfinished exam paper, he let out an involuntary 'Bollocks!'

Heads jerked towards him, distracted momentarily from their papers. Kim visibly stiffened in front.

Gerry saw the headmaster looking over in his direction. Gerry bluffed.

He returned the head's inquisitive gawp with a tight thin-lipped smile. After a fake stretch upwards he folded back to his desk pretending to be immersed in his work.

It would have been so easy to raise a hand and beckon the head over. The head would have gloried in the moment, leaving Gerry squirming at his desk as he made a show of retrieving a spare pencil for him to use and making sure that he reminded Gerry to return it to him at the end of the examination.

There was no way, that was not going to happen, Gerry would rather have failed the exam than give the head the satisfaction of rubbing his nose in whatever particular substance he wanted to rub Gerry's nose in.

A subtle movement just in front of Gerry's desk caught his eye. Allowing himself the privilege of a forward lean he spotted the discreetly offered hand. Kim continued scrawling away on his own paper while reaching backwards with his free arm to offer Gerry a brand new bright yellow and black striped pencil.

Gerry carefully snaked his arm across the top of the desk until his hand was almost in contact with the pencil. Taking a quick scout around the room to check for vigilant eyes and finding there were none he raised his bottom off the chair by the necessary inches and grabbed the pencil.

The scrape of chair legs on polished parquet flooring and the hum of stress-relieving chatter broke the halls sombre mood.

'Thanks Kim. You're a right geezer.' Gerry caught Kim as he was packing his stationery away. His jet-black mop of straight hair shone like the black of record vinyl. Gerry offered back the pencil, worn but intact.

'You can keep it.' Kim said.

Julian felt conspicuous as he loitered in the corridor. Pretending to read the geography display had helped make him feel invisible for a while but examining cross-sectioned sketches of volcanoes complete with their labelled attributes, colourful though they were, became repetitive after a while.

Then when Spud had stopped by for a quick chat as he passed on his way to a sneaky smoke behind the caretakers store, his camouflage was well and truly exposed.

Mr Holness the formidable and stern games master had addressed them in his authority. 'Where should you two be?' His coffee and cigarette breath assaulted their senses. Julian tried to mask a grimace.

'Free period, sir.' Julian tried to blag it. 'Got a tech exam later.'

'Then maybe you should be somewhere putting this free time to good use revising rather than cluttering up the corridor and making a nuisance of yourselves.'

It was not a suggestion as such, more like a directive. The raised eyebrows and stiff posture highlighted his annoyance.

'Oh, and Edwards,' Holness turned his attention to Spud grinning inanely at the games masters shadowing presence. 'take that damn cigarette from behind your blasted ear before I confiscate them from you!'

Holness spun as a youth sprinted past their congregation, the boys blazer spread wide like the wings of a black crow in flight.

'You boy !' He yelled, 'No running in the corridors!' and he set off in pursuit of the fleet-footed urchin.

'Too bloody tight to buy his own cigs!' Spud alluded to school folklore that spoke of Holness never buying cigarettes of his own, happy in the knowledge that he could pick off an endless supply to satisfy his habit by fleecing those unlucky enough to get caught with contraband about their persons.

'What you hangin' around 'ere for?'

'Gerry.' He could see Mr Holness had collared crow boy and was now barking at the unfortunate sprinter. 'He's just sat his English exam.' Julian explained.

'Nasty!' Spud empathised with Gerry's predicament. 'Give 'im my condolences, will yuh?'

Julian watched as Spud swaggered off down the corridor whistling the latest Madness ditty, cigarette perched behind his ear.

The hefty brown doors yawned open and chattering bodies spilled from the halls guts. He spotted Gerry, head and shoulders high above the melee.

He looked humbled, some would have said shell-shocked. His cocky, couldn't-care-less demeanour had eroded; his shoulders looked slumped, soft, limp. His expression was intense with lines of contemplation. He seemed to have aged.

He walked straight past Julian he was so distracted.

'Gerry.' Julian tried to sound upbeat as he fell in beside him. 'How did it go? Did you finish it all?'

'Oh yeah, I finished it alright, no problem. Lucky for me Kim had a spare pencil or I really would 'ave been scuppered.'

'That's great!'

'Oh yeah, really great! That's the only bloody paper I've bothered to finish, d'yuh know that?' Gerry's voice betrayed his agitation. Julian should have left him to calm really. It was obvious that he was close to anger and his face carried the obvious pallor of upset, the blood drained from his skin, his facial muscles taut.

'I'm such a knob. Why the hell did I even bother to sit through all those other papers when I know that I'll be lucky to even get a grade?' Gerry was venting through Julian but it was clear that he was addressing himself; his annoyance being exhibited through gritted teeth and frothing spittle that formed in the corners of his mouth. 'What a waste of bloody time.'

Julian's problem was that he never knew when to leave well alone.

His nervousness, his eagerness to please others, always seemed to trigger a fault in his brain that over-compensated his lack of usefulness with a plethora of inadequate and often inappropriate sentiments.

His attempts to comfort and placate were pretty abysmal given the circumstances.

'Come on, it's not that bad. I'll bet you pass that one with flying colours.'

'Not that Bad?' Gerry was incredulous; his tone had raised in pitch. 'How the fuck could it all be any worse?' Gerry rarely swore and it only added bite to his tirade at himself. 'I've wasted my education. It's taken me four bloody years to realise that but it's too late now ain't it? Gerry Hanlon, this is your wake up call. Time to grow up. Time to take things just a bit more seriously. I've made a right mess of things.'

Despite Gerry's obvious agitation Julian kept trying to lift his spirits. 'You can always go back to sixth form. You can take all those exams again.'

'You are joking!' Gerry looked back towards the hall. 'Them bastards ain't gonna make it easy for me are they? My reputation will put pay to that won't it?'

'Maybe, but they'll forget all about school and the kids over the summer holidays and you could start back fresh next term.'

Gerry shook his head softly. 'Let's just drop it now.' The colour slowly oozed back into his stubbly cheeks.

And yet Julian burbled on, his default triggered.

'It's something to think about though isn't it?' He could hear how patronising he sounded but could not stop the words coming out. 'See, it will all work out in the end.'

It was too much, Gerry snapped. 'I said let's bloody drop it. What part of that do you not understand?'

Julian felt the blood drain from his face. He knew that the he had fuelled Gerry's agitation. Gerry stormed off, left him standing alone.

Julian struggled to disguise his embarrassment. He coolly looked around to see if anyone had witnessed their tiff.

Two second year girls sitting on a low wall sniggered behind cupped hands; his paranoia told him that they were laughing at his predicament.

He gave them his toughest look but they were unfazed.

Julian knew that Gerry did not mean anything personal by his outburst.

He was upset with himself and he had every right to be.

It had taken four years for him to reach the realisation that not only was it important for him to achieve but that, in fact, he had the utmost ability to do so.

The flash of revelation must have felt like a punch in the solar plexus.

Julian reflected that he should feel honoured. After all, it was he that Gerry had chosen to vent his spleen towards. Old folks always said that you lash out at those closest to you. And so he had willingly accepted some of the burden of Gerry's agitation and frustration without argument. It would take more than that incident to divide them. That's what friends were for after all.

In October the previous year, addressing the party loyal at the Conservative conference, Margaret Thatcher had recounted to those attending some advice given to her by a Sam Goldwin, 'never prophesy, especially about the future..'

And she continued putting forward her antecedents as explanation for high and growing unemployment, particularly amongst Britain's youth, one of these being;

'…You can stress that, because of the high birth-rate in the early 1960s, there is an unusually large number of school leavers this year looking for work and that the same will be true for the next two years.'

Old blue was much loved but the constant lack of funds and missing mechanical knowledge meant that ignorance protected them both from worrying about what could happen. And so, one fine day as Gerry, Spud and Julian took turns to take the scooter for a spin around the estate's perimeter, it happened.

Old blue was cruelly taken from them.

Returning from his circuit at a fair old lick, Julian could see Gerry and Spud sprawled out on the grass verge, Spud sucking on a cigarette as Gerry watched his fast approach. The skinny, nutrient-starved saplings planted alongside the scratch of road, like emaciated sentries on parade, whizzed past in a blur. Gravel, shed from the roads surface, spat from the scooter's back tyre. Julian squeezed every micro-millimetre from the throttle.

The speedometer silently read zero, the cable flapping useless in the wind.

It took seconds but adrenalin-soaked senses ensured that he saw the whole thing happening in slow motion.

The original front tyre, its rubber walls cracked, brittle and decayed with age, gave up with an enormous pop.

Julian's wrists were violently twisted as the metal rim of the front wheel bit into the rutted road surface. Like a train on a track, the scooter seemed to follow its own designated path. Julian was powerless to stop its direction.

Squeezing forlornly on the front brake lever, his right foot too busy joining his left in holding the machine upright to make use of the back brake pedal he tried in vain to slow the momentum.

He was acutely aware of the teeth-torturing grind of metal on masonry as the scooters front end made contact with the kerbstone followed the painful abruptness of being flung from the bike as it finally dug in and came to a sudden and metal-mangling halt.

His head was fuzzy. He gazed up at the bright, wispy-clouded sky, the perceived silence around him being enhanced by it following such a cacophony of demolition. The gravel-sprayed surface biting into the back of his head disturbed the tranquillity.

Figures darkened his vision.

Gerry's voice broke the quiet and Julian's body began its complaints as his senses returned to some normality.

Julian's wrists were jarred but not broken. His lower stomach having suffered contact with the handlebars was starting to feel the effects of heavy bruising and his testicles ached. His knee joint stiffened with every second.

'Jesus, you alright, mate?' Gerry leant to help him sit up; he held Julian's crash helmet in his hand. It had been thrown off in the impact.

'Shit me!' Spud was a coarse but simple orator at the best of times.

'I think I'm okay, just a bit sore,' He was careful; mentally feeling out for any signs of serious injury on his body, 'am I bleeding?' Gerry shook his head. 'Can you help me up?'

'It looked really good from here!' Spud was grinning inanely.'Evel Knieval's got nuffin' on you!'

Laughing hurt too much for Julian to enjoy the moment as much as the spectators.

And old blue was in a sorry state. Bent, buckled, scratched and misshapen. It lay crumpled and twisted. The front panels were distorted and its front forks had been bent backwards by the impact which had aided its sudden deceleration.

They never really gave old blue a proper send-off. Left with the abandoned mattresses, fridges and cookers that piled up at the front of the estate, she was taken away by the council workman when they came to do their monthly clean-up.

And as the bruising around Julian's knee slowly eased and became a distant memory so too did the memories of riding around on old blue.

Do Nothing. Summer '80

'You've gotta see this.' Gerry's excitement was obvious; he grabbed Julian's bicep, his face like a euphoric archaeologist stepping out in to the daylight after exiting the pyramids.

And so they ran.

Along the main road away from the estate; past the rows of brick fronted terraced housing with concreted over drives cluttered with the detritus of automobiles and children's playthings.

On past the bus stop at the top of the road and past the small row of shops that generally serviced the estate's community, a newsagents, dry cleaners and an insurance brokers with its dusty plastic plants in its large window and putrid paint scheme.

On they trotted, up the long drawn-out hill towards the high road and its abundant shops, chain stores and eateries.

Julian became acutely aware of rhythm, their feet hitting the disjointed paving slabs as one, like two squaddies on a drill run, keeping time, in step. He noticed that Gerry had shortened his pace, not out of courtesy to Julian's shorter stride pattern but out of necessity as his own endurance began to wane.

Perspiration rolled down the side of his face mingling with the coarse hair of his sideburns slowing the moistures path towards his chin.

The pace slowed to an eventual walk. Then Julian spotted what the fuss was about.

A tall figure about five feet high and of slim build, of very slim build in fact.

A figure dressed smartly in a dark suit with loafer shoes, a trilby hat tipped towards the back of his head and the all-important dark shades.

A handsome fellow he was indeed.

He was standing just inside the doorway of Audio Times record shop. Waiting patiently and uncomplaining, stood as if there to offer greetings and farewells to customers who graced the premises.

'Now that is cool!' Julian gasped.

Gerry stated the obvious. 'The 2 Tone man. What a great idea.'

'Jerry Dammers designed it didn't he.' He knew Gerry would know this fact already but stated it all the same.

Inspired by an early promotional shot of The Wailers, pre- Bob Marley and the Wailers, when the hierarchy of the group had been evenly shared between Bob, Pete and Bunny, the image of a young, dark-suited Peter Tosh had lent the perfect silhouette for Dammer's vision; a perfect mascot and talisman for the 2 Tone movement.

'Yeah.' Gerry was in thought, 'D'you think we could get one from somewhere? I'd love one for my bedroom.'

'Where would you get one from?' Julian was pretty sure that this would be a tough ask even for a person as resourceful as Gerry.

'Yeah, you're probably right.' Gerry went quiet for a couple of minutes.

'I'm gonna go and ask if I can have it when they've finished with it.' Gerry was already heading towards the shop.

He disappeared inside prompting Julian to wander over to the large frontage trying to get a visual on the parlay between Gerry and the shops proprietor through the gaps in the posters stuck to the glass. Gerry's expression and body language looked disappointing.

'He reckons he's already promised it to another lad.' Gerry reappeared, he looked quite vexed. 'Wouldn't bloomin' tell me their name though! I even said I'd give him a couple of quid for it!'

Gerry was pacing about, nibbling the inside of his cheek as he pressed his thumb into his jowl.

Minutes later two young student types entered the shop, probably on a mission to purchase the latest indie release or some other arty-farty, mood-driven nightmare. However their appearance had sparked Gerry into a spurt of positive and direct movement, he headed for the doorway at pace, took a quick peer into the shop to ensure the owner was sufficiently occupied with the indie kids and swept old Walt Jabsco of his feet. The sight of the 2 Tone man wobbling towards him sent him into panicked hysterics, his laughter erupting in a raucous guffaw.

Gerry urged him to, 'Run you wally!'

Julian needed no second directive, he took flight, the pain of having to run while laughing so hard almost too much to bear. The stitch he experienced, a bread knife dug in to his side threatened to bring him to a stop.

The pain showed no sign of easing as it was heightened at the sight of Gerry trying to leg it while trying to maintain control of the large cardboard wind break he was carrying.

When he felt that they were home and dry Julian checked back to make sure the record shop owner was not giving chase before suggesting Gerry he was safe to stop with his newly acquired companion.

'You're a madman!' A grin was etched across Julian's face though his heart was beating so fast he had to lean forward, resting his hands on his knees.

Gerry could not speak; he could just about breathe let alone respond verbally after the exertion of the last few minutes. As his breathing returned to some sort of normality, his face was split by a wide, insane grin triggering a burst into laughter.

'You should see your face! You look like you've been crying!' He pointed towards Julian's tear smeared face with his other arm draped around Two-Tone man's shoulders.

'Yeah,' Julian countered, 'you should have seen your face when you were trying to run with that thing in front of you! You looked like a hippo giving birth to a rhino!'

Gerry laughed harder.

The 'borrowed' cardboard figure made a fitting addition to Gerry's boudoir, really looking at home in the corner of rude boy HQ east end division.

He looked after it, kept wiping off the dark grey mould spores that were attracted to the black and white card just as they also stubbornly appeared on nearly every inanimate surface of the damp flat. Gerry was even brazen enough to continue buying records from Audio Times record store feigning bewilderment and hurt when challenged by the owner about the disappearance of his 2 Tone man Walt Jabsco!

The room was bathed in a flickering orange glow that licked at the anaglypta wallpaper that clung desperately to the cold damp walls. The mood of the dimmed lighting enhanced the intensity of image being thrown out from the television screen. Joe was watching the news, comfortable, his leg folded neatly over the knee of the other. It was a posture Julian always avoided adopting for fear of looking old or effeminate.

''Ello mate.' Joe acknowledged his appearance. 'Ally Pallys going up in flames.' He nodded towards the television.

Alexandra Palace was indeed engulfed in flame. The firemen present at the scene had already lost the earlier battle, that much was obvious, but they were still pumping water at the inferno as it ravaged the guts of the historical building.

The suggested warmth of the flames on the screen gave the impression of having an open fireplace. Julian could have sworn his cheeks grew rosier as if he had spent too much time close to its comfort.

Julian watched the cut-out for the letter box from the safety of an armchair in the lounge. Nervously picking at his fingernails and loose bits of skin, he waited.

The clack startled him despite knowing that it was coming. He had heard the dull pad of the postman's footwear on the landing as he approached the door.

A light-brown tongue of doubled-over envelope pushed its way through the tight gap unfolding before flapping to the floor.

He retrieved it before running up the stairs to his bedroom. Throwing the envelope on to the bed, he flicked quickly through the long players. He chose The Selecters 'Too Much Pressure', an apt choice given the circumstances of that particular morning.

Falling backwards on to his bed, he raised the envelope at arm's length up towards the ceiling.

A jarring ska guitar rhythm and Pauline Black's pained vocals filled the room.

'..it's too much pressure'

'..this pressure got to stop'

'..it's too much pressure'

'..it's getting' to my head'

'..it's too much pressure'

'..it's givin' me a hard time!'

I know the feeling Pauline. Julian eased a finger into a gap and he tore along its length. As he drew the important papers out momentarily he caught his breath. Scanning the words at speed he quickly retrieved the information he desired. The weeks of tentative waiting were over.

He had got A's in maths, physics, technical drawing and B's in art, English language and geography.

He let out a long sigh, feeling all the anxiety of the morning dissipate from his strung-out physique.

The house phones shrill ring cut through the din of the record player. Swinging himself of the bed and jumping down the whole flight of stairs in one fell swoop, he managed to get to the receiver before the caller hung up.

'Well?' The voice implored. It was his mum. He knew it would be

'Well what?' He teased.

'Don't mess me about young man!' The anxiety in her voice was obvious. 'Did they arrive or not?'

'They arrived half hour ago.'

'Well?'

He had to move the phone away from his ear as her whoops of joy threatened to burst an ear drum.

'I-am-so-proud-of-you.' She punctuated each word. 'Everything is going to be fine, I just know it.'

'He says he didn't recognise his attackers but he is sure that it was racially motivated.' Gerry was buried behind the unfurled pages of the paper, his chunky fingertips the only part of him visible as he gripped the edges while narrating the account to Julian.

Lynval Golding, guitarist and backing singer for The Specials, had been attacked by three men while leaving London's Moonlight club after watching a Modettes concert.

He was due to fly with the rest of the band to Switzerland for an appearance at the Montreux music festival in a couple of days.

'Are you going to buy something or not?' The voice of Mr Singh interrupted their musings. His annoyance was obvious. 'You never buy. Always read but never buy!'

Julian heard the hinged counter being lifted and the slapping of the man's sandaled feet on the shops tiled floor as he advanced towards them.

'I know you. I remember your face. You never buy anything.' He pointed at Gerry.

Julian backed out of the shops doorway onto the pavement and into the close heat of the late summer afternoon.

Gerry stumbled comically out after him as Mr Singh nudged him over the doors threshold. Brandishing the stiff -bristled broom like a rifle with fixed bayonet, he gesticulated for them to make themselves scarce before commencing sweeping up dog-ends with vigour.

The rubber soled heels of his Dr Marten boots bounced off the face of the low red brick wall as he absentmindedly allowed his legs to kick backwards in a staccato rhythm against its rough texture.

Swaggering youths murmured greetings to each other as they passed him, sharing disappearing prospects of work and details of any forthcoming house-parties.

Middle-aged men, forlorn looking, made haste, eager to get in and out with as little rigmarole as conceivably possible.

Men in their twilight years went about the routine with an air of acceptance, their age marking them out only for the menial and often degrading scraps of employment left available to them.

Julian had slowly grown tired of watching the constant human stream of bodies enter and exit the job centres lurid-orange skinned entrance. He had seen all represented; black, Asian and white. No colour or creed barred.

Accompanying Gerry had seemed like a way to kill a bit of time but an hour later he was still waiting for him.

Hopping off the stubby wall Julian sauntered over to the job centre. Cupping his hands around his eyes he peered through the film of gritty road-dirt adhered to the huge sheet-glass front.

Those inside drifted amongst the large baize-covered boards spotted with the few white cards offering a chance of employment. Occasionally someone would lift a card off reading its content more closely before either returning it to its place or taking it over to the personnel sat at paper-strewn tables.

'What a nightmare!' Gerry finally arrived puffing with exasperation. 'It's like a cattle market in there.'

Gerry motioned with his head. 'C'mon, let's get out of 'ere.'

'How did it go?' Julian was unsure how these things worked.

'As well as I expected really.' Gerry clasped some folded paperwork in his hand.

'Didn't really 'ave anything for me as such just being just out of school with crap grades an' that.'

'What have you got there?' Julian motioned to the papers.

'Oh, this is some scheme.' Gerry unfolded the papers as they walked. 'The Youth Opportunities Programme.'

'Oh yeah. What's that all about then?' He tried to read the text over Gerry's arm but kept slipping off the kerb into the road.

'Well, it's sort of like an apprenticeship they said. You go and work with someone, learn the trade and the government pay you.' Gerry did not seem sold on the idea.

'Really? Sounds a bit odd doesn't it?'

The Youth Opportunities Programme had been introduced in 1978 aimed at sixteen to nineteen year olds.

It had been described as a; '.. new deal for the young unemployed' by Albert Booth, Labours secretary for the state of employment at the time.

The Conservatives had not seen fit to change anything about the scheme now they had power but never wanting to give any credit to their labour party forebears, in 1980 Norman Tebbit would set out white paper plans renaming the scheme, the Y.T.S, the youth training scheme.

Intended for young people in their first year out of school and described as; '..training on the job ' , it eventually replaced the Youth Opportunities Programme in 1983.

'How much do you get?' Julian was still to be convinced.

'About 16 quid a week.'

Sixteen quid sounded okay to someone who got nothing for attending college. Julian raised his eyebrows.

'They're gonna try and set me up with a building firm. I've gotta go back in a couple of days to see if it's set up then I've gotta go for an interview.'

'Sounds okay.' Julian offered.

As Autumn '80 got into second gear, the Conservative government had been flexing their political muscle for nearly eighteen months. Under Mrs Thatcher's rule, the Tories forged ahead with their radical programme, enforcing reform of the trade unions, restricting their influence throughout and in turn strengthening the power of central government.

They continued to reduce and under-mine local governmental power, controlling spending by rate-capping.

The endorsement and active promotion of individualism, self-reliance and private enterprise saw the gap between the haves and the have not's widen creating a more obvious and affluent middle class.

On the 10th of October in Brighton at the Conservative party conference the prime minister addressed her faithful; 'For those that wait with bated breath for that favourite media catch-phrase, the U-turn, I have only one thing to say; you turn if you want to. The lady's not for turning.'

A strong advocate of strict trade union restrictions and reduced social expenditure, her defiant speech was one of stressed determination to stick to the tough policies already initiated.

Outside the conference, 'right to work' demonstrators protested as the Iron lady continued; 'I am profoundly concerned about unemployment.'

The amount of people in Britain out of work had risen to over two million and showed no sign of slowing.

'Human dignity and self-respect are under-mined when men and women are condemned to idleness.'

Julian was not quite sure what to make of it all.

The cover was a definite break away from the monochrome simplicity of their debut long player.

The scene was reminiscent of a lounge bar setting in an airport, light filtering through the multi-panelled backdrop.

The main members of the band were congregated around a low, drink-strewn circular table. Jerry Dammers and Terry Hall seemed to be enjoying a joke.

Terry looked smart. A blue, knitted polo-top with a cravat just showing above the collar topped off his outfit. His foot was placed on the edge of the table revealing crisp white socks and a splendid pair of brown penny loafers beneath his black trousers.

Jerry sported an oversize chunky knit cardigan with a shawl collar. Julian thought this an odd choice. A pair of black shades framed his toothless grin, he scratched at his chin. Neville and Lynval were next to each other looking serious. Neville with his suit jacket slung over his left shoulder and Lynval gazing into his half of lager. Lynval donned a pair of white moccasins, a pair of argyle-diamond patterned socks beneath his turned-up jeans. Julian wondered where he got the shoes from. He made a mental note to try to find him a pair.

Roddy Radiation was dabbing out a cigarette in the glass ashtray in the centre of the table, his rockabilly hairstyle a nod to his musical and fashion influences. John and Sir Horace helped frame the picture, one nursing an almost drained mug of beer, the other would have appeared overdressed in his white shirt and bow tie had he not rolled the sleeves up to above the elbow.

There new styling seemed more individual. More mature even. Julian felt that they had made a conscious effort to leave behind the regimented look of two-piece suits and trilby hats.

The tracks on side one seemed to have stuck to the formula, that spiky ska sound with a rockabilly energy.

Side two raised eyebrows.

Jerry had soaked the tracks with an easy listening vibe. Apparently influenced by something called muzak, ambient and quite cheesy, Jerry had deliberately tried to revolutionise the 2 Tone sound.

The extended version of 'Stereotypes' morphed into a dub-reggae influenced paranoiac toast. An instrumental 'Holiday Fortnight' and the bizarre 'International Jet Set' were infused with the sweet chimes of Dammer's electric piano and distorted vocals.

Julian had already sampled the delights of the single 'Stereotypes' in September, initially unsure what to make of its bossanova-style arrangement, it had taken a couple of plays to grow on him. Its flip, 'International Jet Set', was a mind-shock, adversely different from anything the Specials had released before, so he had been mentally prepared for the inclusion of that composition on the new album.

Tucked away in the middle of the first side was, in Julian's humble opinion, a nugget of purest gold; an unassuming but supremely gorgeous slice of British reggae, a lilting melody of a composition. Its lyrics simple and yet somehow fitting in the moment.

'Each day I walk along this lonely street,'

The laidback orchestration was perfect as it chugged along behind the vocals, Rico's trombone prominent as its danced its bursts of brass alongside the harmonies. The bassline throbbed forming a solid backbone for the melody.

The previous debut album's sound, the spike and grit, the youthful exuberance of ordering a pint of snake bite and black in a rough pub, seemed to have been smoothed and matured into a smooth-stemmed glass of vin rouge out on the veranda.

Goose bumps appeared on his skin though he was not cold.

'Try to find, find a future,'

'New pair of shoes are on my feet,'

'Cos fashion is my only culture,.'

Lynval Golding had written Julian's all-time favourite song; 'Do Nothing.'

'Nothing ever change,'

On the way towards their prospective homes that night, through the under-lit but overlooked walkways, past the large storage areas housing the huge stinking cylindrical bins that contained the waste of human living awaiting Thursdays collection, past the shadows and moon-lit feline eyes on their nightly hunt among the estates abundant rodent population, Gerry and Julian became remotely aware of a solid, weighty sound. A sound that that reverberated off the steel of the mighty refuse drums and caused their chests to throb along with the booming rhythmic beat.

The sound waves were like an all-enveloping wave of mass that wrapped you up and vibrated through to your soul. It was so thick and heavy it felt like you could touch it.

'I know where that's coming from.' Gerry prompted, 'Come on.'

Julian followed as he always did knowing that whatever or wherever they were heading would be more interesting than sitting watching television with the folks in doors, even if his allegiance to Gerry's escapades did threaten a bollocking and possible grounding.

As they approached the estate's community centre, the sound became more full and rich until it was obvious that it was music, reggae music, played at a level unheard of to Julian's ears.

The bass was cranked quite possibly to the amplifiers full capacity and the vocals alongside were distinctly West Indian, chanting and chatting along to the rhythm in a patois neither Julian or Gerry could begin to decipher, the vocalist throwing in the odd call along the way to which you could hear the response of the crowd echo in a chorus of approval.

'Murdahh!'

The hairs on the back of his neck stood up on end, Julian looked to Gerry for reassurance.

'Ain't no one getting murdered in there!' Gerry grinned. 'Not in the way you think. Trust me!'

The well-lit, slightly elevated entrance to the centre was engulfed by a throng of black men and women with the odd white face speckled amongst them. All were trying to get some respite and cool off in the night air from the goings-on inside.

They were a noisy but exotic display of dreadlocks, afros, and massive colourful crochet hats and leather tams. Dressed to impress in Gabicci knitwear and Farah slacks, they seemed to be having a really good time and, had the landscape not been typically British, they could have been somewhere in the Caribbean.

'What's all this about?' Julian asked.

'C'mon I'll show you but keep quiet!'

'You going in there?' Julian exclaimed, 'You are joking aren't you?'

But Gerry had already moved off and was making his way through the bushes that ran alongside the centre. He pushed his way as noiselessly as he could down the side of the building.

When he arrived underneath a window, the elevation was too high for even him to see through, he beckoned Julian over.

'Get up on my shoulders then you can see what they get up to in there.'

As Gerry bent over at the waist Julian clambered up on to his shoulders offering an excellent platform for viewing being that he was now at the perfect height to see through the window. Visibility was reduced by condensation that clung to the glass and a fog of smoke that wafted around the room inside.

'Blimey, it's like a pea souper in there.' He whispered down to Gerry.

There were groups of people inside bobbing and swaying in time to the rhythm being pumped out of huge wooden speaker boxes the size of domestic fridge freezers.

Some were tugging on large cone-shaped joints, letting out vast plumes of smoke before passing it on to their friends who did the same. Some were sipping from cans of Heineken lager or from hand sized bottles of clear spirits.

Julian could see a wiry looking man dressed in double breasted pin-stripe suit with a tall, black woolly hat circled with red, yellow and green stripes standing next to a set of turntables with a microphone in his hand, his lips were moving as he rocked his body in time with the music. The two men near him were picking records out of a crate and skilfully lifting the previous off the spinning decks before replacing them quickly with another platter. Julian was amazed at the dexterity displayed by the men.

Julian fed all this information to his uncomplaining viewing platform below.

'It's a reggae sound system.' Gerry explained although Julian had managed to work that out for himself. Julian stretched to get another look.

'What a gwan, youngbloods?'

Gerry nearly dropped Julian from his shoulders causing Julian to nearly drop a packet on Gerry's kindly accommodating shoulders. Julian was aware of the closeness of the thorny bushes and fidgeted to keep his balance.

Julian regaining control of his sphincter muscles, plucked up some courage, he peered down anxiously into a large pair of blood-red eyes, the persons face slightly lit only by the glowing tip of the burning spliff hanging from the corner of his mouth.

'Well den? Have fe come fe stir up trouble or come fe join the blues?'

The 'Blues' being a term used by folks of Caribbean origin and descent to describe a party or get-together and obviously in this instance, a sound system clash of sorts.

Thankfully for them, it was Father Augustus, a most respected Rastafarian elder of considerable standing in the estates hierarchy.

He was a conscious man amongst the many players and pretenders who carried their locks as a status symbol or fashion item rather than a devotion to Rastafari.

Arriving as a gift of the windrush years, he had joined the under-manned London transport after the Second World War as a clippie, a bus conductor collecting fares.

At first, having being denied the opportunity to become a driver, he had worked diligently, never a day off sick, carving out a life for himself and his wife in the melting pot of East London. At first they rented a small ground floor flat in Leytonstone joining the other West Indians who had taken the risk of coming to 'hinglan' and setting up amongst the Jewish, the Asians and the gritty working class British folk who also called the East end their home.

Then, after becoming convinced that they would never get to the top of the housing list, Augustus and his wife were offered one of the brand new council flats on a revolutionary housing estate. It did not take much thinking time.

They willingly gave up the damp sagging walls and the backyard toilet for a new start on the estate.

As times changed, Augustus was eventually permitted to take his bus driving exam and became one of the services most professional and committed employees.

A more righteous, sincere, reverent, proud and humble man was hard to find. Augustus was always polite and gracious, always ready with a kind word for the young and old.

Now in early retirement, he was most often seen during the warmer, more familiar climate of the summer months, holding court sitting in a deck chair outside the communal reception area of St Francis block.

Sat there, emitting dense plumes of smoke from his Sherlock Holmes-type pipe which clung to the corner of his mouth, he would offer a raised hand in salutation as others passed and if you were close enough you would often hear an uttered 'young-blood' to personalise the greeting, blessing or however you chose to interpret the gesture.

'Have I and I youth come to hurl stone through window pane or have fe come to lick the chalice with I bredren, heh, heh heh?' Augustus chortled at his own humour, safe in the knowledge that neither would have a clue that he was alluding to the smoking of cannabis.

'Just wanted a look, not gonna cause any trouble, Augustus.' Gerry's voice sounded from between Julian's legs.

'Heh, heh, heh, the inquisitiveness of youth!' Father Augustus smiled, his teeth were discoloured but bright against his dark brown complexion. A complexion that was gnarled with history, like a hundred year old oak tree; his grey-flecked dreadlocks as weathered as the branches of the tree, his beard as wispy and sparse as moss and lichen adhered to the oaks trunk. 'How many years 'ave I yout' graced dis 'ere earth?'

'Eighteen.' Gerry fibbed. Julian looked down at the top of his head quizzically. Gerry could easily pass for eighteen years old if not older but not him.

'Heh, heh, heh.' Chortled the elder Rasta, 'Yuh best mek yuh way back home afore yuh parents wonder where yuh be.' His deep, baritone voice advised. He turned and headed back to the dance pushing through the bush like a natural mystic should, he turned as if he had forgotten something, he offered his blessing, 'Jah protect I and I yout'.'

Gerry rolled Julian down off his shoulders.

'I need a slash now. Keep watch.' Gerry hissed.

Julian did as required while Gerry relieved himself.

'Blimey! Look at this!'

Julian grimaced and refused to turn around.

'Seriously Jules! Look at what I just found!'

Julian puffed and turned taking utmost care to keep his eyes above waist level in anticipation of Gerry exposing him to a hairy arsed moony.

Gerry waved a long ready-rolled reefer under Julian's nose.

'It was under that bush there. Lucky I didn't pee on it!'

'What the hell are you going to do with that?'

'I'm not sure. I've never smoked spliff before. Heard it can make yuh mad!' Gerry looked in thought. 'I've had a cigar and that was well strong, I nearly chucked me guts up though.'

'Get rid of it then.' Julian was worried that Augustus would come back.

'Seems a shame to waste it though don't it?' Gerry looked at him, 'I'll just have a tug and see what it tastes like.'

Gerry lowered himself to the dry dusty earth and leant against the wall of the building.

Julian joined him.

They were both well hidden from passing eyes, sheltered by the head-high bushes. Gerry put the thin joint to his lips and using a box of matches he always seemed to carry about his person he fired it up. Gerry inhaled.

Julian saw the tip glow a fiery red and burn away some of the dry outer skin. He became more curious, eager even, to try some himself as he watched Gerry exhale.

He gave a small cough before looking at Julian.

'It's quite smooth really, not as bad as smoking a bloody cigar.' Gerry offered him the spliff.

'Try some if you want '

Gerry looked okay. Certainly not mad. Confidence restored Julian did not need any more prompting. He took a small lung-full of the perfumed smoke, hearing the joints ingredients crackle with heat watching the miniscule embers float off its fiery tip.

He felt the smoke roam around his chest before letting it out in a tight stream into the night air. He gave a dry hack.

'Yeah, feels alright, don't know what all the fuss is about, do you?' He handed it back for Gerry to have another puff.

Julian watched him go through the process again as he waited for some sort of life-changing revelation to happen. Nothing seemed to have changed.

Gerry passed the joint back to him again and so it went until their lips and fingertips could not bear the heat of the roached end any longer.

Leaning against the wall of the building, the bass of the thundering sound system fed through, solid and real into Julian's body until he felt at one with the sound

waves, a flesh and blood conductor for the invisible energy, feeling it resonate through his limbs to the core of his bones to the very tips of his fingers and toes.

It felt comfortable and soothing. Julian imagined that it was like being back in the womb.

Julian felt the solidity of the walls soften with the rumble. The hardness seemed to dissipate into a glutinous jelly drawing him backwards into its warmth and cocooning him. His blood pulsed in unison with the rhythm in the belly.

'You can see a man's face…'

'but yuh can't know his heart…'

The man's falsetto floated on the sparse ghostly bass line.

The rollercoaster shook violently side to side as it rattled around a corkscrew bend, twisting, turning, flying until it had spiralled through three hundred and sixty degrees.

His stomach tightened, not knowing which way was up or down, lurching with as the small colourful car continued its charge, hurtling downwards towards a steep curve in the track.

Nausea crept into Julian's upper stomach. He could not seem to stop his body from being thrown around like a limp, lifeless rabbit being despatched in a dogs jaws.

The carriage shook again, Julian looked to his side for reassurance, looking for Gerry. He could not focus, where was he?

The car shook again, more vigorously, until he felt as if he might fall out putting an end to the nightmare, albeit unceremoniously so.

Why was Gerry not there? Where had he gone?

'Wake up for God's sake!'

Familiarity registered in Julian's blurred mind. It helped to slow the car.

'Come on mate. Wake up!'

He was there. He could not see him but he was close, he knew Gerry would not leave him on his own.

The car ground to a halt causing Julian to slump forward. He felt resistance, pressure applied to the middle of his chest.

He slowly lifted his languid eyelids until his watery eyes recognised Gerry's concerned features staring into his own. Gerry looked terrible.

'Blimey, you were out for the count, mate.' Gerry had his hand in Julian's chest.

'I didn't think I'd be able to wake you! We both bloody fell asleep, didn't we.'

'What's the time?' Julian struggled to speak. His voice was husky and dry and his mouth tasted foul, like dried stagnant mucus should taste. There was a distinct lack of moisture evident. He desperately needed hydration.

'I'm not sure but the party's finished, they're packin' up, so it must be well gone midnight.'

Julian jumped up with a start, stumbling blindly and unsteadily into the prickly bush that he had forgotten was in close proximity.

'I'm bloody dead meat!' He shot at Gerry as he sprinted off towards home.

The sudden exertion of the sprint and the after effects of the smoking session quickly took hold. Julian realised that his legs were still shaky and that his head was none too stable either.

And so he had to resolve himself with walking slow and steady, resigning himself to the fact that he would be even later home but that he would have more time to regain some composure, to camouflage his elicit dalliance.

It was well gone midnight, quarter past one in the morning in fact and of course, his mum worried to death and about to call the old bill had waited up. She was worried alright, worried enough to ground Julian for a whole three nights.

He eyed the narrow, red strand that stretched out above the man's head. The straightness of the Central line was broken up by the bold, black names of tube stations spotted along its length. From the wild west of Ruislip and Ealing it speared through the heart of the city, Bank and Liverpool street, past the mystical east of Bethnal green and Mile End and out towards the suburbs and the royal hunting grounds of Epping and Theydon Bois.

The gentle rock of the carriage soothed his nerves with its rhythmic rumble as he stroked the fine bristles of the velour material on the train seat. The eardrum numbing roar of enclosure gave way to the sudden brightness of exposure as the train climbed out of the underground and trundled onwards onto the over-ground stretch of the journey.

Gazing out of the window Julian got the feeling of space. Like a rippled expanse of desert dunes, the terraced roof tops of suburban streets, the lichen-speckled slate apexes stretched, the view interrupted only by squat yellow-brick chimneys, spiky television aerials and fat, black crows.

He tugged at the hem of his jacket, pulling it snug onto his shoulders. He fingered the elastic knitted cuff at his wrist. His elongated reflection of earlier had disappeared from the opposite window, the trains emergence from the tunnel into the daylight having destroyed its mirror-like quality. He guessed his appearance had not altered much from his last check.

He smoothed his dog tooth-checked trousers flat against his thighs, the centre crease stood sharp and pronounced. He felt some satisfaction.

The carriage, bustling and claustrophobic earlier in the journey, had already haemorrhaged passengers at the city stops, black polished Gibson shoes and patent leather t-bar heels beating a tattoo as they hurried to their offices. That was before Julian had embarked. Now the remaining few commuters disembarked in drips and drabs leaving behind a smattering of youth sprawled about the seats.

A pretty, shaggy-haired girl, a mobile fabric swatch, swathed in textiles; elaborate velvets, weaves and lace, eyed Julian's brand-new portfolio. She looked like an art school type.

He noticed her eyes flit over the name tab on his black vinyl drawing portfolio. Julian felt a pang of self-consciousness at his personalisation of the tag. He thought the chequer board border had made it seem a bit classier.

She offered a tight smile causing him to flush and look elsewhere.

The train brakes squealed as it slowed into South Woodford station.

The college was angular and modern, a single storey creation of concrete simplicity and practicality. Panoramic windows gave an appearance of openness and light. Students congregated in the general car park, chatting, renewing acquaintances, laughing and petting, smoking cigarettes.

Gone was all the boisterous tom-foolery and banter of the first day of term at McEntee. Pleasingly absent was the adolescent menace and territorial pissings of the tough nuts who had made it their goal to set their manifestos of fear for the coming term.

Julian felt clumsy and awkward, out of his depth. Clutching his empty portfolio, its hollowness flapping annoyingly around his legs, he ambled through the throngs towards the reception area.

Gravel from the car park had embedded into the hard soles of his tasselled loafers and grated annoyingly as he made his way up the steps.

He had visited the college before, attending an open day with his mum and Joe.

Back then everyone they met had seemed like actors in bright and breezy television adverts. All airs and graces and offers of refreshments.

He could not remember having drunk so much tea and coffee in his life but he had thought it was the grown up thing to do.

This time, the first day of term at his new college, he was on his own.

No mum there to hold his hand, metaphorically speaking of course, no Joe and his offered words of the wise or confidence boosting speeches and most ominously of all for Julian, no Gerry.

It was a daunting prospect. He almost turned tail and headed back home.

Julian felt small and insignificant, child-like even.

The other young men around him seemed to breathe a maturity. Their body language expressed calmness and cool, be it forced or otherwise. Shapely girls, all shapes and sizes in fact, anatomically developed and knowingly so, floated amongst the groups dishing out hugs and kissing cheeks of those they knew.

The reception area itself was a swarm of activity resembling a flea market mishmash of styling and fashion statement, a live mass of twisting and turning, to-ing and fro-ing.

Amongst the gathered were the brave, the bohemian and the deliberately provocative.

All manner of exotic hairstyles and radical fashion were represented.

Disorientation threatened to overwhelm Julian. He had yet to completely enter, to step off of the ribbed welcome mat that spanned the width of the entrance.

He scanned the masses for a recognisable face. He searched for a face of some authority, someone that stood out from the youths, someone that stood painfully obvious like an angry purple pimple on a pure white backside. He searched for tell-tale clues amongst the motley crew, something that screamed lecturer, staff or adult, someone in charge.

Time seemed to slow and stutter. Julian felt himself zoom out, dream-like, as anxiety took hold.

He felt the glaring absence of Gerry's presence, the emotional and physical scaffolding that the friendship offered him. Julian missed the everyday support that he felt just by Gerry being there by his side.

He tugged at the hem of his jacket again. It was becoming a nervous tic, a habit.

An approach caught him unawares. He startled. The shock of hearing a decipherable voice amongst the babble and then realising it was aimed at him turned him into a mumbling imbecile.

'Sorry but ..what.. I don't … look… I'm sorry …who?' Julian stammered and stuttered as his eyes became rooted, transfixed by the androgynous appearance of the individual that stood before him.

They only had one eye. Or so it seemed. The other was curtained behind a golden sheaf of long, straight hair that slanted from their scalp, across their forehead and cheek. It divided their face across the diagonal. Their only visible cheekbone jutted sharply from high on their profile and the lips were full and sharp. Their complexion pale but clean.

A moment of studious examination followed before Julian was convinced that 'they', were in fact a 'he' and 'he' was wearing lip gloss!

A smidgen of glitter glinted off his lips wet-look surface.

The lad's Adams apple stood out, prominent, framed by the collar of his sky-blue cavalry shirt, double rows of covered buttons led the eye downwards to his tight white drainpipe jeans and pointy-toed chelsea boots.

The lad angled his head to the side as if to get a better look at Julian. Julian wondered if he was giving him the once over.

Hastily Julian averted his eyes.

'I said, are you okay, mate? You looked a bit lost.' The accent and deep voice were the complete opposite to what Julian had expected. The cosmetic-smeared lips emitted a low bass smeared with a strong London accent.

'Don't worry I don't wanna shag you! You ain't my type!' Julian felt embarrassed by his own lack of tact. His cheeks flushed.

'The name's Jeff by the way. One hundred per cent heterosexual, not that it matters. This get-up is a girl magnet, believe me. Anyway, I've been given the dubious honour of being a buddy for the day and, unluckily for you, you're the first likely candidate I've spotted who looked like they could do with a few pointers on how to survive their first day 'ere.' Jeff thrust out his hand. 'So where should you be headed?'

Despite his new romantic veneer, Jeff was indeed a top bloke, down to earth and very sociable albeit with a suspect fashion sense, a dodgy fringe and awful taste in music; all in Julian's humble opinion of course.

Julian had not heard of half the bands he mentioned or the Blitz club and Jeff had just nodded politely in return when Julian had told him of his passion for the music of The Specials and 2 Tone records.

Julian's futuristic friend took it upon himself to ensure that his induction into college was as uneventful and as seamless a transition as humanly possible and he, for one, was thankful that Jeff had spotted him.

One of the downfalls of the long dark Autumnal nights was spending more time inside.

The jackets that Julian, Gerry and the others coveted and wore as uniform tended to struggle against the persistent bite of the wind as it weaved its way around the base of the blocks whipping up miniature dust devils flicking around crisp packets and carrier bags. How Julian longed for a long black wool Crombie coat with red silk lining, or an even more practical hip length sheepskin coat like he saw the older lads wearing but he knew that these things did not come cheap.

It was only for so long the groups resolve could hold out even with their hands thrust into pockets and their necks pulled down into their jacket collars and knotted football scarves.

Even Gerry's Sid Snot impression from the Kenny Everett show, as good as it was to be fair, was not enough to take their minds of the chill that snuck up the gap between trousers and jacket hems. Now, if he could have perfected his Cupid Stunt 'it's all done in the best possible taste', Julian might have stuck around a while longer but it would have to have been good!

Joe supped his brew from a chunky white mug. Julian's mum had thought it amusing as she had handed him the present she had bought for him. Emblazoned across the white glaze in bold black lettering, the cup bore the drinkers confession.

'I shot J.R.'

Julian thought it cheesy and pointless. He thought it was an awful lot of fuss to make. Great Britain appeared to be in the grip of some media frenzy, a whodunit of unforeseen proportion. The country had immersed themselves in the whole hyped-up drama. The question had gripped the country for weeks.

Who had shot J.R. Ewing?

T-shirts posed the question as you wandered amongst the market crowds. Newspapers pondered the possibilities; columnists dissected the motives of the possible gunpersons with an air of serious deduction.

J.R Ewing, a tough and somewhat disagreeable Texan oil magnate had evidently made a lot of enemies. The list of would -be assassinators was not slim.

Many, apparently, would have been happy to have had the old boy bumped off.

Julian screamed inside, his disbelief at a peak, 'he's not real. He's an actor playing the part of the ruthless businessman in an American soap opera called Dallas. His real names Larry Hagman, for god's sake!'

And yet he had sat that November evening; munching on a packet of roast beef flavoured monster munch alongside his family as the show came to its dramatic conclusion.

It was Kristin who shot J.R!

Gerry jabbed the stop button on the cement mixer bringing an end to its rattling spin. It had been a couple of months since he had signed up for the scheme and he felt that things were going okay. He did not mind the donkey work, the fetching and the carrying, it carried little responsibility and he was generally left alone to get on with it.

That suited him for now.

He wheeled the barrow into position beneath the mixers yawning orange-mouthed orifice pouring the grey slop into the trough.

He picked at the calloused palm of his hand absentmindedly.

His damp t-shirt, moistened with fine drizzle, clung to his pale skin and his body had begun to display the tone of regular manual work. He chose not to wear the yellow standard-issue overcoat he had been given despite the weather. The stiff, rubberised fabric did not breathe and caused him to sweat profusely, he would only end up soaking wet and smelly from the inside out.

Gerry swung the heavy barrow round in a smooth, practised arc, up the plank and into the buildings shell.

The echo of another altercation in full flow made Gerry flinch.

Jacko the guvnor's angry bark rebounded of the naked concrete block walls and around the hard, sharp corners.

'Are you fuckin' stupid or what?'

Gerry slammed the brakes on to avoid colliding with the two men as they appeared. A spade full of cement slapped out and onto the floor by their booted feet. Both men were too embroiled in the argument to notice the mess.

'Don't shout at me. I'm not a bloody kid!' Des stood his ground despite giving away at least six stone in weight to Jacko.

'Don't you tell me what I can and can't do. I'm the boss 'round 'ere in case you've forgotten!' Jacko had turned a vivid shade of plum. Gerry was concerned for the older man's blood pressure.

Jacko was a big man; big neck, big shoulders, big arms. His forearms were huge, like two solid hams, and his gut was voluminous and rotund, the legacy of a six pint a night man. If he got hold of Des, Gerry was worried he might swallow him whole.

'A strong back,' Jacko had informed Gerry on more than one occasion, 'is the best attribute a man can 'ave.' as he had flexed his own thickly-carpeted spine for Gerry's perusal.

'When I tell you to do something it's for a bloody good reason!' Jacko tried to drive home his authority. What good was a site foreman if the labour thought he was a soft touch? 'And I expect you to do it without argument!'

'Jacko, it was a genuine mistake, one I've already apologised for.' Des tried to reason with him. 'You don't even listen, all ready to attack man. I don't need to take your shit. You're so rude. Disrespectful.' Gerry was quietly impressed with Des' calm demeanour. 'You're the one that needs training,' Des continued, 'not me, training in how to speak to people with respect.'

Jacko waited until Des had finished, he leant in towards him, Gerry's nerves rattled. It was like watching a super-heavy Joe Bugner facing off against a welter-weight Sugar Ray Leonard.

'You know, the best thing you can do, Des?' He answered for him, ' Is fuck off. Fuck off back to the dole queue with all your other fuckin' wasters. Go on. Get lost. Get off my fuckin' site!'

Des smiled a tight-lipped smile and shook his head in defeat, knowing that Jacko was never going to concede ground on this issue. 'You'll get yours, Jacko. Believe me. Your day will come.' Prophesised Des.

'Don't you worry, son, I'll keep checkin' up to see if the sky is gonna fall in!' Jacko sneered.

Des turned away, his head shaking softly as he shuffled past a shell-shocked Gerry. Des clapped him on the shoulder. 'Nice knowing yuh, Gerry. Watch him mate.'

Gerry absentmindedly raised his gaze towards Jacko.

Jacko caught him. 'What are you lookin' at?' He snapped. Gerry stayed quiet.

'Do you wanna join 'im?'

Gerry shook his head.

He thought of his dad Stan, hardworking and uncomplaining. Stan could do what Gerry was doing but it was easier to hire younger men, you could shout and holler at them. Get them to do the dirty stuff and play stupid pranks on them that wasted their time.

Gerry swallowed his pride.

He gripped the long barrow handles feeling the liquid bulk shift as he raised it.

'Wasting my time.' Jacko mumbled to himself as Gerry scuffed past the man's stout, stationary figure. He had pulled a pouch of tobacco out of his jeans back pocket. A single liquorice cigarette paper clung to his bottom lip ready for assembly.

'Fuckin' labour exchange, sendin' me mouthy wogs all the time.' He spat.

Gerry winced at the slur. Coldness swam over his body. He was taken aback by Jacko's comment. He had thought Des an able, strong and confident trainee, a bit flash but generally likeable.

Jacko looked awkward now, disturbed and agitated, unsettled by Des' perceived audacity. Gerry had seen the gulf between the two men's worlds, their tolerance of each other over-stretched and torn by an inability to adapt to or respect each other's differences. Gerry was embarrassed by Jacko's ill-thought out criticisms and his vulgar choice of vocabulary. He thought him a relic, a crude caricature of an old England; an England where Jacko's viewpoints and language were not as unacceptable or offensive as they were towards many folks nowadays.

Gerry thought that Jacko's attitude would lead him into trouble one day but he chose to keep his thoughts to himself. Jacko seemed to tolerate Gerry's presence at the moment and it probably helped that he did not have a lot to say for himself.

It probably helped that he was white.

Jacko raised his voice again. 'Youth opportunities, my arse!'

Gerry guessed he was meant to hear it.

'What the hell 'ave you got on your plates?'

Plates. Cockney rhyming slang for feet, as in apples and pears become stairs, boat race becomes face, plates of meat, feet.

Joe, a steadfast East ender and proud, included the full unaffected lingo in his vocabulary every day and without apology.

'They're shoes, Joe.' Julian had anticipated the baiting and ridicule which was now heading in his direction and despite a concerted effort he had not made it out of the front door before Joe collared him.

'Shoes! They're more like bloomin' slippers!' Joe feigned disbelief, he was just warming up, 'Can't go out in your slippers, can you?'

'They're not slippers, they're shoes. See?' Julian lifted a leg and offered Joe a view of the sole, rapping it with his knuckles to emphasize his point. 'Hard wearing, for outdoor use.' Julian humoured Joe, waiting for him to have his fun before letting him get out.

'They look like something a Red Indian would wear though. What they called? '

Julian felt his cheeks redden a touch.

'Moccasins.'

Joe chortled, 'I rest my case, your honour!'

'It's fashion and everyone's wearing them.' Julian attempted to defend his choice of footwear, 'Famous people wear them too!' He spluttered trying to gain some credibility through association.

'Everyone? Famous? who?' Joe had regained enough composure to carry on with the ribbing.

'Terry.'

'Terry who?'

'Terry Hall.' Julian countered.

And this fact was true.

Terry was sporting a pair on the picture sleeve of The Specials latest single release 'Do Nothing'.

'Who the hell is Terry bleedin' Hall when he's at home?' Joe was enjoying himself a bit too much for Julian's liking.

'I didn't expect you to understand.' Julian reached for the front door handle to make his getaway. 'I'm off out to meet people with a sense of fashion, Grandad!'

Joe could not resist a last dig as Julian stepped out.

'Don't forget to ask your mum to take down your trousers when you see her next, it looks like your trousers have fallen out with your new shoes!'

Julian looked down at the perfectly manufactured space between his tan coloured, leather moccasins and light grey sta-prest trousers. A deliberate style choice that exposed his brilliant white terry towelling socks for the general public to admire as he passed by. There was no disputing which side of the youth culture fence Julian chose to graze.

He shook his head good naturedly; thrust his hands deep into the side pockets of his strides and swaggered off down the dimly lit corridor, enjoying the echoed slap of his quick footsteps on the cold mottled flooring.

His picture sleeved copy of 'Do Nothing' held pride of place at the front of his record box. Its glossy black and white shot of the band congregated around a seated Jerry Dammers was the first image to greet him when he folded back the black vinyl lid.

He loved their moccasin-covered feet, their eccentric tartan-checked strides and individual headwear.

He alternated between playing the album and single version just in case he wore one copy out with his new-found ritual of playing the song at least once every day.

It was slowly sending Joe around the twist. 'Can't you play something else for a change?'

The reverse side, a rendition of a Bob Dylan composition, 'Maggies Farm', was brought up to date Specials-style, turning it in to a raucous rocking rant.

Its vintage message was hauntingly apt for the time.

'I ain't gonna work on Maggies farm no more…'

It was murder. Plain and simple. Joe had said so and to be fair Julian could find no reason to disagree with him.

'To use the term assassination implies that there was a point to be made by the act.'

He went on, venting his agitation in his familiar way and closing his statement.

'It awards justification, a meaning, and there's none, not ever, not for such a brutal and cold-blooded act.'

John Lennon's music, his spirit, filled the airwaves that grave day in December.

And quite rightly so.

The glossy skin of the door flexed with the impatient thumping it was receiving. Julian deliberately tried to ignore the bounce of the thin veneer and the muffled shouts from the other side. The small fixed bolt held for the time being.

'I know you've got it!'

Julian grinned at his mischievousness as he chose to keep quiet, his silence designed to cause maximum distress.

'I heard it. You took it in there with you! I heard it!'

He grinned at the commotion his teasing had caused. He twisted the block roughly, clicking the multi-coloured cubes backwards, forwards, vertically and horizontally.

He had given up trying to solve the thing properly minutes after locking himself in the toilet.

In his opinion it had to be the most time-wasting invention ever.

The clacking was loud and definitely audible from outside as evidenced by Jessica.

'Stop it, it's mine!' Jessica's voice was an agitated shrill. 'You said they were rubbish. You said no-one normal would want a Rubiks Cube for Christmas. I need it back. I nearly finished it and now you're messing it up on purpose!' She paused for some sort of response from Julian.

He gave the cube a sharp twist again.

'Mummm!' Jessica had given up trying to appeal to his better nature and screamed for parental reinforcements.

Julian stood, dragging his crumpled trousers up over his thighs, the toilet seats imprint was etched on his buttocks. Flicking the bolt across and swinging the flimsy door open he was met by the pouting and expectant Jessica, one skinny hand was outstretched to receive her Rubiks cube while the other was engaged in pinching her nostrils tightly together.

'You stink!' She bleated, her finger-clamped nostrils making her sound like a dalek.

Julian was happy to be under house arrest for Christmas day. He liked to be around the family. There was something magical about that time of year for him. Maybe it was the escapism? The change of routine? It was nice to pamper yourself once in a while and Christmas seemed as good a time as any to indulge.

That said, by Boxing day he was chomping at the bit to get out, to feel the sting of winter on his ears and to fill his stagnant lungs with frigid, urban air.

He walked quickly across the estate; his neck was shrunk into the raised collar of his jacket in an attempt to protect his quickly numbing ears. His football scarf knotted under his chin scratched his soft skin dusting it in claret and blue fluff.

He spotted Gerry bowling along. His dark wool 'benny' hat seemed hardly worth wearing. Rolled tightly into a skullcap and perched on the back of his head it did not cover much of his scalp.

'Alright mate!' He called out. 'Great minds think alike!' He had been on his way over to call on Julian.

Linking up, they walked on together, blowing away the cobwebs of their previous incarcerations, oiling their stiffened joints. Steam jetted from their noses and mouths as they ambled around the estate, catching up on news. They had not seen each other for over twenty four hours!

'God ! If I had to listen to St. Winifreds school choir one more time I swear I would have gone mad.'

Jenny had asked for and received the chart-topping single as one of her Christmas gifts and she insisted on playing it on rotation before and after Christmas dinner.

'Aren't you bored with it yet?' Julian had pleaded.

The looping lament of the choir had him near breaking point. He had even stuffed his tissue paper crown in his ears to block out the torture. All that had done was turn his ears green.

'Not yet, I haven't learnt all the words!' She had snootily informed him.

Gerry laughed at the re-telling. 'Sisters! Who'd 'ave 'em?'

After a thoughtful pause he spoke, 'Actually I'd have loved to have had a brother or sister or even both.' He nodded. 'Yeah, it must be nice to 'ave someone else around.'

It was another view for sure. Julian realised that he took his extended family for granted, whether he meant to or not.

His home had become a station that he passed through a lot of the time. He, being a heavy goods train, a through train, not stopping at all stations. Occasionally Julian would stop long enough to refuel and pass pleasantries with whoever was around but he was normally too self-absorbed to digest any of their conversation.

He made a silent resolution to take more of an interest in his family and spend a bit more quality time with them.

'Yeah, you're right. I am lucky I suppose.' Julian elbowed him playfully. 'Anyway, feel free to borrow them for a couple of days; you might have a change of heart then!'

VI
Do The Dogs. Early '81

'We do have a vision of the sort of society we want for Britain: one in which there will be no sharp differences in prosperity between one part of our country and another' ; The Tories vision of hope for the forthcoming year was put across by Thatcher's 1980 end of year speech '1981, our way forward.'

Their aim; '..a happier and more united country.'

'They got the bastard!' Julian looked up from toast he was slapping marmite on to. Joe was hidden behind the black, white and red of his tabloid newspaper. 'About bloody time I reckon.'

Peter Sutcliffe had finally made the mistakes the police had been waiting for.

Found in the services of a prostitute in a brown Rover with false number plates, he had stuttered and stumbled and fallen.

Initially claiming that the streetwalker he had picked up was his girlfriend, when asked for her name he was stumped, 'I don't know, I haven't known her that long.'

Then, after asking for permission to relieve himself behind a nearby storage tank before being taken to the police station, one of the arresting officers, working on gut feeling, returned to the scene later and found a hammer and knife Sutcliffe had stashed behind the tank.

The lucky woman was intended to be his fourteenth victim.

Sutcliffe wasted no time, offering a full confession in a fifteen hour statement. He admitted to thirteen murders spanning several years. The police had finally nailed the Yorkshire Ripper.

'Well it's me,' Sutcliffe referred to the Yorkshire Ripper pseudonym he had been given. 'I'm glad it's all over.'

He was given a life sentence at his trial at the Old Bailey.

Joe folded his paper with finality before flapping it down onto the table sending spilt sugar everywhere. 'Hope they throw away the bloody key.'

Jacko leapt from the van, its throbbing diesel engine coughing to a halt. He grasped the keys in one of his meaty fists. The driver side door was left hanging agape in his rush to exit the vehicle.

Jacko could really shift when he had to and when he had spotted Des leaving the Job Centre he had jammed the yellow panelled transit van into the kerb before setting off in pursuit of the otherwise oblivious Desmond.

Gerry remained in the passenger seat, momentarily stunned by the turn of events.

One minute, they had been cruising along the high road headed for the builder's merchants, Jacko sucking on his tight roll-up and leering at the young mums pushing babies in prams, and the next his mood was shattered by the unexpected sighting of his former employee.

Gerry had quickly realised what it was all about.

He saw Jacko roughly grab Des' shoulder causing the younger man to whirl around on the spot. Reacting instinctively Des stepped quickly backwards. He looked confused but tense, tightly-sprung and ready; a man who looked used to situations just as this. He appeared streetwise and alert. His posture was defensive but ready to attack.

Gerry trotted up behind the two men.

'You're mad, Jacko. I ain't been near your site since you told me to get my arse back here.' Des nodded back towards the job centre.

A curious crowd was starting to gather outside the entrance filling the pavement and slipping off the kerb and in to the road.

'I know it was you, you lying fucker! You warned me, said I'd get mine.' Jacko jabbed his calloused finger in Des' direction.

The two men's opposites were glaring. The youth of Des, his lean, sinuous frame, gave the impression of athleticism. His clear, smooth, brown skin, his glossy, tight afro hair, his crisp, thought-out street attire were in distinct contrast to Jacko's overweight but powerful stature.

Jacko's white skin was crazed with the red hair lines of capillaries, the blood rush of exertion had brought splattered colour to his fleshy cheeks. His plain white t-shirt, grubby and washed-out, clung tightly to his boulder-like shoulders and flabby belly. His low-slung jeans exposed the hairy cleft of his upper buttocks.

'So that's all the proof you need is it?' Des challenged.

Jacko inched toward him. Des flexed. Ready.

'Easy now, Jacko. Back off. Cool yourself down, man!' He warned.

'You're all the same your lot! Bite the fuckin' hand that feeds you!' The tone had become more vicious, more threatening as Jacko hissed his anger at Des. 'Hundreds of pounds your little prank cost me the other night.'

Two nights previously a group of men had accessed the site and vandalised equipment and work. They had poured sugar in the petrol generators, put hammers through the newly plaster-boarded walls and stolen the ready-made window frames, probably selling them on for a nothing price. They would have stolen the generators and mixer too had they not been well secured.

The police had said it was becoming a common occurrence but it was unlikely that they would apprehend the thieves and vandals. They were hoping that they might pick up a lead when the thieves tried to offload the stolen windows.

Jacko though, had his own theories about the break-in and Des figured strongly.

The crowd from the job centre had congregated around Gerry. They took no notice of him, only having eyes for the stand-off between Jacko and Des. Gerry felt their bustling presence. He could hear the hum of their excited chatter.

He smelt the fug of alcohol and tobacco.

They smelt the blood.

'I ain't listening to your crap any more, Jacko. You're so bitter and twisted, it's unreal. So back off and let me go about my business, man!' Des was starting to look vexed. His neck muscles were rippling beneath his drum-tight skin.

'You'll stay right here and fuckin' listen, you black bastard! I don't work my balls off, so's some jumped-up wog can come and try and ruin it all for me!' Jacko ranted. His fury had made him oblivious to the crowd that had surrounded the incident; a mixed crowd of different nationalities and colours. The crowd closed in on the pair.

Gerry felt the atmosphere around him thicken, the menace growing, stirred by the incendiary language Jacko chose to use.

Des started laughing at Jacko. 'You are such a fool, man.' He shook his head in disbelief before continuing.

'You're like a caveman. Catching me up and cussing me like this. You've got no proof but you've got plenty of enemies. Man, I could write you a list of people you've pissed off.' Des paused. 'You come 'ere, grab me up, abuse me and on what? A hunch? This ain't your site. This is my manor, my yard. This is my stomping ground. I live here!'

Gerry had deliberately squeezed himself free from the squash of the gathered men. He knew it was impossible to help Jacko now. This was a mess of his making.

Gerry had never suspected that the man's anger ran so deep. His language was usually coarse and his personality volatile and objectionable but the spite of his comments towards Des displayed another more sinister attitude.

That of a racist.

A bitter racist man; a man whose bitterness that run deep, hidden feelings that spewed out unchecked when the man was rattled.

Gerry felt he should do something to stop it all but there were too many angry men now and Jacko had gone beyond reasoning.

Gerry saw Jacko's face go a deeper red. He heard him unleash a guttural bellow as he launched his huge frame at Des. Des was quick though, his right fist snapped out catching Jacko on the nose.

It was like shooting a rhino with an air rifle.

Before Des could fire another shot, Jacko had enveloped him, steam-pressing his small head and neck in his powerful arms.

It was a scene of bedlam. Other men allied in some way to Des willingly joined the fray and engulfed the bulk of the man like a swarm of ants in a feeding frenzy on a blob of chewing gum. Their arms winged blows and their legs swung viciously as the roaring figure within bucked and lurched in its fury.

Jacko was lost beneath the overwhelming odds.

Gerry ran to the job centre and muscled his way inside where he found and yelled at a member of staff to 'call the bloody police'.

By the time he ran back outside to the scene, Jacko had been felled. Like King Kong he had eventually succumbed to the greater volume of firepower and fallen from a great height. Passers-by stood over his crumpled, bloodied figure. Most of their faces bore little emotion at the sight before them.

Gerry walked back into the job centre. 'You'd better call an ambulance as well.'

Gerry retold the whole story with a quiet sadness. He seemed disappointed.

Julian wondered who he was disappointed with.

Jacko?

Des?

Himself? Maybe he felt he could have done more to avert the incident.

Julian thought that it was an inevitable happening. He reckoned that once things are said and done, something's were only heading one way.

'If you live by the sword, you die by it.' Julian voiced.

Gerry grinned at him. 'Where did you pick that little gem up from?' He teased.

'Joe.' And he had. 'What I mean is, you can only go around upsetting people for so long, it all catches up with you in the end.'

'That's probably true I suppose.' Gerry pondered. 'Some people just seem to get away with murder though '

'What goes around comes around.' Julian chirped divulging another of Joe's pearls.

Gerry sniggered. He levered his prone form off the floor onto his elbows reaching for his mug of tea. Julian peered down at him from the vantage point of his bed.

'How's it going at college?' Gerry enquired.

'It's alright. There's a good crowd there and everyone seems friendly enough.' Julian grinned a toothy smile. 'At least I don't have to worry about psychos loitering in the corridors anymore.'

'And that was just the teachers!' Gerry quipped, 'You'll just 'ave to watch out for all them new romantics now instead!' Julian laughed at Gerry's reference to his first day encounter. 'Pretty boy like you, should be very popular!'

Julian lobbed a pillow at him.

'Are you going back to the site?'

'I don't see how I can, do you? It wouldn't be the same.'

'I suppose not.' Julian agreed. 'What are you going to do now then?'

'Go back to the exchange and apply for another training post I suppose.'

Gerry quaffed the remainder of his beverage and wiped his mouth with his forearm.

'Come on, let's get out of 'ere.' He rose quickly, gesturing for Julian to join him. 'Must be something we can get up to! '

They smelt them before they saw them.

Mooching along the high street, the group, Julian, Gerry and Terry were heading nowhere in particular and would probably have ended up in the record shop again, where they would have looked at the same long players that they had gazed at and discussed at length the week before while also finding strange comfort in knowing that they were still there in the racks, had they not been otherwise distracted.

Their journey to nowhere particular that fine day was abruptly interrupted by a gangly individual called Itchy and two nameless associates.

'Alright girls!' Very witty was Itchy.

It had no chance of being a courtesy call, Itchy being renowned around the area for being a conniving, spiteful opportunist. He was also a coward who always relied on some form of back-up when executing his nastiness hence the skinheads guarding each of scrawny his shoulders. He was an opportunist with a sizeable chip on his puny shoulder. A chip that could be moulded from whatever issue he had that particular day.

'What's matter, cat got yuh bleedin' tongues.'

Julian swallowed hard in an attempt to consume the Marathon chocolate bar he had jammed into his mouth, the caramel and un-chewed peanut chunks clogged and scratched at his throat.

Gerry spoke for the group.

'How's it going, Itchy?' A good start, always best to be friendly in the circumstances.

'I'm fine.' Itchy appeared almost civil. Julian remained suspicious.

He wore a smile, a crooked forced smile.

His frayed denim jacket was stained dark at the collar by his grease-laden quiff, a checked work-man's shirt barely soaked up the recognisable waft of body odour. Itchy had always worn the dated fake rocker look.

Itchy had never owned a motorbike in his life though he had stolen plenty and the only rock and roll he was familiar with was the East end rhyming equivalent, rock and roll; the dole; the dole queue.

His image was made all the more bizarre by the choice of company Itchy had chosen that day. Julian had never seen these two cohorts before and their presence was intimidating to say the least.

'What's all this 2 Tone rubbish?' Itchy dismissively flicked the badge pinned to Julian's jacket lapel. The gesture made Julian flinch, causing a trickle of sweet gooey dribble to hang precariously from his bottom lip. He sucked it back in before it lost touch.

Itchy grimaced at the performance.

'The Specials, Selecter an' all that. Proper music mate.'

Gerry went through the motions of explaining Julian's choice of accessory but it was obvious Itchy was already acquainted with the famous 2 Tone philosophy when he retorted, 'What? All that black 'n' white unite shite?'

He continued, sneering and twisting his features to emphasise his points.

'Look, it don't take no Einstein to work out that they don't need us an' we don't need them. Far as I'm concerned send the lot of 'em back where they come from, bleedin' muggers an' scroungers getting' off wiv our women and creating a race of 'arf breeds,'

He pounded his chest.

'England for the English that's what I say!'

His two henchmen nodded in appreciation of Itchy's rant, the odd grunt of approval being heard from their rotund features reinforcing each of his points.

Julian felt anxiety creep in to his spine as he realised that in their naivety his group had allowed the accompanying skinheads to close the space between them all.

The skinhead's scalps were devoid of hair, like hard-boiled eggs, the wrinkles and creases of skin around the base of their skulls looking like neatly folded wet ham.

They had bleached their jeans giving them a bird shit effect. Their boots were high lacing, at least fourteen-holers Julian thought.

One of the goons had written 'B O M' in black marker pen, a cross dissecting the 'O', turning it in to a rifle sight on the cuff of one of his jacket sleeves.

They were the recognisable initials of the British Movement.

They were close enough that he was sure he could detect the unmistakable aroma of vomit on their clothes.

'Aren't they over 'ere 'cos we were over there? The inherited benefits of the late British empire an' all that. What about the black kids an' Asians that were born 'ere?'

Julian looked at Gerry in stunned silence, his jaw to dropping in shock. He must have given the impression of a chocolate-stuffed goldfish.

'You being funny or what?' Skinhead one exhorted, allowing them to hear for the first time his sinus-infected drone. A sound, Julian surmised, that may have been created by his nasal passages having to secrete enormous amounts of protective mucus to protect his linings due to a prolonged dalliance with sniffing glue.

'They're British though, aren't they? They were born 'ere after all.' Gerry challenged. 'Probably got British passports.'

'Yeah, well, they shouldn't have.' Skinhead two attempted to close the debate. His logic was alarmingly simple.

Itchy, looking slightly more confused than he usually did. He thrust his hand in to the back pocket of his jeans and pulled out a booklet. The cover bore the title The Bulldog; the fanzine of the young National Front.

'You lot should read this.' Itchy held the curled tea-stained booklet towards them.

'It's our last hope before we end up drowning in our own blood, the victims of a savage uprising from within our community.' Itchy had obviously read some of the print within and not just scanned the pictures.

Julian was waiting for a rendition of Enoch Powell's classic 'rivers of blood' speech but he reckoned that would have taken up too much memory space in Itchy's brain cell deficient storage.

'It's about time we got our England back from the pakis and coons so's our old people can walk around wiv out being mugged an' stuff. Go on take it, I can get another one, the perks of being a fully-fledged member now, ain't it bruvvers.' Itchy looked to his new-found brothers for confirmation.

Gerry took the literature from Itchy's bony nicotine-stained fingers and flicked through the pages as if giving it some serious perusal. The blockade around them was reluctantly lifted by Itchys' cohorts, allowing them to squeeze past the ample frames and to continue on with their intended plans for the day.

When they were sufficiently clear of danger, Gerry turned, holding the booklet aloft waving it at Itchy and his mates.

'Thanks for the fascist wank mag, Itchy, I've run out of bog paper at home and I need something to wipe my arse on, you Nazi prick!'

Julian had no time to fret; momentum drove him forward as Gerry pulled at his jacket forcing him into a sprint.

Terry, who had hot footed it as soon as Gerry had started his taunt, was already ten metres ahead of them and not looking back.

Julian heard the clump of heavy soles contacting the paving behind them, not daring to turn and check how close they were for fear of slowing the pace.

He became aware of Gerry beginning to struggle.

So sure that his youth, despite his considerable weight handicap, would be sufficient enough to escape these older and brain-cell compromised sociopaths, he had miscalculated badly.

Gerry appeared to put the brakes on as he ground to a messy halt. Julian stumbled on a few metres as he tried to slow and turn to see what had happened to Gerry.

His heart leapt as he realised the brakes had been roughly applied by skinhead one who had managed to get within reaching distance of them. He had shot out a beefy paw grabbing Gerry's jacket collar wrenching him backwards, causing both of them to come together in a frightening melee of fists and footwear. Gerry's arms were flailing like a windmill in overdrive as he attempted to match his assailant's assault.

Within moments, Itchy and skin two had arrived at pace to add their violent opinions to the physical debate.

Gerry was now trapped, pinned against the bus shelter as the three laid about his person ensuring that their boots, fists and knees made destructive contact with the parts of his anatomy where they would cause most pain and distress. The sheet-steel shelter shook and rumbled noisily with the assault taking place beneath its canopy.

A shop keeper emerged from the butchers shop but understandably afraid to physically intervene, could only yell at the attackers to stop.

Every second Julian pondered his next actions, Gerry took more punishment.

Refusing to bow or collapse, holding his ground stubbornly, the three upped their effort, their grunts and groans of effort discernible above the din of their attack. Gerry was well outnumbered and only his considerable physique was stopping him for being taken to the ground where he would no doubt receive a sound kicking that would help them spread fear of their violent supremacy.

Itchy was gritting his teeth sadistically as he put in repeated knee blows with his bony appendage.

Julian took a couple of terrified steps towards the jumble of bodies still lashing out at their static target in gratifying blood lust, Gerry was almost completely hidden by the bodies of the aggressors.

Then he caught the awful glimpse of Gerry's bloodied face between the pumping, clawing arms of the two skinheads.

'Run, you bloody idiot!' He managed to croak between blows that rained about his person, a gash on his forehead released rivulets of blood down his face to be sprayed off his lips as he yelled obscenities at his attackers.

'That all you got, you wankers!'

Feeding on the rush of emotion that had stirred the normally passive blood in his being, fired a surge of adrenalin triggered by anger, fear and loyalty, Julian leapt forward and unleashed a huge hay maker of punch to the back of Itchy's head, ignoring the mire of copiously applied grease that controlled the man's fifties inspired hair style.

He followed that initial contact with an almighty swing of a kick, burying the toe of his Dr Martens boot into the crack of Itchy's bony arse. The force of which would have launched a football across to North London and back again.

Itchy swirled around in a blind panic and instinctively grabbed Julian close in an effort to slow his assault, a bid to gain him time to regain his composure. He drove his slimy cranium up into Julian's face sending him backwards towards the butchers shop window. Blinded by the impact from a headful of Brylcreem, Julian grabbed for Itchy's hair, entwining it in his fingers, feeling hair roots pulling free from his scalp. It was with some relief Julian found that most held sufficiently as he wrenched Itchy's head downwards and forced his knee up and into his weasel-like face.

Julian heard the crunch as bone met bone and repeated the action before letting go. Itchy slumped to the floor in an agonising heap. Foetus-like, pathetic-looking, Itchy clutched his battered face.

Quickly Julian turned.

The two skinheads were showing signs of intense fatigue as they continued their demoralising quest to bring Gerry down.

With a hop, skip and leap Julian managed to throw his forearm around skinhead two's fat neck linking his hands to lock the choke hold. Skin two writhed beneath his ten or so stone trying desperately to shake off the limpet-like grip.

Julian realised that Gerry had been gripping the clothing of both the bald assailants, holding them in some kind of death grip not allowing them the option of leaving the scene unscathed.

Julian could hear skinhead two's breathing begin to labour as his airways tightened under the unrelenting assault. In a last ditch effort for survival skinhead two swung a blind punch over his head and found his target, his club of a hand connecting viciously with Julian's nose triggering a cascade of blood to pour out of his nostrils and down the back of the skinhead's sweating neck.

Despite that success he sank slowly to his knees, like a dinosaur giving in to the inevitability of extinction, as his strength ebbed and his attempts to free Julian's grip became feeble and ineffective.

'Let him go, young un' before he carps it.'

The calming, kindly voice filtered through Julian's blood-red rage, a light touch of a hand on his shoulder brought him back to reality. 'You've done good. Let 'im go now, there's a good lad.'

Julian released his hold and turned nervously to look at the butcher. Regaining his senses and remembering Gerry, he leapt to his feet to see Gerry, having turned the tables, giving skinhead one a taste of his own medicine as he banged the bald bloodied head against the bus shelter post with a surprising rhythmical quality.

'Leave it, Gerry. I think he's finished.'

Gerry allowed the obese figure to slump onto his backside whimpering and cradling his claret-marbled skull in his round, fat fingers.

'You boys get yourselves off to the hospital before the old bill arrive. I'll clear up this lot.'

The butcher gestured dismissively with a wave of his hand. 'Go on, get.' He ordered.

They straightened their clothing and Julian shoved scraps of an old tissue, salvaged from his jacket pocket, up his nostrils before 'going on and getting'.

Gerry nodded back towards the butcher standing over the scene as they head away. 'A bit of blood an' guts ain't gonna worry 'im now is it!'

It was funny but they were far too sore to laugh.

Before they parted company that day, they agreed that it would be the best thing to do if they both told the whole truth from beginning to end. They were sure that their parents would respect their honesty and see it as a mature gesture, offering sympathy and sweet tea after they had heard their tale of woe.

Besides, they could not think of anything else to make up.

Suffice to say, neither Julian's parents nor Gerry's dad believed a word of it and they were both grounded for the following day and night. The only consolations to this sanction being that Gerry was so deeply bruised that he could hardly move anyway, his bones and joints aching from inside out after the sustained pummelling he had received. Julian at least got to watch the sexy and titillating hospital soap 'Angels' while the bruising around his eyes and nose cured to a deep shade of yellow.

The young, attractive, starch-uniformed female characters were the perfect antidote to the throbbing pain that spread across his face and provided ample subject matter for his daydreams and fantasies even if it did mean having to watch it with his parents.

The National Front had been targeting the younger white community for some time. Tapping into the communities insecurities about rising unemployment, inadequate housing and the lack of housing in general, perceived depletion of British culture and traditions and escalating street crime, they fed embellished, exaggerated and often fictional information, statistics and facts through the tabloids, word of mouth on the street and through their own network of pamphlets and fly-posting.

Often seen outside football grounds and concert halls, 'The Bulldog' sellers would encourage young, disenchanted, testosterone-driven men to join their ranks by promoting 'patriotic', anti-socialist, anti-intellectual, racist diatribe and promising benefits of honour, comradeship and notoriety in return for loyalty and commitment to the cause.

Agitating socialist and communist rallies, recruitment of peers, vandalism of recognised ethnic and religious buildings and a bit of 'paki-bashing' were all deemed as suitable strategies in pursuit of a better and safer Britain.

'Bulldog' editor, Joe Pearce had been jailed for inciting racial hatred within its content. The slogan 'Free Joe Pearce' had become a common sight daubed across bridges and decaying walls around the East End.

What was a young National Front?

Was there a middle-aged National Front?

A geriatric National Front?

Or a pre-school National Front?

No, it was exactly what it was; a thoroughly transparent attempt to attract the disenchanted, the weak-willed, the bitter and the gullible to join its shallow membership. Part of the recruitment of aggressive and expendable storm troopers to be easily-led and deployed on the streets, making their presence felt and heard with provocative marches through sensitive areas, in sinister back alley beatings and covert arson attacks on family homes and businesses.

The East end of Bow, Mile end, Stepney and Bethnal green were fertile recruiting grounds for the National Front and the less well-known British Movement; a fringe organisation that endorsed street action from its members.

These areas had once been known as 'Irish areas' before a large influx of Jewish settlers moved into the vacated slum dwellings; more than forty thousand by the 1880's, and helped build and man the predominant rag trade around Petticoat Lane E1.

Those dwellings, decaying and in dire need of modernisation, vacated by the upwardly-mobile Jews, became home to the poorer, more vulnerable and, some would say, less-integrationist Bangladeshis.

A recognisable and organised movement against immigrants settling in the area was first seen by the appearance of the pre-second world war black shirts, followers of the fascist Moseley, leader of the British union of fascists.

They quickly made their presence felt with their provocative marches through the community making big news.

The legendary Battle of Cable Street on October 5th 1936 saw left-wing, socialist and communist groups attempt to block the proposed march by the B.U.F by barricading the streets. This tactic resulted in street-fights erupting between the police and the anti-fascist demonstrators as the police tried enforce the legal right of the marchers. The march was eventually diverted towards Hyde Park, a bitter-sweet victory for the anti-fascists.

The legacy of the BUF presence in the area had been crudely replaced in modern times by their contemporary skinhead off-spring who sought out the opportunity for violence, normally venting it towards the passive, compact-sized Asians or careless homosexual men.

Occasionally the young fascists also found themselves facing the angry and organised Anti-Nazi League and Socialist Worker paper sellers who were more willing opponents.

The Sunday morning appearance of the infamous National Front paper sellers at the top of the famous Brick lane had become as every-day-a-scene as the oppositional graffiti adorning the red brick walls nearby and the traders laying out their blankets on the ground to display their wares for sale.

The East end borough of Tower Hamlets would become front page news in the 1980's when the British National party would win their first ever council seat in a local election.

Julian and Gerry had met their first storm troopers; stereo-typical in dress and attitude; a bastardisation of their original skinhead forefathers.

It would be naïve to say that the original late-sixties skinheads were all tolerant and peaceful. Evidence is clear that the originals boasted a taste for violence that they carried with them to football matches and though evidence also shows camaraderie existed between the early skinheads and Jamaican youths the skinhead's tolerance for others differences was less apparent; Asians and hippies being particularly marked for aggression.

In the late seventies the skinhead fashion had seen a huge revival amongst working class white youth, particularly in the inner cities, some, certainly not all, had taken the style a thousand miles away from the smartly turned out, reggae-loving roots of the late-sixties originators.

Some chose extreme right-wing politics, a more extreme dress sense and preferred the street-punk thrash of Oi music; a genre of music that would suffer an association with violence and politics that it could never successfully distance itself from despite the efforts of many and evidence that most Oi bands were not racist.

These off-shoots had created a Frankenstein monster; a sub-culture within a culture; an adverse opposite to the skinheads who chose to stay close to their original roots and followed the 2-Tone movement.

They were a thuggish vision that became synonymous with the cult as far as the general public were concerned and one that the National Front sought to nurture and develop.

Along with those who made their opinions clear there were those that appeared confused; those that listened to the new ska music, subliminally absorbing black culture, while continuing to display aggression to non-whites. The whole ethos of 2-Tone's racially harmonious message seemed to be lost somewhere for these few.

Fear of reprisal faded with time as word on the street spread that Itchy had been given six months inside for allegedly snatching a pensioner's handbag as she exited the high street post office after picking up her pension. The seventy two year old widower had given an accurate description of her mugger, right down to the greasy quiff and noxious body odour and there was only one Itchy.

The girl's jeans looked like they had been sprayed on. Her nicker line was visible through the light stone-wash of the stretch denim.

A sharp jolt from Gerry's elbow into his ribcage woke Julian from his lustful day-dream.

'Don't let 'er slap'ead boyfriend catch you looking at 'er arse!'

The girl's tall skinhead companion glanced back towards them in the queue. Julian pretended to study his loafers for blemishes.

'Alright mate,' Gerry cockily asked, ' 'ow long before they let us in?'

Skinhead frowned and shrugged before squeezing his hand into the tight back pocket of the girl's jeans.

Gerry lent in towards Julian's shirt collar. 'Lucky bastard!' Julian looked quickly to see if skinhead bloke had heard before allowing himself a grin.

The architecture of the Odeon cinema was art deco, straight, angular and simple lines.

Cylindrical pillars stood guard on the long entrance steps to the three heavy brass-framed double doors. The granite steps had been worn hollow with the traffic of history. The magnolia masonry paint was peeling in places. Thick and crusty, it was losing its battle against the grubby, polluted air, the acidic rain and the probing, picking fingers of queuing children.

Remnants of discarded chewing gum, blackened and hard, mottled the pavement.

Cinema tickets and wooden ice cream spoons were scattered amongst the forest of feet as they waited for the doors to be opened.

They had been eagerly awaiting the showing of Dance craze for weeks now, a 2 Tone film of concert footage, the brain child of American film producer, Joe Massot.

The film was a shaky and grainy compilation of twenty-seven live performances featuring The Specials, The Selecter, The Beat, The Bodysnatchers, Madness and, for their first and only appearance on a 2 Tone production, Bad Manners.

The Odeon was showing it for one week only and with that day being the first screening, the queue was heaving with youthful exuberance and high expectations.

The following day's screenings would see the crowds thin out alarmingly as it became obvious that the film was not going to attract big gates.

Sadly, its release was six months too late, music and fashion were already moving on and the 2 Tone train appeared to be running out of steam.

On vinyl at least, the film soundtrack met expectations. While the film flopped, the album steamed to number 5 in the charts.

Was 2 Tone was getting its second wind?

'The truth about this Government is that they deliberately engineered 2½ million people on the dole—the figure is still rising, and will probably rise to well over 3 million in order to subjugate the trade unions and the workers, through fear. That is the policy of the Government, and that is why we shall eventually get the right hon. Lady out of power, either in this Chamber or outside.'

In another of the many verbal skirmishes that centred around trade industry and unemployment figures, Mr Dennis Skinner, M.P for Bolsover, attempted to rattle the Iron Lady Margaret Thatcher, as the House met to consider a motion from the Conservatives ; the motion being put forward that;

' ...this House approves the economic and industrial policies of the Government; welcomes the continuing fall in the rate of inflation, greater realism in wage bargaining, and increasing awareness in industry of the need to be competitive; and recognises that lower inflation, higher output, an expanding private sector and better industrial relations provide the only secure basis for more jobs. '

Quick to respond, Mrs Thatcher defended the motion and met Mr Skinner's accusation head on;

'That is not the truth. It is just plain rubbish. It is the sort of rubbish that we expect from the hon. Gentleman...'

Expanding on her defence of Governmental policy, she elaborated;

' ...Another of the reasons for declining profitability has been that companies that have invested have often been unable to use their new machinery efficiently because of restrictive practices and resistance to change. Clearly, companies will not invest unless unions allow them to use the new equipment and machinery for the benefit of the companies and of all those who work in them...'

'I turn to the vital need to be competitive if we are to get more orders to our factories...'

'Our competitiveness will decline further unless management and work force share an understanding of the need to earn sufficient profits for investment, for development and for innovation. It is not enough to look only at next week's wage packet if one wants job security.'

To the men rolling up to the factory gates at Morgan Electrical fittings, the unseen governmental shenanigans were a million miles away, as they clocked on as usual. The brown envelopes that awaited them, formally addressed and looking ominous would ensure that things would never be quite the same again.

VII
Ghost Town. Early '81 (Extended Dub)

Julian was slightly puzzled. He looked up to check the sky. It was by no means tropical but a pleasant late-spring day nonetheless. He looked across the dry, dusty concrete to where Augustus normally sat out front of the tower block, watching time pass, talking stories with his congregation, playing dominos with spars on a flimsy card table.

It was too quiet. Doors were shut and human traffic was minimal. There was no-one around, not even any of the youngsters that played tin can tommy and run-outs under the Jamaican-born elder's watchful presence.

It was an unusual occurrence, not exactly earth-shattering but one that left Julian feeling a touch bemused anyway, he carried on homeward.

Joe had already switched the evening news broadcast on as Julian flopped on to the sofa beside him.

'Bob Marley, Jamaican reggae superstar has today died, aged thirty-six, after losing his battle with cancer.'

The estate had been buzzing with the rumours all day Friday that April.

Julian had been hanging around as usual with Gerry and a couple of like-minded individuals monkeying around and discussing the latest record releases and news, when Twiggy had turned up around seven thirty. He excitedly told them of the troubles he had heard about that were brewing over in Brixton, across the Thames, South London.

Julian knew of Brixton. He had seen it written, it punctuated the end of the bright blue Victoria line on the London underground tube map like a full stop at the end of a sentence but to him it could have well been a million miles away, another world, let alone another borough in London.

All he really knew was that it was home to a large West Indian community much like his own estate but also bore a more militant community. He had heard of the Brixton frontline on the urban grapevine, just as there were rumoured to be frontlines in most major British cities such as Birmingham and Liverpool. There was reputedly a frontline, a no-go area for police, in Hackney.

Brixton's supposed frontline, Railton road, was rumoured to be a no-go area for the metropolitan police force too.

'It's kicking off lads! Whites versus the blacks! The old bill are over-run.'

Always a simplistic orator, Twiggy was not renowned for his in-depth analysis of anything.

However not being any the wiser at that point in time Julian and the others were not in a position to contradict or challenge his statement.

'There's people dead already and the army are going to have to go in!'

Realising that the best part of restraint had been thrown to the wind and Jackanory had arrived in its place, they decided to break the little tête-à-tête and head home to catch the late news.

That weekend, all news broadcasts were dominated by the ferocious battle for control amongst the immediate community of what was known locally as 'the triangle' and the police force.

Railton road, Brixton's alleged frontline, was part of that triangle.

The area mainly inhabited by black council house tenants and some politically motivated white squatters had become a meeting place for many, inheriting a street culture despite England's particularly fickle weather.

Earmarked for demolition which had never been completed due to funding running out, some of the empty houses had become drinking, smoking and gambling clubs with all-night blues parties being common. This was their social space and no bull man, street slang for the police, were going to encroach upon it.

'There were no signs of them (the police) keeping a low profile.'

A Railton road resident was to comment to journalists with hindsight after the rioting had ceased.

Operation Swamp 81 had been initiated by the top brass as an attempt at re-enforcement of police authority amongst the predominately black youth of Brixton. There was a heavy police presence on the streets, the policy tending to be containment and harassment.

The universally hated SUS, Stop under Suspicion laws; being stopped and searched with good cause and with not so-good cause, many finding themselves inconvenienced by being stopped for absolutely any petty, fictional reason, were used and very abused. The operation saw over one thousand people stopped and searched, most were young black men. Police hatred amongst the defiant black community burnt fiercely, fuelled by the inadequate and insensitive approach endorsed by the police command.

Brixton was simmering.

On that Friday, 11th April 1981 an incident that appeared to be a concrete example of the lack of communication between the police and the people served to ignite the beginnings of the troubles to come.

Allegedly attempting to assist a youth who had been stabbed in an argument and was fleeing the area of the triangle, policemen came under attack from a group of youths.

The incident prompted a swift show of strength and an attempt at enforced control from the local constabulary.

'… there were so many (police) I thought they were on some sort of exercise.' A resident of Dulwich road had described the scene at the time.

By the time a young man was arrested outside a mini cab office at one end of Railton Road, battle lines had been drawn. The youths steamed the un-prepared police present at the scene pelting them with a hail of brick, stone and glass forcing them to radio for immediate re-enforcements.

In the aftermath of the riots, the ferocity of the attack caused some officers to question their duty and regret their adherence to the recent community tactics that helped trigger the violence.

A local Methodist preacher called the riot 'a fireball of anger.'

As the disorder continued in to the weekend, white people were seen visibly taking an active role in the looting and aggression towards the police laying waste to the rumours of a race war.

The violence, administered by brick and baton alike, drawing blood and bruise, causing broken bones and laceration, was heightened by the need for supremacy of the streets. The police and the locals were drawn into a fight for authority of territory. Shops and local businesses became targeted and ransacked leaving empty disembowelled shells in their place. The Windsor castle public house was one of at least two of its kind to betorched, it collapsed in eventual surrender as the flames ate and weakened its structure from within.

The director of a West Indian venue opposite Brixton police station commented. 'It's been coming a long time. I don't think it's a set-back for race relations.'

Five thousand people were estimated to have been involved.

Tension amongst some of the community on Julian's estate grew, becoming 'in your face', brooding and threatening. Words were not minced.

Suspicion, paranoia and ugliness spread like venom through the veins of the youth, their anger ascending through their bodies like a burning fuse fizzing its way to the powder kegs stacked within their skulls. The elders looked on with increasing concern and familial empathy.

All looked over their shoulders, avoiding the darkness. Deliberate wide berth was given to areas that normally felt safe through familiarity.

Groups of young black men congregated in the stairwells, corridors and outside the estate's betting shop and pub, debating and reasoning with occasional raised voices and exaggerated body gestures.

'Dem bombaclaat!'

'T' rass!'

'Burn don Babylon!'

The curses flowed, a mix of genetic patois and inherited cockney.

'The NF are gonna march down the high street?'

'Not on my fuckin' watch mate!'

'They're gonna pass the end of the road!'

'They want to march to the estate!'

'They ain't gonna get past the top of the road, believe me!'

The believable and ridiculous became inseparable as truth and fiction spewed from over-eager mouths merging to create the heavy cloud of fear, uncertainty and resentment that was casting a dense doom-laden shadow over the estate.

The cloud was about to break.

By Saturday, most were convinced that the National Front did indeed intend to march in numbers through the high street and, quite possibly, onto the estate where it was rumoured that they intended to hold a rally.

Their spokesman, it was believed, a man who apparently held some standing in the hierarchy of right-wing fascist politics, was to make a fire and brimstone speech to the disgruntled white masses, or, in reality, continue preaching to his already converted minions who might have managed to get on the right bus that morning.

It was a spurious rumour without a doubt but one that seemed to solidify by the hour until it eventually became the gospel itself.

Gerry called for Julian around ten o'clock, he looked quite dapper that morning in his ice-blue Strides and lovingly-shined, black tasselled loafers. Julian felt scruffy in comparison but was waiting for his favourite items to be washed and dried, so Fred Perry polo shirt and jeans it had to be.

'Where are you lad's headed?'

Joe was leaning on his shoulder against the lounge door frame, his hands thrust in his jeans pockets. He had cut them off at the pass, not allowing them to vacate the flat without passing border control and experiencing a little interrogation first.

'Not sure yet.' Julian lied, ensuring that his eyes avoided Joes.

Gerry shuffled self-consciously beside him rubbing the toe of his shoe against the back of his trouser leg before checking its glossy shine.

'Well, you've heard the rumours no doubt.' He paused for confirmation from them but none was forthcoming. 'Stay clear of it. If there's trouble it won't be pretty and the last thing your mother needs is a phone-call from the old bill or accident 'n' emergency saying you've been hurt or arrested. Get me?'

Julian nodded, again avoiding Joes stare.

They headed straight for the estates main frontage, where the blocks and maisonettes and the voluminous concrete skirt gave way to the main road to and from the area.

They had heard that this was where the welcoming committee for the royal racists visit would be congregating.

The road was already blocked with a small crowd.

From their vantage point suspended on the concrete apron above the road they observed the main faces, faces they knew, heads up, chests out, as they milled about among the parked cars, chatting with associates, acquaintances and cohorts and looking mostly serious.

It felt as if they were watching a theatre production.

There was no merriment, the small muster of youths were tense and volatile, the adrenaline they secreted and other stimulants they may have consumed working their way through their systems, heightening the anticipation of confrontation and battle.

Strangers, almost definitely not from around the estate seemed to keep a quiet back seat on the fringes allowing the natural leaders, the generals therein, to mingle amongst the ranks and offer encouragement and reassurance to those whose bottle wavered. Some had scarves tied around their mouths and noses in readiness.

Gerry gave a nudge and gestured up towards the high road. Julian twisted his upper body to achieve a better view, expecting to see a marching parade of Nazi boot boys heading towards the estate and instead found a line of policemen in front of dark transit vans kitted out with steel meshed windscreen shields. They carried a mixture of long, transparent, rectangular-shaped shields and compact, round shields among them and wore protective headgear much like a half face motorcycle helmet with a visor. Some had already drawn their long batons.

'Shit, it's the SPG!'

The SPG; Special Patrol Group.

A centrally organised mobile police squad originally set up nearly twenty years previous to combat serious crime and problems which were unable to be controlled or dealt with by local divisions. Within ten to fifteen years the patrol group had become folk devils, urban legends, spoken about amongst the general public, especially the young, with an exaggerated dread. They were often compared to storm troopers with little empathy for anyone unlucky enough to be in the way when they executed a well-drilled baton charge or sent in a snatch squad to grab agitators.

In recent years the group had been brought into increased and often controversial use to control demonstrations, football crowds and large public disorder. Tasks for which they would became forever associated.

A jingling of milk bottles caused Julian to turn and face three young men who had appeared from behind them unexpectedly. He looked down at the crate held between two of the men, the intoxicating fumes of petrol crept up into his nasal passages making his head swim.

'What you doing 'ere, lickle bwoys?' The soul boy looked a touch vexed, Julian did not recognise him. 'Dis 'ere ain't no place for you. Best move along an' let us do our t'ing.'

Julian glanced at Gerry. He was already moving around the group without comment; Julian hurriedly joined him as they made themselves scarce.

'It's okay we'll find another spot.' He insisted, once out of earshot.

Gerry planned to stay and watch the fireworks regardless of the risks involved. Julian was shaken up a touch by the interruption of the petrol bomb crew but found the lure of curiosity too great to resist.

Leaning on the railings of the outer fire escape of Basil block they had found a panoramic view of the whole road and the nervous stand-off between the two groups.

Through the crowd of youths, two older men eased their way to the front. One was instantly recognisable as Father Augustus, the other was a youth worker from the club which was held at the community centre. From there, they advanced without falter up the road until they were standing in front of the thick blue line which cut off access to the high road. Augustus asked to speak to someone in authority. A hard looking sergeant-at-arms shouldered through his ranks from the rear, the shields parting to allow him through to parlay with the two negotiators. He looked stern and stubborn, standing legs apart, arms folded. At best, he looked impatient.

'Why the heavy presence?' It seemed like a fair question from Augustus, there were an awful lot of police present.

'Why the mob?' The officer retorted, nodding past Augustus' shoulder towards the crowd.

'The NF are not welcome 'round 'ere.' Augustus kept cool.

'You lot don't decide who goes where and who does what.' The officer motioned to his men with his thumb. 'That's our job.'

'But this is their home, feelin's is running high. The yout' getting' restless.'

Sporadic shouts and curses flew in the police direction.

'Back off, Babylon!'

'fuck off, bullman!'

'SPG burn t' raas!'

'Let us manage our children and settle down the pressure.' Augustus was asking for a tactical withdrawal. 'Take your men back up the road, give us time to talk do'n an' disperse dem. They will soon tire and hunger.'

'Are you 'aving a laugh, old man?' the officer shook his head. 'Tell the kids to get their arses off home and get on with their homework.'

The youth worker made a plea for clemency and cooperation but this fell on deaf ears as the officer turned and made his burly way back through the line to his position. Father Augustus stepped forward in an attempt to get closer to continue the negotiations but was blocked by the solid plexi-glass of a riot shield which, had he been younger and more steady on his legs, he probably could have absorbed but in this instance it sent him backwards a couple of stumbling steps before he fell back onto his bottom with some drama.

The youth worker struggled to help him to his feet while the line of grim-faced officers remained impassive and firm. As the two made their way to the side of the road for Augustus to regain his composure, the first half brick hit a shield about head high.

The initial bombardment of the police lines was short-lived as the youths in their eagerness used up their supplies of missiles quickly. This prompted a strong organised baton charge from the ranks who punished the brick throwing stragglers by targeting their legs and arms, caning them with long batons before leaving them groaning in the road or having them picked up and unceremoniously speared into the back of the waiting containment vans.

The petrol bombers were frantically trying to light the rags that acted as fuses for their home-made molotovs. Soul boy hurled the first primed bottle of flammable liquid which shattered just short of the advancing line, spewing its napalm-like contents over the bottom of the riot shields. The line paused in its tracks for a moment, the appearance of petrol bombs warranting more caution.

A small group of officers with smaller circular shields peeled off the back of the line, despatched by the command in the direction of the bombers. Quickly alert, the bombers fled into the maze of the estate, leaving the remainder of the missiles behind to be confiscated by the snatch squad.

Julian watched the riot fizzle out to a standstill as throughout the rest of the day and into the early evening the police and the few remaining obstinate youths fought minor skirmishes through the walkways and underpasses of the estate. As darkness descended, rumours of a fight back or night time assault came to nothing as the estates youth dispersed, slipping off to the sanctuary of their family homes and the safety of their beds.

The police command kept a small contingent of officers parked up the road in case of any further re-occurrence. They looked bored and restless as they drank lousy coffee out of Styrofoam cups and told lewd jokes to one another in the dimly lit interior of the riot wagons.

The local papers reported a distorted and inaccurate piece on the disturbance, blaming delinquent black youth and outside anarchist agitators for triggering the violence. And though there were certainly delinquents and anarchists present amongst the locals present they could hardly be credited for designing or starting the disturbance.

Those seeds of revolt had already been sown and nurtured in to the psyche of those in society coming of age. Seeds that had been planted by the actions and policies of the insecure old guard who tried to enforce their out-dated values and principals upon the young with their iron fists and puppet police force.

And of course, as expected, the rumoured right wing march was found to be a work of complete fiction as well.

Its haunting relevance and apocalyptic vision were uncanny. When 'Ghost Town', The Specials latest release flew to the number one spot in the charts, the sound of sirens and splintering glass continued to disrupt the everyday life of inner city communities after those riots erupted in the late spring of '81.

The banal chatter of the geriatric deejay-cum-television presenter clasping his foam-headed microphone like a ceremonial phallus and surrounded by jostling flick-haired females, interrupted the promotional videos ending.

Julian felt like kicking the screen in.

Gerry broke the stunned silence.

'Terry looked well different.' He was right, Terry had looked different.

Older, more mature. Jazzy in his dark-blue pin-striped zoot suit. His hair was longer on top than usually wore it. Neville had also donned a wide-lapelled suit, with his hair twisted into short dreads he looked like a medusa-headed gangster.

'What do you think of it all?' Gerry looked across Julian's lounge. Straddled across the seat of a reversed wooden chair, his arms folded across the back rest, he looked over at Julian awaiting his insight.

Julian's mind rewound. Back to the dark foreboding of the video, remembering the subtle menace of the cinematography, the simplicity of production thoroughly complimenting the message within the song's lyrics and instrumentation. Watching the band joy-ride a large jalopy around in the suggested dereliction of the streets of wherever, the action escalating to a maniacal peak of hysterical wailing, had certainly had an impact. Julian's synopsis though was brief.

'I really liked it.'

Gerry's expression seemed to demand more in-depth analysis from him.

'Best video they've done?'

Neither of them was to realise the finality of the moment.

Ghost Town was destined to become the bands triumphant swansong, creating an almost unsurpassable peak, the jewel in their crown as far as most critics were concerned.

All the clubs are being closed dooown...

Dis place...

Playing the extended version on 12 inch later in the dusk-lit interior of his bedroom, Julian studied the tiny mites flurrying around the moist black-mould rooted in the corners and creases of the window frame. He wondered what on earth they could find there.

What attracted them?

Leaning on his bare elbows, feeling the cold flatness of the metal sill, he gazed out at the deserted expanse below the window.

All the kids had drifted off to their homes, leaving the painted goal posts on the planters and the concrete pitch, where imaginary goals had won the cup for the Hammers or the Spurs, to the coming night and its creatures.

Rico's mournful trombone oozed out from the small speakers as the record segued into its second phase; a seamless dub. Like a ghostly wail it lamented off the peeling wood-chip covered walls.

A woman across the way busied herself un-pegging laundry from a line stretched across her balcony and cradling it in her crooked arm. Her legs were blurred by the wire-strengthened glass of the balconies rail.

Movement around the base of a planter caught Julian's eye. At first suspecting a cat he watched the creature's movement with a lazy disinterested gaze before he recognised that the animal's snout was long and also boasted a tail of fluffy brush. Looking more attentively he recognised the snap, alert movements belonging to the fox, its pointed ears and its head flicking sideways at the smallest sound, movement or whisper of scent. Searching amongst the blown detritus of human life it sought a morsel, a tasty tit-bit tossed aside by an individual too lazy to search out a bin. Julian watched as the foxes persistence seemed to have paid off. After a quick glance about, it burrowed its narrow wet nose into a discarded bundle of grease-stained take-away wrappers.

After a quick root, it withdrew triumphant, the remains of a red-skinned saveloy clenched firmly between its teeth.

Snappily, as if realising that it had been watched, it raised its head up towards Julian's window, its eyes glistening and the sausage-shaped delicacy hanging from its mouth like a fat cigar, before trotting off towards the outer perimeter of the estate.

The audible pop of the needle lifting of the record stamped a full stop on the moment.

They were in the kitchen. They spoke quietly as if to avoid the youngsters overhearing. Julian recognised the sounds of his mum preparing Joe's nocturnal lunchbox, the metallic rustle of tin foil and the snapping of the tupperware lid being pressed into place on the plastic container.

It was seven o'clock in the evening. Joe had been moonlighting for a good month. Taking on some temporary security work, he drove around in a small sign-written van, checking on specified premises, making sure there were no unsolicited visitations in the lonely hours of the night. This was all on top of his regular job driving the trucks.

If he was fortunate and timed it right he could sneak cat-naps throughout the shift, parking up out of sight and setting the alarm on his digital watch so he could check in at the required times.

'It'll be worth it in the long term, love' Joe reassured her. Julian heard the kiss Joe pecked on to her forehead. 'It's the only option at the moment, if we want do what's right for the kids and ourselves the dough's gotta come from somewhere.'

'I know, Joe. I just wish I could do more.'

'You do plenty.' Joe reassured her, 'Don't you worry about that. Bringing up this family amongst all the crap that goes on around 'ere is a miracle in itself.'

There was a pause in their conversation. Julian guessed they were hugging.

'We'll soon have that deposit saved an' then we can start the ball rollin'. We've gotta stay strong, we never thought it would be easy, did we?'

'No. It's just hard when you're not here that's all.'

Julian heard his mum hand Joe his lunchbox.

General maintenance and up-keep of the estates fixtures and fittings had long become a thing of myth and legend. As funds had dwindled, the council's money belts were tightened and maintenance had suffered. The promise of a complete refurbishment to include new front doors, central heating and UPVC windows had evaporated as Conservative policy eroded local governmental power and therefore local spending by rate-capping.

Strikes by public sector workers in retaliation to cuts in hours and redundancies had left a backlog of badly needed repair work around the council estates of London.

And so windows remained smashed, doors hung injured from hinges, graffiti merged into one great unreadable scribble.

Once shiny and new, the intercom systems haemorrhaged brightly coloured wire innards from their vandalised fasciae; they had been assaulted soon after they were installed, never to be repaired.

Originally intended to minimise undesired access to the blocks, they had become a nuisance as the angry buzz of a pressed button breaking the quiet became a common and nightly occurrence and, more often than not, was found to be an irritating prank by bored youths. Foul-mouthed insults often accompanied the interruption through the intercom speaker.

Inside the flats, the wind and moisture forced its whistling presence through the badly designed window frames and the seemingly unbeatable black mould broke the will of even the most fervent, bleach-welding, scrubbing brush-armed house keeper.

Do you remember the good old days before the ghost town..,

We danced and swayed and the music played in a de boom town…

Their limbs were tingling with excitement. Conversation was difficult in the roar of the train carriage and yet they still chattered away. Gripping the sprung teardrop-shaped hand-holds to keep balance as the train flew along the rails of the London underground was an art in itself. Julian wondered what bright spark had invented such useless aids.

He caught their distorted reflections in the glass of the curve of the tube door. The pork-pie hat perched on the back of his head topped off his outfit of burgundy Fred Perry polo shirt, braces and jeans.

Gerry had also opted for a more casual look for the evening and had opted for a black with yellow trim Fred with white Sta-prest. Julian questioned the folly of wearing white trousers to a concert but Gerry was his own man.

He fingered the paper ticket stashed in the back pocket of his denims just to make sure it was still there. He could visualise the bold lettering, stating the name of the band they were on their way to see.

The Beat had once been part of the 2 Tone stable but after an initial hit on the label with 'Tears Of A Clown' had decided to go it alone. Spawning their own Go Feet label complete with dancing girl mascot, they continued to receive the adulation of the 2 Tone faithful with their calypso-tinged take on the sound.

Julian really liked them but he secretly wished it was The Specials they were going to see. That would have to wait. He was sure they would tour soon after the success of their recent release. After all it had got to number 1 in the charts.

Arriving at Hammersmith station they disembarked, slipping in among the throng of late commuters and colourful concert goers who made their way towards the yellow-lit exit signs.

Flashes of rude boy styling caught their attention as the crowd snaked and slithered slowly towards the escalators that carried them back up to the earth's surface.

A trilby hat here, a Harrington jacket there, button badges and cropped hairstyles.

A tall, sinewy youth passing nearby gave them both a knowing nod as he and his crew eased their way through. His olive skin and tight afro hair gave away his mixed race roots. He looked cool in his plum tonic suit, an underlying petrol-blue hue appearing in waves of movement through the material. A crisp white, button-down shirt emphasised the look. Julian gave Gerry a nudge with his elbow.

'Now that's smart.' He offered in a hushed voice. Gerry nodded his approval.

Exiting the fluorescent brightness of the tube station into the darkening skies of the evening they joined the hordes heading towards the venue for that nights gig, the Hammersmith Palais,.

The concert goers were a good mix of rude boys, skinheads, mods and the usual student types. Excited chatter and the clatter of lager cans floated on the exhaust-stained air.

The queue was long and seemed to be a law unto itself as friends and acquaintances blagged their way into more favourable positions in the line. Beer cans, flyers and chip wrappers littered the pavement around their feet. Plumes of cigarette smoke puffed from the queue like the steam from the funnel of a train. The anticipation was building, youngsters in the line were buzzing with adrenalin.

'Ruuudeboyyys!'

The shout from somewhere nearer the front of the queue made the hairs on the back of Julian's neck stand to attention, an involuntary grin spread across his face. Gerry gave him a nudge.

Before they had a chance to get bored with the wait the line began its workhouse shuffle towards black-jacketed gorillas waiting, ready to manhandle who and how they pleased.

The heat inside the ballroom was intense, causing sweat to trickle down Julian's forehead. Gerry's top was already wet through as if he had showered fully clothed. In the darkness the crowd swayed from one side of the auditorium to the other as one, like a human sea, it was futile to resist the movement. Julian made sure to stay close to Gerry, luckily he was easy to spot being so tall.

The music piped through the rooms personal address system was barely audible above the hum of conversation and banter. Sporadic chants were instigated by unseen songsters.

'Stand down Margaret, stand down please, stand down Margaret!'

The crowd sang, the lyrics flowing around the huge room like a football chant.

Julian felt sorry for the support band, out of place and out of their league they attempted to play their brand of jangly pop but the partisans were unreceptive, having none of it.

A deafening, drowning chant of 'We want The Beat!' ensured that no-one present could hear their set. Finally, with resignation, the support band left the stage before they were due; their heads hung low with disappointment as they helped the roadies drag the gear off the stage.

Julian felt he may pass out the heat was so immense. The atmosphere felt volatile, on the edge, teetering between frustrated hostility and expectant euphoria. Luckily for Gerry his height meant his head was held well above the furnace that Julian was enduring below his own shoulders but he was also perspiring in litres. Julian felt droplets splash on to him as the crowd swayed.

Then at last the lights dimmed, a spine-tingling roar went up from the crowd.

Shadows entered the stage from both wings; Julian could vaguely make out figures picking up instruments and somebody climbing behind the silhouette of the drum kit. Spotlights snapped in to life and exposed the stage.

'Y'alright?' Rankin' Roger addressed the crowd, wearing his characteristic black felt fedora hat and a check shirt. 'Take it easy y'nuh, look after your breddahs! Yeah?'

The band launched into 'Mirror in the bathroom'.

Dave Wakeling's vocals, the saxophones melody and the chugging rhythm sent the crowd into a communal skanking frenzy, you had no choice but to join in.

It is said 'that time flies when people are having fun' and Julian surmised that their time must have been travelling on Concorde that night.

All too soon it was over and they were back on the train scoffing the remnants of a greasy chilli-sauce-laden kebab and analysing the gig. The sweat from their bodies dried to a clammy film as a breeze drafted in through the open slits of a tiny vent in the carriage.

'When they did 'Twist An' Crawl',' Gerry slurped a piece of doner meat into his mouth, 'the crowd went mental!'

Julian belched. 'Yeah mate and 'Hands off she's mine' was ace too.'

'Wonder who's got your hat?'

Julian rubbed his cropped hair. His pork-pie hat had disappeared off his sweat-sodden head approximately three songs into the set and he had not seen a glimpse of it since. He hoped it was with someone who appreciated style.

He shrugged then looked down at Gerry's stained trousers.

'Shame about your strides, do you think you'll get them clean?'

'I don't know but you know what?' Gerry looked at him. 'It was bloody worth it.'

'I know what you mean.' Julian agreed. 'Now for The Specials!'

Gerry heard the familiar scratch of a key in the front door lock as Stan arrived home that evening. Gerry filled the kettle and placed it on to the gas ring of the cooker to heat while his dad settled in. Stepping into the lounge from the kitchen, Gerry greeted the saturated, bedraggled figure of his dad standing in the doorway.

'Nice weather for ducks!' He chirped. Stan returned a short, pained grin.

Gerry helped his father remove the sodden wool coat from his slumped shoulders. Water dripped from the corners of the coat which smelt heady as the moisture reacted with the wool. Collapsing with resignation into his favourite chair, Stan offered a weary attempt to remove his work boots. He raised his eyes to Gerry.

'Son?'

Gerry needed no more prompting. Kneeling before Stan, he untied the sodden boot laces, using his teeth where necessary to loosen them before hauling the boots off Stan's feet, the leather squeaking and secreting rainwater in his hands. Stan's socks were soaked through and stained. Pulling them off exposed ghostly-white wrinkled feet, evidence of too much time spent immersed in water.

Handing the hot mug of tea to his father, Gerry asked,

'How'd it go today, dad?'

The factory workforce had been given recent notice of enforced redundancies.

The government's policies that endorsed and encouraged individualism, private enterprise and, in turn, sought to weaken the trade unions power base, had allowed space for the boards at the head of industry to seek ways of ensuring that the workforce was run with economic efficiency and with discipline. New competition in the marketplace created bidding wars. This meant that firms had to fight dirty for orders. By saving on production time and expenditure and offering the best price on their product they could protect their profit margin and, maybe even, the survival of the firm itself.

Conservative policies had stunted the growth of union power initially with a moderate response to what they perceived as indiscipline in the public sector. Targeting those weaker public sectors such as the education and health department where they could exercise direct control, tight limits on pay increases were imposed. This tactic proved to be a lot tougher to implement where stronger senior unions, such as steel, the railways and coalmining were concerned.

The government were forced to back down when their 1980 coal industry act which reduced subsidies to the pits threatening immediate closures, caused a furore.

The miner's union may have presented the illusion of impregnability.

But Margaret Thatcher bided her time and as history would bear witness, once consolidating her position after the success of the Falklands war campaign, she would even up the score.

A bonus for the government in the rise in unemployment figures was that it helped weaken the trade unions strength. A government-induced business recession had increased unemployment to over two million by the end of 1980. With the skilled use of persuasive language, the Tory government had pointed an accusing finger;

'The economic problems that Britain was experiencing were partly due to the unions restrictions on the labour market…' they said.

The government outlawed the union's customary methods of regulating employee or employer's behaviour, in particular, pushing through a reversal of the legislation that favoured collective bargaining. In future, any union's interference of individual choice would not to be tolerated. The proportion of the workforce membership in the trade unions fell.

Cleverly, any restrictions on trade union activity and effect that came in were usually presented in tandem with the trumpeting of voluntarist tradition and the promotion of the individual right to choose. Closed shops, where it was obligatory to be a member of a union in order to be employed at that respective workplace, now required 80 %

support in ballots to set up any new arrangements.

Public funding was made available to support secret trade union ballots that were held, for example, to elect full-time officers and in votes for strike action. The number of strikes decreased as did work days lost due to industrial disputes.

The Conservatives first employment act in 1980 attempted to reduce the chance of mass picketing by limiting strike action only to the employee's place of work.

Stan had fronted the picket line at Morgan electrical fittings for a day the previous month when the first rumours of redundancies and other cost-saving drives had first ruffled feathers and caused concern amongst the five hundred plus employees that worked there.

But this day had been tougher.

Having received the official declaration of intent from the board and after attending numerous union meetings after work, listening to the uncertainty and fear of most of those present turn to militancy and anger, the picket line had seemed like a war front this time.

As the sky emptied its heavy load over himself and his comrades, Stan had envied those continuing to work through the strike action as he imagined them getting on with the job in hand, taking their breaks in the canteen and smokers room, reading their tabloids and enjoying the banter. Yet Stan knew this was not about a day's wage lost.

This was about the future.

The future for himself, his colleagues and the youngsters due to leave school.

It was a matter of honour, the working class standing side by side, protecting their right to work that day and for the future.

He had watched as his fellow strikers had aimed insults up towards the windows where he knew those inside the building would be supping their brews. He had shown restraint when the lorries had come and gone from the site, their trailers heavy with full loads, crossing the picket line.

He could not deny his companions their venom as they launched their fury at the driver's windows but it was just not his way.

'It's not looking very positive at the moment, Gerry.' Stan puffed, he stretched out his bootless feet wiggling his numb toes. 'Lads are breaking the line every day. It's as if they've already accepted their fates and are just resigned to earning their crust day by day with no thought for the immediate future let alone the years to come.'

'Will you be pushed out, d'ya think?'

'I expect so, mate. I'm older than most, can't lift like I used to, they probably view me as a bit of a liability even with my experience. New machinery means constant re-training so apart from time on the floor I'm no more knowledgeable than the next. I'm not far off me pension neither.' Stan paused with the thought, 'No, I can't think I'll be one of the lucky ones.'

Stan's eyelids drooped as they grew heavy with fatigue. Gerry watched them fight against the inevitable before they closed and the man's barrel chest began to rise and fall into the rhythm of sleep. A whistle broke the silence as expelled air passed through Stan's hairy nostrils. Perched on the broad arm of the chair, Gerry leant in, laying his arm across the chairs back and resting his head softly next to his dad's. He found comfort in the smell of his damp hair and tobacco smoke. It wasn't long before he dozed off too.

A frown was carved into Joe's brow; he appeared to have aged some years.

'Why don't you put some clothes on!' The bark startled Julian. 'And sit down while you're eatin' will yuh!'

Julian stopped spooning the cornflakes into his mouth. Nervously flicking a lone flake that clung to his lip like an orange scab back into the breakfast bowl, he watched Joe cross the kitchen.

'You alright, Joe?'

Joe paused at the opened fridge door, still for a moment, his hand resting on the chrome handle.

'I'm sorry, mate. I'm bloody knackered, that's all.'

Julian gazed down at his milk-white bare chest and yesterday's strides he had slipped into after getting out of bed that morning. A pair of thin black braces hung like elastic serpents around his buttocks. Julian's hairy-toed feet spread out in front of his body as he leant back against the melamine worktop. 'Do you want me to go and put more clothes on?'

Joe gave a forced tight-lipped smile, it looked painful. 'No, you're fine as you are.'

He poured hot water onto his instant coffee with two sugars, whitening the beverage with a splash of full-fat milk. Supporting himself against the worktop opposite, he took a slurp of the coffee.

He had already taken off the clip-on tie on his way home, allowing the light-blue shirt collar to flare out at the neck. Epaulettes sat on each shoulder in an attempt giving the garment a military feel, a look of authority, dark blue embroidery on the left breast pocket proclaimed the name of 'Securichex'.

'A hard night?' It was a question not a statement.

'Not hard, son, just long. Long and lonely. You almost wish for a bit of excitement, a break-in or something to break the monotony!' Joe shook his head lightly and gave a little laugh. 'I'd probably shit meself if I had to deal with a real alarm call!'

The red, white and blue bunting fluttered ever so gently in the whispered warmth of the summer's day. The open area around the estates community centre and its adjoining scattering of block-built planters were a hive of human activity.

The smell of burgers, hot dogs and fried onions mingled with the exotic spice of Jamaican patties, goat curry and jerk chicken. An ice cream van was handing out ice creams to eager children clamouring around its colourful panels. The elders, accessorised with union jack imagery, gently chided the over-boisterous youngsters who were beginning to make nuisances of themselves amongst the tables of food, drink and set-up activities. It was a day meant for relaxation and fun.

The announcement of a national holiday meant that most of the country had been looking forward to this day for weeks now, since February 24th in fact, when the couple's engagement had been announced publicly.

Doreen had watched the news broadcasts intently as they fed updates regarding arrangements for the royal wedding of Prince Charles to Lady Diana Spencer; or Lady Di as the commoners tended to allude to her.

The gig was to be held at St. Pauls cathedral on the 29th of July with an invited congregation of 3,500.

'She's so beautiful.' She had chirped and Julian had to agree with his mum, Diana was a pretty woman. Shy looking but radiating a sweetness, Lady Di , a 20 year old kindergarten nurse, daughter of Earl Spencer, seemed to be the perfect choice of bride for the man who would one day be king. Time would tell.

She appeared to genuinely want to be in contact with the public and displayed affection for the young, the old and less-able.

Julian secretly developed a bit of a thing for her though he was glad to say that it soon passed!

Julian had even had to endure the fictional soap marriage of Ken Barlow to Deidre in the Manchester-set soap Coronation street, a well-planned warm-up to the real thing, he had laughed along with Joe as his mum had blubbed when the on-screen duo finally tied the knot.

600,000 people filled London's streets on the day to celebrate and hopefully catch a glimpse of the young bride as she and the Earl Spencer made their way to the church in a glass carriage. Her Emmanuel designed dress boasted a train of 25 feet in length.

Charlie was there waiting, looking rather dashing in his naval dress uniform. Julian wondered if he knew how to sail a boat let alone a battleship.

The wedding became the most popular ever broadcast on television as 750,000,000 viewers worldwide tuned in to watch them get hitched.

The collective clangs of a troop of steel drummers rattling out a calypso rendition of 'Oh when the saints' helped complete the carnival atmosphere as Julian and Gerry fed their way, amongst the fancy dress adorned kids waiting for judging to commence, towards the fairground rides that had been set up for the day.

Julian scraped around a girl melting in her cardboard box Rubiks cube outfit and bumped into Hilda Ogden welding a mop as she tried to devour her quickly melting ice cream cone before the judges appeared.

Movement on top of the community centres single story roof caught his eye.

Budgie and Alfie, the estate's friendly skinheads had climbed up on to the flat surface and were now perched on the edge, their boot-clad legs dangling over the roof apron as they sat sharing a bottle of cheap but no doubt potent cider, swigging straight from the large bottle. Already slightly inebriated, they were gyrating comically to the catchy Caribbean sounds of the steel drummers and were sporting custom-made t-shirts bearing the portraits of Charles and Di, complete with royal crest. Large block letters spelt out their good wishes to the soon-to-be-weds.

Passers-by underneath shouted up returned pleasantries as the two friendly characters called out to the mixed bag of faces below. Spotting them below, Budgie gave a thumbs up as he hollered, 'Awight, rudies!'

Julian worried for the tipsy patriot's safety but they seemed unconcerned.

Julian checked out Gerry's outfit of 'Specials' transferred t-shirt and denim strides, a pair of opaque wrap-around shades covering his eyes as they waved back at the loveable rogues.

Competing with the rabble congregated around the waltzer was a test of endurance but good-natured. As the previous ride came to a slow halt, it was all the attendants could do to stop the impatient hoards clambering onto to the cars before they had safely stopped and dispensed the previous occupants.

Tucking themselves into one of the cylindrical cups, the hard bench seating quickly numbing buttocks, they were about to pull the chrome bar down into position when the attendant, resplendent in his teddy boy outfit of white cap-sleeved t-shirt, Elvis tattoo and crepe-soled brothel creepers, his long elephants trunk quiff dangling in the middle of his forehead, grasped the bar, gesturing for others to join them.

Julian glanced across nervously at Gerry, his favourite shades now held safely in his palm, as the two girls squeezed in beside them. The sweet, buttery aroma of coconut oil filled the compartment and Julian felt the smooth velvet of the girl's skin as their upper arms made contact. He tried to look cool and collected as he attempted to relax despite being sandwiched between Gerry and the lithe figure of the girl. Straining his eyeballs to the corners of their sockets he could see that the girl was pretty, her features elfin, boasting full, glistening lips. Looking down he could see her jeans hugged her narrow legs, her bare feet exposed in her rubber flip-flops.

His embarrassment was temporary as the fairground ride jolted into life, the noise of its grinding mechanics vying with the amplified pop being emitted from various tinny speakers.

Tears rolled from his eyes as the cars and their occupants caterpillared their way around the circular track. Given the occasional helping hand by the attendants, the cars would spin ferociously as momentum and gravity combined forcing the bodies of the riders into the backs of the seats and into unintentional contact with the other passengers depending on which way the car was spun.

Gerry's features were a picture of distortion as his face unwillingly grimaced with the g-force. The girls screamed and laughed, the thrill of the moment taking over.

Julian's grimace threatened to split his face in two. It was a job to stop the snot flowing from his nostrils never mind the flow of his tears.

Cherise was the gorgeous result of a liaison between a West Indian man and her Irish mother. Of course, Julian did not discover the facts that day and they were not relevant to him then.

The ice having been broken by the involuntary exposure of ones emotions on the waltzer it had been a relatively easy task to initiate the start of courtings with the two girls.

Julian felt a bit guilty as Gerry's intended was a bit aggressive and resistant to his manly charms but being the great mate he was, he stuck in there allowing Julian the privilege of time with Cherise.

The attraction had been instant and despite her subtle teasing about still being a 'rude bwoy' they got on like the proverbial house on fire.

The gang of four hung out for the rest of the day, enjoying the festivities and entertainment, allowing the sun's rays to gently toast their skins as they lay on the scratch of grass left on a sloping bank near the fairground set-up.

That night Julian experienced the coolness of Cherise exposed skin in a more intimate closeness as they pressed against each other on the landing of the fire escape stairs to her block. Her moist lips felt voluminous against his own, the lingering hint of juicy fruit chewing gum sweetening the taste.

She was assertive and pulled away from him before he got too clever.

'Can I see you again?' He asked as she turned and pushed open the fire escape door, its hinges complaining through lack of lubrication.

'Yeah, why not.' she smiled back at him, 'You know where I live now, don't yuh'

Julian shrugged his shoulders in the yoke of his Ben Sherman button-down shirt ensuring it was hung right on his frame before rapping his knuckles on the varnished front door. Standing awkwardly he squeezed his hands into his trouser pockets. Deciding this could look too cocky he pulled them back out again.

Then finding that his arms felt nervous and superfluous flapping around by his sides he chose to clasp them behind his back instead.

He could not detect any movement coming from inside number sixteen, at least he could not hear anything that is. Spotting the crudely fitted doorbell on the door jamb he reached and gave it a good firm press with his finger.

Right at that precise moment the door swung open startling Julian into momentary paralysis. His finger stayed put, glued on to the white button for longer than was necessary.

'Where's the bejeezus fire?' The strong looking woman's Irish brogue cut through the annoying ring of the bell like a hot wire through butter.

He let go of the bell quickly.

'And who might you be?' The question caught him by surprise. He thought he had been expected. He stuttered as he tried to recall his own name.

'Ah,' The Irish lady nodded sagely, her dark red hair bobbing with the movement 'You'd be the young scallywag that's been taking advantage of our Cherise!'

'Err, umm!' What could he say?

'Alton, Alton!' She hollered back into the dark corridor of the flat, 'The young man who's been takin' a liberty with our daughter has saved you the job of having to track him down, he's right here fresh-faced and looking pretty pleased with himself. Do you want a word, like?'

Julian's eyes widened with fear as he imagined what creature lay beyond the door at the end of their hallway. He got ready to sprint.

'Rose, will you leave the boy alone, you cruel woman. Fetch him in, where's your manners!' The deep baritone of the man's voice boomed through the narrow hall. Rose grinned at him.

'I was only having a bit of banter with the lad, a bit of a joke that's all.' She called out. Rose opened the door fully. 'Come on in darling, Cherise will be down in a minute.' She guided Julian into the hallway with a gentle hand on his back closing the door behind him. 'Go on in, he doesn't bite.'

Passing a mirror that boasted a colourful beaked toucan peering out from a Guinness advertisement, he felt warmth, homeliness to the flat that the outside disguised. He eased the door of the lounge open.

Alton was sat in a green foliage-embossed armchair that matched the rest of the suite.

The room was meticulously clean, everything in its place and not a speck of dust floating in the window-lit air of the room. A display cabinet housed small china figurines and Julian found his eyes drawn to a brown and white glazed china shire horse pulling a Gypsy caravan.

There were bottles of spirits collected neatly on a shelf with cocktail and shot glasses stacked regimentally next to them.

Alton was watching horse racing on the television. Julian noticed a copy of the Racing Post on the arm of his chair.

Alton looked him over. 'Sit yourself down, son.'

Julian was surprised though he tried not to show it, he had been expecting a Caribbean accent. He did not mean to stereotype but he did that sometimes. Alton had a strong cockney accent.

Catching Alton's eyes he noticed that the man appeared to have a lazy one. Julian tried hard not to focus on it.

'Nice shoes.' Alton gestured to Julian's tasselled loafers. Julian was glad that he had taken the effort to shine them for the occasion.

Alton was a big man but definitely not fat, he looked strong. His short afro hair was peppered with grey, a bald patch glistened through a thinning crown.

'Nice to see a young man makin' an effort these days.'

'Any luck?' Julian enquired as he plonked himself onto the firm seat of the sofa. He nodded towards the racing on the screen.

Alton laughed a deep laugh. His face stretched with good humour.

'Won a penny, lost a pound.'

'It's a bloody fools game, that's what it 'tis!' Rose ambled into the room interrupting the merriment.

As she sat on the other end of the sofa she turned slightly to address him.

'Tell me a bit about yourselves.'

Alton raised his eyes at Julian, Julian tried not to alert Rose to the act.

'What do your mother and father do?'

As he gave Rose the heads-up on the family history he noticed the gold crucifix she wore, its patina, its harsh edges smoothed with a thousand caresses. It hung between the three undone buttons of her white blouse nestling at the top of the deep cleavage of her ample freckled bosom.

Realising that she may have thought he was staring at her breasts he quickly averted his eyes, peeking over at Alton to ensure that no etiquette had been breached.

'Ahh, it must be nice to have sisters, especially ready-made ones!' Rose heaved herself up off the chair causing him to sink back in to it.

'I'll go hurry Cherise up. Probably making herself beautiful for yourself.'

'Could be a while then!' Alton joked.

Julian laughed then stopped himself quickly.

Alton was watching the horses being paraded around the paddock before the race. Julian guessed he was checking their posture, gait and form.

All the nag's looked the same to Julian!

Cherise arrived in the doorway and she looked stunning.

She had parted her straightened afro hair down the centre of her head, drawing both sides together in bunches. The puff-balls of black hair stood stiffly off the side of her head. Her skin was flawless, not a spot or blemish.

She wore a broderie anglaise blouse tied at the back and tight figure hugging black velvet trousers.

He stood up. It felt the right thing to do. He had seen James Bond do it when a lady entered the room.

'Dinner will be around thirty minutes. Do you like toad-in-the-hole?' Rose asked.

'Sounds great.' He smiled.

'Good 'cos that's what you're getting anyway!' Rose left for the kitchen.

'I'm gonna give mum a hand.' Cherise looked at him. 'Will you be okay for a mo?'

'Get on,' Alton waved a hand, ' He'll be fine, won't yuh, son.'

Alton had arrived in England in the fifties as a young boy with his parents from Jamaica. His parent's stoic stubbornness had helped them survive the early years; that early pain of isolation, the fear vented towards them by some of the community, that fear manifesting itself through direct hostility, ignorance, uneducated comments and dirty looks.

Alton remembered well the bullying and put-downs at school he received from teachers and pupils. In geography and history lessons he was always asked to point out the pink bits, the British Empire, on the maps. He was reminded constantly of what Britain and its pioneers had done for the uncivilised world including the West Indies.

Thankfully the arrival of the Sixties heralded a new era of revolution, of experimentation and of integration. Alton found that his colour and culture became exotic, in demand even. Young folk, curious, tolerant, inquisitive, less prejudiced, the Modernists of the East end, Jazzers and brave adventurous women sought the company of himself and his kind.

Frequenting the Roaring Twenties club in Carnaby street long before the street became the clichéd fashion centre of swinging London he partied with his peers, among sussed white men, plenty of pretty black and white women dancing to the blue beat and rhythm and blues records spun by resident dee-jay Count Suckle.

At a basement shebeen in Islington, North London, early one summer morning as the party was in full swing, Alton had found his attention stolen by a girl with flame-red hair, her milk-white freckled skin a distinct contrast to the dark complexions of most of the clientele, including his own, who were at the illegal drinking club.

After politely interjecting in the conversation between Rose and her friend who had dragged her to the party, he spent the rest of the evening in her company.

Normally quick and eager to bed the ladies he chatted up in clubs, instead he found himself enveloped in her sharp-witted, intelligent personality. Her self-confidence and assertiveness were attractive qualities.

Rose made Alton laugh.

Rose was a student nurse. Hailing from Enniskillen, in the county of Fermanagh in Northern Ireland, she had come to England with a long term friend Sheila to fulfil their dreams of working as nurses in the National Health Service.

Her friend Sheila had missed Ireland and her family awfully, eventually deciding to return home leaving Rose alone in London.

As if to ward off the possibility of loneliness, Rose busied herself with study and work. By the time she returned to her digs at night she was so exhausted that it was all she could do to get herself undressed before closing her eyes.

It was not long before Rose fell pregnant with Cherise.

Alton was thrilled and proposed marriage immediately. He hoped his job as a plasterer would provide enough for their immediate needs.

Music and laughter filtered through from the kitchen, Alton raised his eyebrows. Julian got up and opened the door. The blast of oven-heat and hearty home-cooking smells caught him full blast.

'we got a good thing going..'

'a real good thing going..'

'that girl and me..'

The soft reggae of a lovers rock tune was chugging out of the radio, its sweetly-sung romance accompanied by two self-appointed backing singers, Rose and Cherise.

He leant on the kitchen doorframe partially hidden by the plastic streamers that were designed to keep the flies out. They always seemed to get tied back in most of the houses he had been in that had them. It was such a pain to pass through their rainbow web as you often got caught up in the multi-coloured tentacles all the time. Julian wondered why bother putting them up in the first place.

Rose and Cherise were gyrating around the kitchen to Sugar Minott, a potato masher and wooden spoon as microphones. They were oblivious to his presence. Julian thought it was a lovely scene.

Later as they lay on top of Cherise bed, their stomachs full with batter and sausages, he found himself wondering how bizarre and unpredictable the world could be.

How much was down to design? How much to planning? How much to chance? How much of it was fate?

What was it that drew a black boy and his family from the West Indies and a Northern Irish girl across the sea to a dingy basement party in London, England where they would meet for the first time?

Was it accident or design that saw Cherise and her friend clambering onto the same fairground ride that Gerry and Julian just happened to already be on?

'What you thinking about?'

'The world of cause and effect, the great wheel of life.'

'Heavy, man!' Cherise tucked her head back into his chest.

Arriving home that evening, he crept in quietly, slipping off his hard-soled loafers in the hall aware that the girls were already in bed upstairs avoiding wanting to make too much noise.

The lounge was mood-lit, the television flickering, its sound turned low.

'Hi darling. Did you have a nice evening?' His mum looked up. She was cradling one of the cushions off the sofa, her legs folded up onto the seat pad.

'It was really nice, thanks. Alton and Rose are really nice.'

'Oh, that's good to hear.'

'Are you okay?' He looked at the cushion.

'I'm fine it just gets a bit lonely sometimes after the girls go up, you'd think I'd be used to it by now, your nan and grandad were always early to turn in when we lived there'

Julian felt some guilt for going over to Cherise's for the evening.

'Rose is a good cook, we had toad-in-the-hole. Not as good as yours though!'

'Flattery will get you everywhere.' Mum put aside the cushion giving it a pat. 'Would you like a cup of tea?'

'Stay there, mum, I'll make it.'

After placing the cup of tea on the sideboard nearest, Julian sat on the floor next to his mum's knees.

The hardness of the linoleum tiles under the thin cord carpet gnawed at his buttocks but he endured the discomfort enjoying the closeness the position offered.

Juliet Bravo was on the beat, the familiar theme tune of the police drama accompanying the opening credits.

He felt his mum's finger tips contact his bristly head, circling, stroking and massaging his scalp with affection.

'You're growing up so quick. I don't know where the time goes.'

His nerve endings were tingling with her gentle scratching.

'Pretty soon you'll be off and doing your own thing, maybe even getting married.'

Julian gave a small laugh. His head, neck and shoulders were beginning to relax into submission. He vaguely remembered letting his head collapse onto his mum's legs then the lights went out.

The lorry's cab shook aggressively in time with the huge engines throb as it waited, gearstick jammed in to neutral, it was hard to hear the stereo on the dashboard.

Joe waited patiently and, somewhat, apprehensively for the two large galvanised steel gates to be opened by the factory security guards.

He had a good idea of the reception he was likely to get on the other side of the gates but it still made him a touch nervous. Emotions could play havoc with a man's common sense, driving him to do the most ill-thought-through acts.

The lorry was heavy with the load of electrical fittings Joe had just collected from the despatch department. He had been surprised by how solemn the blokes in the loading bay had been, normally chatty and up-beat with a well-aimed joke, they had gone about the task of loading up, efficiently but with a sense of weariness.

Morgan's had been suffering the nasty business of industrial dispute between the employer and employee and Joe was still not used to running the gauntlet of ugliness that waited outside the factory gates. He had locked his doors.

The guard had checked the paperwork Joe had handed him and was entering the small hut adjacent to the gates where he activated the opening mechanism.

Joe could understand the strikers upset and anger.

He empathised with their cause.

Put in their position, he liked to think that, he too, would stand up and be counted.

But he guessed he was a realist.

He believed their protests were wasted energy, a feeble irritation and minor problem that the fat cats, the bosses with their cosy offices, with their swanky boardrooms, with their Epping residences and with their highly polished executive cars, would slowly break down until the numbers at the gates were fewer.

After all the government was on the boss's side.

The toughened windows of the truck's cab and the throbbing engine noise blocked out most of the vented obscenities and angry voices aimed at him but he wished they would not gob phlegm on his side windows and mirrors.

He could use his wipers and washers on the large front screen but the spit on the side had to be removed by hand and that made him nauseous.

He did not mean to upset anyone but if they would listen they would understand his need to continue crossing their picket line, earning an honest crust and providing for the present and the future of his family.

He would explain that they were in the process of saving for a deposit on a house.

He would explain the need to get the kids off that rundown hell-hole and to give them all the comfort and safety they deserved.

He was even working two jobs, he would tell them.

Joe didn't think the workers would be very receptive though.

The gates parted slowly with the odd stutter in their mechanised movement. Joe waited as he always did for them to reach the sides of the road before engaging first gear and allowing the truck to advance.

The men in the gate hut did not give their usual raised salute as he left the premises. Joe wondered if they sympathised with the pickets.

Unfamiliar faces, contorted in anger, hurled abuse at the truck's cab. Placards and fists beat a tattoo on its bodywork like a roll of distant thunder. The side windows became fogged and smeared with mucus.

An egg exploded on the passenger side windscreen, its sticky contents adhering to the glass.

Joe applied the brakes as a striker tumbled in front of the huge vehicle despite the efforts of two clearly out-numbered policemen to stop the man doing so.

He checked his doors were locked, they were.

Joe glanced out of his side window at the group of men stood on the pavement. He was glad he did not see anyone he recognised. He felt guilty enough as it was.

Most looked completely fed up with the situation as they stood with their hands buried deep in their pockets. Some glared in his direction and others were already turning away, their point having been made, saving some of their insults for the next traitor or scab who dared to cross the picket line.

A lone figure stood out from the crowd.

He reminded Joe of somebody but he could not place the face.

A stout, bull-like man, his size elevated him above his colleagues. His hair was full and dark but it belied his age, Joe thought.

He looked up at the truck's cab with a dignified air allowing a plume of cigarette smoke to jet from his pursed lips.

He did not shout, spit or attack the lorry but stood impassive.

Their eyes locked for a moment.

Joe felt the communication.

Stan was feeling fatigued, he had stood the line for hours and was running on empty but still he stayed.

Bound by his principles and his sense of duty, he served his time alongside his comrades, a flesh and bone reminder of the real and human impact of impending man-power cut-backs at the factory.

He had watched men he had respected, he had once counted as friends and colleagues pass through the steel spiked gates that morning. Heads down, they had hurried past the small group of cold, wet and angry strikers who fired their barbed comments towards them.

For greed or necessity, Stan was not sure. They had made their own choices as was their right to do so in his opinion.

Stan had chosen his way, as he always had, and that way was to stick to his beliefs, his principles and carry them through despite the consequences.

The crowd around Stan became restless, bustling, agitated, as they realised another truck was about to bring its load out of the factory gates.

'Fuckin' slag!'

'Scabby bastard!'

'Ain't 'e got no fuckin' morals?'

The men were descriptive in their anger, Stan winced at their explicitness. No prude, he never felt comfortable with personalised verbal abuse even if people were upset.

The atmosphere thickened as the gates began to open slowly peeling back towards the kerbside.

Stan reached into the inside pocket of his donkey jacket pulling out a pack of cigarettes. Placing one between his wind-dry lips, he lit it.

As the truck crept forward through the gates, the burst of noise enveloped Stan, the foulness of its content a reminder of the emotion that fired in the striker's bellies.

Stan saw a pink orb fly and splat against the driver's windscreen leaving fragments of smashed shell and glutinous yolk stuck to the glass.

Johnny Osgood stumbled into the road despite the clear requests from the police present to stay on the pavement for safety's sake.

Stan's eyes lifted, drawn to the driver's side window where his gaze made contact with the occupants own. He forced the cigarette smoke through his lips.

He looked like any other man.

Dum de dum de dum de dum de dum…

It was not often that he got the chance to be alone with Cherise. Trying to divide his time between Gerry and his love life was becoming increasingly more difficult for Julian as the hostilities between the two became more divisive and common-place. She objected to Gerry as he objected to her.

Dum de dum de dum de dum de dum…

Her tongue wove its magic in his mouth smearing his palate with pungent aniseed-ball flavoured juices. The settee complained at their combined weight as they wriggled around on the seat cushions.

Dum de dum de dum de dum de dum…

Being asked to baby-sit the two J's would normally have been a real chore but inviting Cherise round to keep him company helped make the evening far more interesting.

A bottle of cherryade and a bag of penny sweets was enough to convince the girls to adjourn to the upstairs allowing him and Cherise some quality time together.

Dum de dum…

Feeling that Cherise was nicely warmed up Julian slipped his hand into the gap between her velour sweater and stretch jeans feeling her baby-soft skin, goose-bumps erupting on her with his touch. Slowly, he smoothed his palm along her side, upwards until he felt the hard edge of her cotton brassiere; the border control, the Berlin wall.

He chose to take his chance, he was going over! For death or freedom!

She allowed his hand to slide along the material until he cupped her warm, firm breast snuggled tight within.

Dum de dum..

A tribal-type chant mingled with the hypnotic drumbeat from upstairs.

'Ant music!' Cherise started, she craned her neck, twisting her head to hear it better. Any sexual tension was dispelled abruptly, any hint of libido quashed by her curiosity.

Julian suddenly felt compromised and conspicuous; his hand was still planted firmly on her breast. Like a schoolboy caught peeking, he eased his hand out, her breasts shape now nothing but a memory imprinted in his moist palm.

'Ant what?' He had difficulty hiding the frustration in his voice.

'Adam and the ants. Ant music. Stand and deliver. You know, The dandy highwayman.' She said this to him like it was obvious, something he should know instinctively. The penny dropped. Julian conceded defeat.

'The girls are playing it upstairs.'

Freeing herself from his clumsy embrace, she straightened her shiny top, pulling it downwards before getting up.

'Where are you going?' He was perched on the edge of the seat, waiting for the outward expression of his excitement to abate before daring to get up from the sofa himself.

'I'm gonna see what your sisters are doing up there.'

She headed off, up the short flight of stairs across the small square of landing to the girls bedroom. The music leapt out, the rhythmic beat and yelping vocals filling the interior of the flat, as Cherise pulled open the door.

'Oh my god!'

Cherise loud shriek and her following incredulous, shrill laughter startled Julian into movement. Leaping the stairs in one go he was soon at the door.

Moving Cherise aside, the two J's grinned up at him.

It took a moment before he registered the broad white stripes emblazoned across both girls faces; glaring, bright, brilliant white stripes across the bridges of their noses and cheeks.

'Jesus Christ, what the hell have you done to your faces?'

Cherise's accompanying laughter distracted him momentarily.

Regaining his composure he attempted to take control, his hands on hips and chin jutting towards the girls in authority.

'Turn that racket down.' He ordered. 'Now explain yourselves.'

'We're antz!' Jenny declared. Her face exuded a pride in the statement.

'You're what?' He spluttered.

'Antz, dummy!' She repeated.

'Ants with a zed.' Jessica explained. 'Antz.'

'Right, okay, ants with a zed, will you explain why you've got white lines daubed across your faces!'

'To show we love 'em, stupid! Adam has one so if you want to be an ant you should do it too. Haven't you seen the video to Stand And Deliver?' Jenny shook her head slowly widening her eyes at Jessica as if to emphasise his stupidity.

Julian pondered her response a moment, absorbing the situation and the information overload he had experienced. The memory of Cherise's pert boob faded with each painful second.

He wondered who was the more stupid, him or them.

After all, he was not the one standing there with a bright white stripe across his nose.

It occurred to him that he had better ask though he feared the answer.

'And with what did you paint yourselves with?'

'This.' Jenny held out a small white bottle towards him.

Its red label bore the Tipp-ex logo, a quick-drying white liquid correction fluid.

He groaned. 'How are we going to get that lot off?'

Cherise, who could no longer contain herself, doubled over with laughter again.

'And that's not helpful!' He barked.

Only after dragging the protesting ants to the bathroom sink and subjecting them to a variety of cleaning methods, of which a pan scourer he had unearthed proved most effective, did he feel happier.

Though a red blemish now replaced the white line he guessed that this would fade with time, before morning he hoped, avoiding the interrogation of his parents at breakfast.

Unfortunately for Julian by the time they had cleaned the girls up and got them to bed, Cherise had gone off the boil. He had to content himself with a peck on the lips goodnight when Alton passed by to escort her home after he had finished at the pub.

Knowing that he had probably played cards there, Julian enquired politely. 'How was your luck tonight, Alton?'

'Not so good tonight mate, not so good.'

'I know the feeling.' Julian agreed.

Stan saw it coming but it still hurt. He was pragmatic and thought he would be ready for whatever came his way. Enforced redundancies were handed out and his name had not been far from the top of the pile. It was logical really.

Stan was a long-serving, hard-working foreman but he was also a proud union man and his philosophies were well known. He was sure that this had a lot to do with who got the nod nowadays. His skills were quickly becoming redundant. The new machines tended to regulate themselves and setting them up was so much simpler than it used to be. One man could do the job of five and it was cheaper to pay off the old guard with redundancy and then to employ younger, less-skilled, less-opinionated men on new contracts at a lower yearly pay.

The problem now was that having a few quid in the bank from the redundancy would be handy but it would not last forever and now Stan was faced with the uncertainty of finding alternative employment. He could not rely on Gerry to contribute much to the running of the house, the boy already gave more than he could afford from his meagre supplement from the training program and the boy's tight-fisted employer was not too generous with the cash I hand opportunities either.

He was in his twilight years. That was inarguable. Still strong and capable by anyone's standards but he was definitely on the downhill leg and even Stan knew the chances of him finding permanent, meaningful employment were now pretty slim.

Big-name factories were closing, priced out of the game by overseas competitors and others were being bought out by rival companies who then had to skeleton down the workforce, moving production lines up north where labour was cheaper.

And worse still, some businesses, despite desperate attempts to compete in a world market, would go down the pan anyway, going into liquidation before redundancies could even be taken. No funds left in the coffers to placate the unlucky.

Stan felt lucky on that score.

Some got nothing.

He scanned the local paper weekly, hopelessly seeking the opening, a vacancy that would end his worries. He applied for working on the bins as a refuse-truck driver but had been gob-smacked when he had turned up for the interview to find twenty other applicants, all younger, fitter men, who had been short-listed for interview as well. He wondered how many had originally applied in the first instance.

No explanation was given as to why he was not successful.

Hard as it was, Stan was a realist.

It was the grey waffle-effect slacks that finished it. Cherise had handed him the carrier bag in her bedroom, its instantly recognisable logo print made his stomach juices squirm. He hoped that it was an old bag she had pulled out of a kitchen drawer and that whatever it contained had been placed in it for safe keeping.

The trademark logo of Farah menswear printed below the retailers name and address reinforced the shops statement as being; 'purveyors of clothing for the discerning gentleman'.

'I got you a present.' She looked really pleased with herself. 'Go on open it.'

Sliding the trousers out of the bag he felt static discharge tingle the hairs on the back of his hand. The bag was crisp and straight; it was new.

Feeling the squares of dimpled cloth, he knew instinctively what was coming. Allowing the trouser legs to unfurl downwards he held the slacks out in front of him.

'Oh wow, thanks Cherise!' He prayed she would not see through his fake pleasure. They repulsed him.

'Try them on then!' She prompted, bouncing on the edge of her quilt covered bed.

'What? now?' He stalled, wondering if she picked up the quiver in his voice. He dared not look in her eyes for fear of alerting her to his discomfort.

'Yeah, go on.' She forced her excitement on him. 'They'll look well smart.'

'I don't think they'll go with my top though, do you?' It was feeble.

'So?' Cherise face changed. A quizzical frown appeared, creasing her smooth, shiny brow. 'Just want to see if they fit, that's all.'

'What if your mum comes in or something?' He was desperate, forcing him to clutch at non-existent straws. 'They might think we're up to something.'

Cherise stared deep in to his marrow, lips pursed, she was getting cross. He had been rumbled and he knew it. His sphincter muscles tightened.

'You don't like 'em, do you?'

His brains working gear came to a grinding halt, the question was too direct to skirt around.

'Sorry, Cherise, they're not really my sort of thing.'

What else was there to say?

Cherise stood up quickly, her whole demeanour turned feisty, she folded her arms tight across her bust.

'Oh yeah! Then just what is your sort of thing?' Her head wobbled dramatically with the challenge.

He could not respond, his eyes were now firmly fixed on Cherise, threatening and aggressive. She appeared to have grown six inches in height.

His imagination ran amuck. He allowed the pretty-faced slim-build of his girlfriend to distort and morph into a cartoon image of a huge busted, big-armed, intimidating, heavy-set woman, her hair strapped up in a headscarf and pinny tied round her ample waist.

'You wanna go on wearing your old man clothes, do you?' Cherise fell into her stride.

'You're a cartoon character now. Can't you see, things 'ave moved on. You gonna be a rude boy when you're sixty?' She kissed her teeth loudly, a look of disgust spread across her once-attractive face.

She paused to allow some sort of response from Julian but the force of her tirade, oozing with the sneer of sarcasm and put-downs, had left him shell-shocked. He had never thought about what he would wear when he was sixty.

'I suppose you'd prefer me in Pierre Cardin tops and Farah strides.' He hit back.

'Well come on Julian even you've gotta admit your get-up is kinda old-fashioned now, innit?'

'Maybe it is in your eyes.' He kept his voice at a respectful volume, choosing a dignified approach to neutralise her overt aggression. 'But I like the way I am.' He paused. 'And so did you once.'

As he turned with finality and let himself out he heard Cherise's venomous verbal attacks echo after him as he raced down the communal staircase.

'Go on den, rude bwoy. Go back to your cave. Go on back to your boyfriend. I'm sure Gerry still likes your old man clothes!'

He was upset. That was undeniable but he never cried about Cherise. He never felt that unmistakeable pain of loss in his gut that usually accompanies a break up.

Cherise words had already erased any fondness he had once felt for her. Like corrosive acid on baby-soft skin, her verbal spite had burnt away any feelings he had ever held. The pain he felt right then was different from the discomfort of a relationship ending.

It went deeper; deeper in to his core, in to the marrow of his very being.

After leaving Cherise flat, his anger had slowly morphed into the turmoil of doubt. As her vicious words swirled in his head and refused to fade, uncertainty grew in him. Walking back towards his own block, he felt the creep of self-consciousness prompt him to check his walk, his streetwise gait tightened to a stiff normality.

Glancing around himself with a paranoiac urgency, he looked out for odd stares and listened for shouted insults as he passed adults and kids going about their business.

But no-one seemed to acknowledge his even being there, barely raising an eye in his direction.

At first he was relieved that they had not seen fit to object to his parade. Then just as quickly this relief flipped over to become a feeling of disturbance. He was disturbed, disturbed that they had not noticed him either.

Any reflective surface passed became a tool for checking his appearance. The curve of a car's wind-screen only served to increase the distortion of appearance his mind had already made so he avoided looking in them.

Grubby, unwashed ground floor windows had the effect of adding age to his reflection. The hazy mirror image evoked a dusty relic pulled from a rack, a strong blast of breath required to remove the long settled dust to expose its true form.

Arriving home, unable to play out the usual pleasantries required, Julian called out to his parents before heading up to his room.

'Hi, I'm going straight up, I've got a terrible headache.' He felt bad but knew that it was for the best. They would know something was up anyhow.

Opening the black box, he sought solace in his collection of records. He flicked through them, occasionally pulling out a contender for the turntable before dismissing each one and returning them back to the box.

Closing the clasp with a snap, he rose and stepped across his room to the wardrobe door. A full-length mirror spat his image back at him.

He stood motionless, studying, staring at his reflection.

He looked so much older.

He had allowed his cropped hair to grow out slightly, more by accident than design, and the skin around his jaw-line bore the evidence of roughening brought about by his amateurish shaving regime.

His outfit looked too casual.

The shirts stiffness had been washed and worn away with time, its colour lacking the usual sharpness. His jackets vibrancy had dulled, the black twill faded matt by exposure to the urban rain and bleaching sunlight, the tartan lining frayed and holed in places.

He stared intently into his opposites eyes, allowing his focus to centre on the deep black of his own pupils. He stared, searching, seeking, something, nothing in particular.

As if embroiled in a bizarre subliminal staring match he continued, refusing to submit until something spoke to him, until answers were forthcoming.

His body tensed as frustration welled up in his chest. He fought the urge to lash out at the image. He imagined his fist crunching into the mirror, the impact triggering a spider web of splintering silver glass, droplets of deep crimson blood seeping from his sliced knuckles.

His hot breath passed through his flared nostrils with a deep rhythm until the snap of a heavy blink broke the spell and he averted his gaze.

Defeated.

'This isn't just about you!'

Julian flinched at the sudden rise in volume.

Anger was an emotion that his Mum rarely displayed. It was unusual for her to have to be this way.

Always careful to avoid exposing the kids to unnecessary trauma she would usually contain any upset feelings within and, if needed, release them later in more private and less sensitive surrounding.

Tears, disappointment, frustration, Julian had witnessed all of these before, only now he was receiving all three emotions married together with some good old fashioned anger. And it was all fired in his direction.

'I'm not bloody going, I like it here. My life's here. My friends, everything. I cannot believe that you would do this to me! I don't give a shit, I am not leaving!'

He recognised his tirade was not the most mature response to being told that his parents had finally managed to raise the funds for a deposit on a house.

'Why are you are trying to ruin things for me!'

'I never had you down as being such a selfish person!' She glared at him as she scolded. 'When did this happen? Come on tell me. When did you become so self-absorbed?'

He shrugged his guilt-heavy shoulders. It felt another childish and completely inappropriate gesture.

His Mum confirmed his feelings. 'That's it, is it?' She mimicked his shoulder action.

'What does that mean?' She shrugged again just in case he had missed the point she was making the first time. 'Don't know? Don't care? What? Come on Julian, enlighten me!'

Julian could not recall having seen his Mum's skin ever taking on that shade of red before. He squirmed, his experience in familial conflict was sadly lacking.

'I just want to stay here.' He instantly regretted the comment as he heard its pitiful tone.

'I'm sure you do! That's as maybe. Unfortunately for you, you are not the only person of importance in this house.' She paused with the reprimand, allowing her volume level to lower to a more amiable pitch before continuing.

'You have two younger sisters now and it's of utmost importance that they can both grow up in a safe and nurturing environment. Sadly, this estate does not fit that bill anymore.' She looked at him. Tears had settled in the bright-red canals formed by her lower lids.

'They won't survive here.' She flopped onto the nearest kitchen chair. Its vinyl-covered cushioning wheezed as expelled air was forced from a small hole in the seam.

'I'm alright though, aren't I?' He reasoned. 'Living here hasn't done me any harm, has it?'

'No it hasn't.' It was a concession of sorts. 'But you were older, more capable, less vulnerable than the girls when we came here. The area has changed. I don't just mean the superficial structure of the estate, the mess, the neglect, the vandalism and all that sort of thing.' She wafted her hand around in dismissal. 'It's the people, the community. These places are becoming dumping grounds for thieves, drug dealers, prostitutes and even paedophiles. Good people move out and the council move in the troubled, the criminal and the antisocial. Do you know why they do that Julian?'

He shook his head. He was pleased that the emotional rant had run its course, job done, point made.

'Because it's easy. Because it offers camouflage. They bank on folk not knowing, not noticing, not questioning'

He must have frowned, as she elaborated on the statement.

'Look at the size of this place. How many of our neighbours do you actually know?'

'Not many but a few I suppose' Julian offered. He tried to picture their faces.

'How many of their names do you know?'

He thought quickly but he struggled to fit names to the faces he could picture.

'Not many.' He admitted.

'Well. I'll bet that's a few more than I could name. And if I was to ask you their surnames or what they do for a living that would probably really stump you. People can disappear here Julian. No-one asks questions, who's who? No one cares. Not once they have shut their doors.'

She lifted her head in contemplation towards the long lounge window.

Smeared with grime, she had long ago given up straining to clean the outside of them when the acrobatic performance required to reach the uppermost corners had nearly sent her tumbling down to the concrete four stories below.

'I love you so much and I would go to the ends of the earth for you, but I love those two girls like they are my own too. Surely you can understand that?'

He nodded.

The sound of the front door opening, its security chain rattling, broke the atmosphere. Joe appeared in the lounge, shrugging off his anorak. He looked perturbed.

'The bloody lifts out of order again!' He barked.

He pondered his wife's emotion-strained expression before looking towards Julian searching him for a clue to the atmosphere.

'What's been going on 'ere then?'

'Twenty two grand!' Julian's expression oozed disbelief. 'Twenty two grand for a bloody house!'

It was, in fact, a three bedroom Victorian house requiring some tender, loving care in a lively, terraced street.

The street boasted mature poplar trees, knuckled and scarred, their roots erupting through the split tarmac of the pavement at regular intervals.

Small gardens, some with crusty railings, some with ornate concrete blocks crowning their low red-brick boundaries, fronted the properties.

The space allowed children, black, Asian and white, to play together in relative safety, riding bikes along the pavement, organising impromptu cricket matches and playing football, yards from the safety of their front doors.

Vandalism was virtually non-existent, there was nothing to vandalise.

Everything seemed to belong to somebody and mostly, everyone seemed to know everyone else.

'Twenty two grand! Can you believe it?' He implored Gerry to empathise with his incredulity.

'Don't know.' Gerry pondered for a moment. 'Don't know what a house should cost do I.'

The white pages fluttered and flipped as they were strewn from the open window in handfuls.

They floated on the streams of air that weaved amongst the upper floors of the blocks, like a flock of white doves, until their papery wings became too heavy with the October drizzle and the moisture dragged them downwards.

Gerry wrenched another fistful of his typed notes from the familiar black binder as Julian made haste across the bedroom floor. He latched onto Gerry's arm. He felt the tension in Gerry's man-sized forearm soften as he became aware of Julian's concern.

'Pack it in, Gerry. What are you doing?' He blurted.

Gerry turned his head. His eyes were fiery red with spent emotion, his face set in a mask of upset and confusion.

'What?' He challenged. 'This?' Gerry gestured with disdain to the screwed remnants in his hand with a nod. 'This don't mean shit no more!'

The words were accompanied by flecks of frothing spit through gritted teeth. Pulling his arm free from Julian's feeble grip he launched the remainder of the journals out of the window to the mercy of the wind and the rain.

'What the hells happened? Why are you so mad?' He pleaded for some coherence and explanation.

'You really don't know do you?' Gerry shook his head lightly; a wry grin appeared in contrast with his emotion-scrawled face.

'Know what?' Now he was worried. 'Don't mess about Gerry just tell me what's happened?'

'They've left, they've split.' Gerry's tension seemed to dissipate with the words. His head, his shoulders slumped. The stripped carcass of the folder bounced off the floor with a hollow clatter as it dropped from his grip.

'Who's left, split, whatever?' Julian gazed imploringly at the devastated figure in front of him.

'The Specials.' Gerry held out his palms in resignation. 'Terry, Lynval and Neville have called it a day.'

The group had just returned from a tense and turbulent tour of the United States.

The Specials boasted quality singers and songwriters amongst its ranks though inarguably Jerry Dammers held the title of chief song-smith and, most importantly it transpired, saw himself as the admiral of the good ship 2 Tone.

Disagreements over song inclusions for the album and ideas for musical direction, to name a couple, did not harmony make.

When a collective of egos and personalities as varied and as talented as The Specials line-up met it was bound to be a volatile mix.

The band as a whole had become bored with the touring, the huge fights among the audience and the show-stopping stage invasions.

Since the beginnings of the 2 Tone campaign, violence and disorder had tarnished the philosophies espoused by the bands and the labels personnel.

As early as October 1979, at a gig at the Hatfield Polytechnic, gate-crashing thugs attacked concert goers, injuring ten and causing nine hundred pounds worth of damage before Hertfordshire Police eventually gained control. Eleven of the yobs were eventually arrested.

The troubles were not only confined to Britain.

That same year when The Specials performed at the Bilzen Jazz and rock festival fighting broke out between security and fans.

The Specials concerts continued to be blighted by violence amongst a minority of the audience. Football, territorial, fashion and political rivalries were fought out on the dance floor.

Right-wing supporters made their presence felt at numerous venues despite Two Tones radical racial harmony message.

The 2 Tone publicity machine had issued a public statement through the pages of the New Musical Express; 'Those who come looking for fights are unwelcome…'

But still they came.

At Cambridge on 9th of October 1980, large disorder and a stage invasion found Terry Hall and Jerry Dammers arrested and, somewhat bizarrely, charged with provoking crowd trouble. They were fined £1000.

At home as abroad.

At a Specials gig in Paris, French mods battled with English skinheads.

Some of the band members had also been taking time out and pursuing side projects, dipping their toes in other waters and experimenting with new ideas.

There were rumblings of discontentment amongst the members about 2 Tone marketing and its vision for the future.

All this eventually came to a head in August 1981.

The Fun Boy Three, that is; Terry, Lynval and Neville, informed the rest of their intention to split from the band. Allegedly the deed was done in the dressing room after a Top of the Pops appearance promoting 'Ghost town'.

Roddy Radiation resigned from the group a week later.

They both stood still as statues. The moisture-licked draught from the still open window coated their faces. Julian raised his hands with deliberation before bringing his palms down with a loud stinging slap onto the window sill.

As they shuffled across the concrete Julian had to swallow hard to contain the ball of emotion that threatened to slip out of his throat and trigger the exposure of his true feelings.

He kept his neck bent towards the ground, avoiding eye contact, his hands sheathed deep in his pockets.

Occasional wisps of breeze lifted the familiar scent of soap from Gerry towards him and he sucked up the pungent comfort into his nostrils, allowing the aroma to momentarily lighten his sombre mood.

Things felt fuzzy and distant, unreal and dreamlike. Julian felt off-balance.

He wanted to speak but he was afraid that he might betray the boy inside him. Every time he tried to initiate speech the lump almost slipped from his emotion-wracked airway.

Gerry spoke first. 'It seems a bit weird don't it?' He paused. 'I mean. You don't seem to have been here very long but it feels like I've been mates with you for years. D'you know what I mean?'

Julian nodded. He allowed a small smile to crease his face but had to contain it as he felt the blur of tears begin to cloud his eyes.

'Time seems to 'ave shot by don't it?' Gerry looked across at him. 'You alright mate?' He enquired, concern creasing his brow.

Julian shook his head. The lump in his throat threatened to choke him. Breathing was difficult.

He kicked out hard at a discarded milk bottle, enjoying the explosion of its fragile form as it impacted against the hard base of a concrete planter. The shards of clear glass lay scattered around its base like cheap diamonds. Gerry did not flinch.

'I don't know what else to say.' Gerry apologised. 'I'm really sorry, mate.'

Julian felt angry with himself. Angry for allowing his self-absorption and upset to mar the little time they had left together.

His anger at his selfishness gave him some strength and composure. 'It's not your fault mate.' He blurted. 'It's no-ones fault, it's just got to be this way that's all.'

Gerry nodded softly. 'Don't mean we've got to like it though, does it?'

Arriving at the removal van seemed to ease the pain a touch. Maybe it was resignation to the fact, recognition that all was set, wheels in motion.

The vans side boasted the bold moniker and contact details of Joe's employer who had kindly lent him the use of the van for the weekend. Hi parents hovered around the van trying to look inconspicuous as they eyed the two boys approaching.

On the occasion his eyes met hers, Julian's mum squeezed out a guilt-laden smile in desperate support. She raised an awkward hand of greeting to Gerry.

'I never know quite what to do in these situations, do you?' Julian admitted.

'Never 'ad to do it before that's why I suppose.' Gerry grinned. 'It don't seem real. You can a have a man-hug if you want but no tongues!'

Julian laughed, enjoying the relaxation the moment of mirth brought.

'See yuh then, mate.' Gerry offered his big paw. 'Good luck an' all that. Not that you need much luck boffin!'

Julian felt the need to reassure, not for Gerry, but for himself. 'I'll keep in touch. I'll come over as often as possible and you can come and visit us. Yeah?' He promised, holding tight, reluctant to separate their palms.

'Sure, mate.' He comforted giving Julian a couple of strong slaps on the shoulder blades encouraging him towards the waiting van.

His mum rubbed his lower back in consolation as he clambered up and onto the vans bench passenger seating before following him up and slamming the heavy door behind her with a loud boom.

As the engine spluttered into life Julian felt the great wobble of the diesel engine. He stared intently out of the side window. Gerry stood by, solid, his face masked, any emotion hidden.

His hands were buried in his jeans pockets.

His familiar flight jacket was unzipped allowing the flash of bright orange lining to catch the light.

As the van pulled away Julian craned his neck around to offer a feeble wave. Gerry tugged a hand free from his pocket to raise a solitary salute before turning away and walking back up the slope towards the estate.

Julian noticed Gerry's head and shoulders slump, a hand reached up towards his face. Julian's own tears fell unhindered.

VIII
You're Wondering Now. 2002

The scene was reminiscent of one of those bizarre Japanese-produced Godzilla films.

An apocalyptic vision where enormous mechanical dinosaurs moved destructively amongst the urban landscape belching noisy bursts of black emissions from their nostrils; snapping out their heads in a feeding frenzy and taking huge great bites of the crumbling decrepit masonry they devoured, the metal reinforcing rods once encased in the concrete shells hanging from their jaws like long ferrous bones. The tails of other just as monstrous, diesel-guzzling behemoths swung, blasting the edges and corners off the grey inanimate prey send great clumps of concrete plummeting towards the ground in billowing gritty dust clouds.

Watching this destruction of a once familiar landscape from the safety of the footbridge that spanned the busy dual carriage way nearby it was an understandably distant and somewhat unreal moment for Julian to take in.

The phone call had come early one morning jolting him from his slumber with a frightening start and not without some danger as he groggily tried to slip a twisted and knotted pair of boxer shorts that he had hurriedly grabbed over his nether regions. He stumbled and skidded as he angled towards the telephone threatening to ring itself off the stand in the hallway of his one bedroomed flat. He was disturbed. Only a few close friends had access to his landline number.

'Yeah, hello?' He snapped as he flicked on the lights. A full length mirror told a story. He noticed he had his shorts on back to front and inside out. His balls were caught up like chicken giblets in the leg hole.

'It's me, Gerry.' There was only one Gerry so no need to ask which one.

'Shit.' He had recently taken to using occasional expletives in his communications; it was the company he kept these days he supposed. 'What's going on, what's happened?' With his spare hand he struggled to free his snared gonads.

It was a complete shock. They had not spoken for a long time.

Life just seemed to take over making keeping in touch with friends and family an easily forgettable chore in his life. He felt guilt ridden.

'Why are you ringing me at …' He looked at his wrist but his watch was still ticking away to itself beside the bed.

'Six o'clock in the morning.' Gerry filled in the blanks. There was a short silence, 'They're pulling it down today.'

Julian was obviously supposed to appreciate the magnitude of this bombshell but it really had been a long time.

'Pulling down what?' Julian racked his sleep deficient brain trying to engage first gear.

'The estate,' Came the reply. 'they start the demolition today.'

'Wow,' Julian was not sure what Gerry expected him to say, 'that's kind of sad, isn't it?' He was unsure if his response was enough but it was all he could come up with at that time of the morning.

'Yeah, I suppose it is.' Gerry went quiet, Julian could feel him thinking even though he could not see him.

'Would you meet up with me Jules?'

'Christ, mate. For sure.' And he meant it. ' When? At the weekend or something? I can get some time off. I'm owed time.'

'Actually, I meant today.' And Gerry meant it.

It felt the right thing to do.

Historically Gerry's insistence that Julian join him on his spontaneous escapades had led them to experience some pretty interesting, usually life enriching and quite often, downright dangerous adventures. There was also the argument that they had been 16 years old at the time but Julian ignored that fact.

'When? Where? What time?'

And so he had phoned Timmy his right hand man at the firm asking him to cover for him for the day and promised him a couple of pints and the number of a bird that he fancied that in return.

After waking himself up with a good firm shave and a long, hot shower, Julian set out on the journey from north to east against the heavy flow of commuter traffic that was heading into the city.

He made good time aboard his scruffy scooter, weaving like an expertly welded darning needle, in and out between the white commercials, four by fours and countless Japanese saloons. He enjoyed feeling the hypnotic metallic pop of the small two-stroke beneath the Vespa's panels resonate as he accelerated through the gaps between the other road users keeping a watchful eye out for careless lane changers and leg breakers.

Gerry was sitting watching a foreign pop music channel on the cafe television set, nursing a large cup of coffee and drawing on a cigarette as Julian arrived in off the dusty, litter-strewn street.

As he approached the table, Gerry called for Ahmet to bring an expresso for over for Julian, there was an air of familiarity between the two men. Julian wondered if Gerry spent a lot of time there.

'How did you know I'd like an expresso?' He smiled, squeezing himself into the plastic bucket seat opposite Gerry.

'All you North Londoners drink posh coffee, don't yuh?' Gerry joked.

'An expresso will be fine for this honorary East ender, thank you!' Julian countered, no offence taken.

'A good journey?' Gerry made small talk, 'I suppose riding a bike helps cut through it all, don't it?'

'Yeah, it does.' Julian cut to the chase. 'How are you Gerry?'

Gerry's looked down in to his cup.

'Fair to middlin'.'

'Family all okay mate?'

'Fine, kids sending the missus round the twist as usual.'

'How old are they now?'

'Billy's eight and Jonny's nearly ten.'

Julian felt the unmistakeable pangs of guilt in his belly rise again.

'Time goes too quickly Gerry. Before we know it we'll be in our boxes feeding the worms!'

Julian drained the expresso.

'The old man. How is he?' Julian remembered Stan with fondness.

'Older!' Gerry quipped. 'His back and knees are shot. Needs a wheel chair if he goes out, so he tends to stay in most of the time.'

This rang true. Julian knew that as a proud man, Gerry's father would want to be as independent for as long as possible, never to be looked at as a burden. He would be embarrassed to have others think of him as feeble.

'He's got a zimmer,' Gerry referred to the quad footed aluminium frames that people who have difficulty walking can use. 'but he gets knackered real quick, his arms are not as strong as they used to be.'

Gerry nodded in Julian's direction. 'What about you?'

Julian had been waiting for that question. He knew it would only be a matter of time before Gerry began asking about his love life.

'Has a woman threatened to make an 'onest man of yuh yet?'

'You know me Gerry; too busy, too self-centred and too used to being my own boss.'

Gerry laughed and leant back in his chair.

'Too bloody fussy and too bloody frightened, more like!'

Julian squirmed a bit. Gerry was quite correct in his crude analysis of Julian's love life. He was currently enjoying the company of one young lady in particular, they had a lot in common, but he was far too used to living on his own and answering only to himself to make anything more permanent of it.

Coffees drunk, Gerry paid the bill before they made their way towards the estate. The estate where they had first met twenty years previously; just two fifteen year old sparrows spreading their wings all the way back then.

'What's all this about mate?' Julian asked looking sideways at the large man.

He still looked like the Gerry he had always known and grown to love like a brother, his face still oozed pleasant demeanour though his dark black hair was slightly flecked with grey now and those great bushy side burns still smothered his jowls.

He looked world weary, tired and thoughtful, his youth now hidden beneath a thick layer of hard, manual labour and cruel knock backs.

Life had been tough on Gerry.

'I don't know.' He replied.

They eventually arrived at the road-grime and graffiti smeared bridge over the dual carriageway. Experience had reminded them both that it would provide a perfect viewing platform. A platform from which to witness the dismantling and destruction of the blocks of dwellings they had once known as home.

They walked to the centre of the bridge, the soles of their shoes scratching against the textured surface before stopping and turning to support their forearms on the cold handrail.

It had been repainted; who knew how many times? They had a long time ago added their own names in permanent ink before proudly underlining their signatures with the bold statement, 'rude boys' to make the connection, the link between them complete.

The rail felt scarred and disfigured now, a hard white gloss crust and indecipherable hip-hop style tags burying a decade of history.

'I suppose they'll pull the small blocks down first and bring the towers down with explosives later on.' Julian surmised.

'Yeah,' Gerry agreed, 'that'd make sense I suppose. I'd like to see that. I bet that would be a sight to remember.'

Gerry looked across his shoulder at Julian. 'Did you know that when they erected the estate it literally arrived on the back of lorries flat-packed, like an enormous concrete jigsaw to be put together on site.'

Julian actually knew this fact but allowed Gerry to carry on with the story.

'And then they realised years later, that there was a major flaw in the planners vision.'

'Why? Was a piece missing?' Julian joked. Gerry gave a short snort of laughter.

'If only it was that simple, mate.' He shook his head lightly. 'The problem was poor build quality. None of the lips of the outer skin interlocked properly with each other. This in turn allowed the wind and rain to get into any gaps causing massive damp problems in the flats; they sucked the moisture in like a sponge. You can probably remember what that was like? '

Julian nodded allowing memories of his mum to enter his head, memories of her scrubbing furiously at the stubborn black mould that clung to the ceilings and exterior walls with diluted bleach in an attempt to halt the spores multiplying.

'So fighting the mould and damp problem was always gonna be an impossible task for anyone but the thing that really put the icing on the cake was the damage done by the winters. The moisture that got trapped in the gaps froze and unfroze, expanded and shrunk, causing cracking and concrete fatigue in the outer skins. Eventually, over time, lumps of concrete began detaching themselves from the sides of the buildings and falling off. It's amazing that no one was bloody killed. You, me, my kids, we all wandered around that place without a care in the world not realising that a time bomb was tickin' away above our heads.'

Julian listened politely to it all.

As he listened and reflected he came to understand that Gerry was well informed. That they were all just expendable pawns in any of the major political parties housing policies; inconvenient and expensive human burdens that they, the supposed parties of the people, had to grudgingly bear and seen to be doing something with.

'And do you know what makes the whole bloody thing so sickening?'

Gerry had turned to face him, leaning to one side and resting his elbow on the railing.

Julian gave him his attention.

Gerry was agitated, ready to ram his point home. He waited for an articulated lorry, its roar making conversation temporarily impossible, to pass underneath before answering his own question.

'They bloody well knew about it all. The council, the building firms, the government inspectors.' He was purse lipped, his chin pulled in towards his throat in indignation.

'They knew about the poor manufacture of the skinning blocks, they knew about the inadequate construction and they knew that problems were imminent from day one.'

He paused. 'Yet they chose to say and do absolutely nothing, encouraging unsuspecting, naive families to move from their houses and streets to concrete boxes and balconies with promises of a revolutionary and futuristic housing experience. It was criminal.'

Julian could find no reason to disagree.

'They talked about taking down the estate down for years but I never really believed it would happen in our lifetime, you know.' Gerry continued, allowing his emotion to filter through. 'They're saying they're gonna build more humane and architecturally pleasing terraced housing. They think that by doing that the people who move back into them, including my family, will take more pride in their community and environment thereby decreasing crime, vandalism and the general despondency that, apparently, plagues our waking hours. 'But times they are a changing' as Bobby Dylan once sang. Society's unrecognisable from what it was, even from when we were young let alone from the fifties and sixties; more competition, more selfishness, more resentment. Not a healthy formula.'

Gerry allowed himself a moment to breath.

'I'm at a loss to fathom as to how re-housing the drug dealers, addicts, car thieves, fences and sex offenders back in amongst families in, albeit, lower level and more eye pleasing terraced bloody housing is gonna create a rosy and crime-free utopia. Some sociologist somewhere made a good few quid churning out that load of blinkered claptrap, I'll tell yuh! Should've come and spoke to me and I'd have saved 'em some bloody money!'

He gave Gerry some time to settle back down before continuing the conversation. Julian could not remember ever seeing him as agitated about anything except for that horrible day that The Specials announced they had split up.

'How's the work front looking?' He enquired.

'Just signed up for some temporary graft with a road gang I've worked for before.' Gerry was renowned for his durability and strength, just like his dad. 'They've had their contract extended, so I should be okay up until next Christmas. Always plenty of overtime that comes in handy for paying off debts.' Gerry let out a puff of air. 'We're resurfacing part of the M11 at the moment.'

'I don't suppose you get many new roads built nowadays. The anti-road lobby seem to get themselves heard.' Julian always tried to keep up with contemporary issues. 'I suppose somebody's got to defend what little countryside we have left.'

'It makes you wonder what's more important though, don't it? The middle classes and their Sunday walks in the country or the working man's need to make a living?' He did not look at Julian. 'Bloody little Englanders if you ask me; terrified that some oiks might be housed near them and lower the tone of the area.'

Julian felt insensitive. He recalled all the petitions he had signed in support of campaigns to stop road building particularly in the south west of England.

'Sorry, mate, I wasn't thinking.' It was the best he could offer in the circumstances.

'Don't be.' Gerry looked sincere. 'It's not your problem.'

And yet it was.

Julian had thought about Gerry's situation often when sat at his high-specification drawing board or in front of the computer screen. He had often been tempted to line him up some work with one of the many contacts he had made in the field but he knew and was positive that Gerry would have said; 'Thanks but no thanks'.

A proud, stoic individual, Gerry would be unable to accept what he would regard as a hand out even from his oldest and closest friend.

'How's your business doing then?' Gerry showed no resentment following Julian's earlier comments.

'Pretty well at the moment. As you probably know the development of the Docklands went absolutely ballistic. Everyone seemed to want a slice of the yuppie pie. Warehouses were being converted quicker than I could get the plans printed off. Not much time left in the day to enjoy the money though!'

By 1979, the docklands area of the old East end lay derelict and abandoned and forgotten. Huge warehouses, docking yards and storage depots, once full of the hustle and bustle of a proud industry employing thousands of men between them, now stood neglected and forgotten. Weeds and tough grass pushed up through any available openings and fissures. The Thames rats multiplied in their thousands as they made the barren wasteland and uninhabited shells of buildings their own.

Until that is, 1981 and the formation of The London Docklands Development Corporation.

Instilled with the ability to circumvent housing and planning controls, the LDDC was given the role of selling and leasing the redundant areas of land to entrepreneurial developers.

Compulsory purchase orders cleared out the old and the stubborn who resisted the clear out of the proposed development areas. Resistance was futile. All it did was slow the inevitable. Money spoke louder than any sentimentality.

Apartment blocks and studio flats now lined the bank of the old river Thames, sparkling visions of glass and chrome, a plethora of balconies, seating areas and canopies overlooking the wide, murky tidal waters.

The rich and the famous. The criminal. The chancers and city kids. The yuppies.

The spawn of Thatcherism. The products of free enterprise all clamoured for that periods ultimate sign of affluence; ownership, part or full, of a pad in the heart of the Docklands.

History would bear witness, that the true locals of the East end, British or Irish or Bengali or Jewish or otherwise would not be amongst those who benefited significantly from the gentrification of the Docklands.

Julian though had done very nicely out of it.

'Must be nice to draw pictures for a living!' Gerry offered.

'Yes, I suppose it is.' He paused for thought, 'It's a lot of hard work, pretty boring, very time consuming and way too much responsibility sometimes.'

'That I don't doubt mate but it's obviously worth it.' Gerry pushed himself away from the handrail by straightening his arms. 'You've done really well for yourself. I knew you would. '

'I was lucky, I got the breaks.' Julian conceded.

You're wondering now…

What to do…

Now you know this is the end.

'Thanks for coming today.' Gerry held out his shovel-like calloused hand.

Julian took it in his own, allowing Gerry to draw him into a smothering embrace.

Julian recognised the scent of Imperial leather soap. Some habits die hard he thought. Gerry released his affectionate hold on him, opening a space between them until only their two hands, Julian's dwarfed in Gerry's, remained entwined.

Julian saw a hint of resignation in his eyes. He squeezed Gerry's hand firmly.

'I wouldn't have missed it for the world, rude boy!'

IX
Rudeboy Outa Jail. 2002

Julian allowed his thoughts to settle and become solid once more, back to the now and then. The mesmerising spin of the seven-inch single on the turntable signified movement and time, the world revolving and life evolving.

He raised his misty eyes up on to the detritus strewn counter reacquainting his eyes with his surroundings. He was unsure how long he had been daydreaming.

The semi-circular pulpit in which he stood bore the disturbing appearance of an administrational apocalypse but was, in fact, a bizarre example of eccentric organisation.

He knew where everything was if he needed it.

Pens, copper coins, cigarettes, chewing gum, record middles all mingled with the untidy piles of flyers announcing gigs, clubs and events that were spread across the melamine counter.

The shelf immediately beneath housed an archaic cash register which shared the space with a robust set of Technics record decks, bombproof kit as far as Julian was concerned. The decks were coupled to a hefty home-built amplifier that any Jamaican producer would have been proud to polish. The set-up was all connected to numerous speakers thoughtfully positioned to offer the most complimentary sound distribution.

Beneath the hardware, long, skinny crates packed with forty-fives were parked, their clearly labelled fronts facing out for easy identification.

Julian focussed on the faint indigo remains of ink that had been rubber stamped in a moment of distraction on the counter.

'Rudy's Records, 11 Camden High Rd, Camden Town, NW1.'

The words brought an involuntary smile to his face, the warm satisfaction of contentment threatened to overwhelm him.

Rudy's .

What else could he call a record shop!

The large floor to ceiling glazed frontage of the shop served its purpose;

'Specialists in Reggae, Ska and Rocksteady, includin rarities and deletes. Vinyl bought & sold.'

Julian tolerated the missing 'g', accepting it's omission as a mark of authenticity. Besides he knew that the native Camdenite who had painstakingly carried out the sign writing for him in return for a couple of Jethro Tull long players and a few bevvies at the Elephants head public house would have probably argued for artistic license.

Better to do and regret than to regret not doing.

After he had left Gerry the day the estate had been torn down, Joe's ancient piece of wisdom had plagued Julian's thoughts. Filed away in that corner of his brain under 'no regrets' it had been unearthed by that day's events and the emotions he had experienced.

It had not gone away. That niggle kept returning like a persistent organic groin rash to gnaw at his feelings of uncertainty. Feelings that had been brought into play by the risings of dissatisfaction that had been appearing more frequently of late, arrived like pangs of hunger in his gut, like angry moths flapping madly, scratching, against the walls of his stomach.

Two nights and one long day later, after the endless hours of turmoil, of deep soul-searching had frazzled his senses into submission he knew there was only one decision he could possibly live with.

Throwing back the sweat damp sheet off his clammy skin, he sat upright in his bed.

He felt the spirit-level in his brain shift and activate an alcohol-induced wave of pain that assaulted his moisture-starved cranium. The bottle of scotch by his bed was a bone-dry reminder of last night's meditations.

He staggered to the kitchen slipping on irresponsibly scattered album sleeves like ice skates. He did his utmost to keep his head from moving too much.

Grabbing a packet of paracetamol he wolfed a pair down his parched throat. They stuck, like two great chalk boulders clinging to the inner rock-face of his gullet, releasing their bitter taste and burning his throat. He flushed them down with a whole pint of London's finest tap-water.

He arrived at the office of 'Aitchison and Partners' before official opening up time. As he had anticipated, the man he wanted to see was already swinging in an expensive leather executives chair in front of a great expanse of a desk. His steaming mug of filter coffee clouded his glasses that framed his moon-like face. He was deep in conversation on the telephone. Spotting Julian standing in the doorway, he grimaced exaggeratedly.

Julian looked down at himself. Not exactly office attire.

His jeans were stained and creased and only his wax-oil motorcycle jacket hid the inside out, armpit crusty t-shirt he had been wearing since meeting up with Gerry two days previously.

Tony Aitchison put his hand over the phones mouthpiece for privacy.

'You look like shit! Go and get a coffee or something, I'll be with you in a minute.' Tony's tact and diplomacy had not got him where he was today.

His business head and entrepreneurial spirit plus a lust for the finer luxuries in life had.

Leaving his helmet in the room, Julian went to the office kitchen. Already busy with the laughter and retelling of weekend stories amongst the junior staff and secretaries he decided against making a drink and gave it a swerve. They made him feel older than he really was and his patience was not at its best that morning. He wanted to do his best to avoid the interrogations of the office gossips.

After a quick slash in the toilets, he splashed cold water over his face, flushing the crust of sleep from the corners of his eyes. He drank greedily from the tap in a bid to subdue the hangover assaulting his head. After checking for loose bogeys clinging to his nostrils he returned to Tony's office, walking quickly and looking too busy to stop and talk to passing colleagues.

'Come in mate. Where the hell 'ave you been?' Tony stood to shake his hand. He was distracted, busy as always. Julian found no space to offer a reply.

'I was gonna send out a search party! Have you had a coffee yet? No?' Tony pressed a button on his desk top intercom system. 'Sharon love, bring us another couple of coffees when you get a minute, cheers darling.'

Tony reclined back in his chair; it gave a low long squeak. His fingers were linked across the stomach of his crisp, lemon-yellow shirt. He slowed himself. He eyed Julian's appearance.

'Christ, man. Have you been ill or something?'

'You could say that I suppose.' Julian started to relax a little; Tony and he were old friends and associates. There was not much that one did not know about the other.

'I've been doing a lot of thinking the last couple of days.'

'Don't want to be doing too much of that, mate.' Tony gently rocked back and forth. Sharon arrived with the coffees on a tray.

'Hold the calls for a bit, please love.'

Sharon swished off back to her station, Tony's eyes watching her backside sway beneath her pencil skirt as she departed. 'Like two boy scouts scrapping under a blanket.' He quipped.

'The old ones are the best ones, Tony!' Julian raised his eyebrows.

'Anyway…you were saying, dear boy?' Tony gave Julian his full attention at last.

'Like I said, I've been doing a lot of serious thinking about the future, my happiness and ambitions, what exactly I want from all this.' Julian checked to see that he was still listening.

'We all get like that sometimes,' Tony leant forward. 'You've been working all the hours lately. Get a holiday. Take that new bit of stuff you've been hanging out with to Barbados. A week of sun, sea and shagging will sort you out. You'll come back like a fully-charged teenager!'

Julian felt guilty as he remembered the lady friend he had rudely and selfishly neglected of late, ignoring her messages left on the answer machine and avoiding her other attempted communications. He was quite fond of her and he knew that she lived in hope that he would settle down enough to go steady with her.

'It's more serious than you think, Tone,' He paused, Tony waited.

'I want to pack it in.'

Tony looked shell-shocked. He thought for what seemed like an eternity before speaking.

'Yeah, okay, ha ha, hilarious, pack in a top-end five-figure salary, nice one.' The sarcasm was light-hearted. 'Like I said 'ave a week off then come back and see me again!'

'No, Tone. I'm serious. I've done nothing but think about it all. For days and bloody long nights I've looked at the pro's an' cons. I've even tossed coins! I've made up my mind mate, I'm calling it quits as from today.' He looked for Tony's dark round eyes. Tony returned the stare.

Recognising Julian's sincerity he let out a long blast of air in resignation, shaking his head gently at the same time.

'Blow me! You are serious, aren't you! Who you gonna sell your share to?'

Good question. Who was Julian going to sell his stake in the business to?

The gift of shares, a bonus awarded when the turnover and status of the firm had skyrocketed during the mid to late eighties, had seemed insignificant all those years ago. He stood to make a substantial profit from the sale if the right buyer came along. Aitchison and partners had become a far reaching and continually expanding architectural design firm with contracts worth possibly millions already in the bag, as it were.

'I don't think I'll have trouble finding a suitable purchaser do you?'

Tony looked at Julian with his hard, stony business stare.

'You ain't trying to shaft us are you?'

Julian pulled the cup away from his mouth in mock shock. 'Tony! How could you even think that!'

'Well, you can't blame me for asking, can you? For all I know, you could be planning to set up on your own, nicking our clients in covert gazumping raids!' Tony held his hands out, palms up. 'It does happen you know and I've got a lot to lose.'

'I'm serious, Tony.' Julian implored 'I want out, out of the whole thing. No more of any of it. I couldn't care less if I never see the inside of a drawing room again.'

'You're bloody good at what you do, you know that. I hope to god that you've thought this through as much as you say you have. It's a fuckin' massive decision to make mate.' He clasped his hands behind his head.

Tony reluctantly accepted that Julian was not going to change his mind. 'Well okay mate. If that's what you want I can't stop you. So what you gonna do now then? Travel the bleedin' world?'

Julian looked out through the window across the busy market square below the office, over the railway arches and the small businesses that nestled in them, past the local primary school and small play park with brightly coloured apparatus and on until he could not see any further across the vast expanse of North London.

'I don't know yet.'

After a few convivial meetings and a couple of heavy sessions at the Hare and Hound public house Tony and the rest of the partners happily gave Julian what he expected.

All he had to do was decide how to invest it.

He recognised the balding, bespectacled figure in urban camouflage flicking deftly through the funk and soul section. The man would occasionally slow to lift a twelve inch record from the rack to peruse its content even slipping the vinyl from its sheath to check condition and playability.

His long-strapped record bag already looked heavy with the weight of earlier finds.

A classic bill poster of James Brown in cool sixties garb, promoting a re-issue of 'Funky drummer', looked down on the man's glistening pate.

The familiar shape of Walt Jabsco the 2 Tone man, dog-eared with age, its lustre lost to the years, stood guard over the voluminous racks of reggae, ska and 2 Tone long- players. Gerry had eventually dragged it out of the loft space from where he had stashed it in his new home so that it could join Julian in his new venture.

Julian regarded Walt as a kind of good luck charm for the business.

Julian unfolded his arms bringing his hands to rest on the shop counters surface.

The fresh young face on the other side of the counter studied the black and white sleeved disc in his hands intently.

'Sorry mate. I was miles away mate.' Julian apologised. 'What did you say again?'
The youth looked up from the seven inch he was cradling.
Julian smiled. 'Gangsters' The Specials AKA.
'Were you a mod or a skinhead?'

The End